THE MANCHINEEL

A Novel

Jessica Carrasquillo

ISBN:
979-8-35093-136-5

The Manchineel is a work of fiction. Names, characters, places, and incidents either are products of the author's imagination or are used fictitiously. Any resemblance to actual persons, living or dead, events, or locales is entirely coincidental.

For Jacob. You are the inspiration for all the good things a man can be in any story I'll ever write; for Monica, my elder sister who has been my biggest cheerleader since I was a little girl. Without your faith and support, this work would not have been possible.

Special thanks to my editor Elizabeth A. White whose keen eye and invaluable insights elevated this work to its final form.

Author's Note:

Please be advised that the following work contains themes and scenes that may be triggering to some readers, including domestic violence, strong language, and references to sexual abuse. It is important to approach this work with caution if you find these topics particularly distressing. Remember to practice self-care and seek support if needed.

x x x x x x x x x x x x x x x x x x x x x x x x

"They're here, though; not a creature failed—
No Blossom stayed away
In gentle deference to me—
The Queen of Calvary—

Each one salutes me, as he goes,
And I, my childish Plumes,
Lift, in bereaved acknowledgment
Of their unthinking Drums –"

— Emily Dickinson

x x x x x x x x x x x x x x x x x x x x x x x x

Chapter One

"See this beauty? It may seem innocent, but this invasive species is a killer." Elyse's fingers glide over the plant's red, spiked fruit. Her smile drips with honeyed charm, golden eyes gleaming in the afternoon light.

A tripod holding her battered iPhone rests in the grass. Turning to the camera, she speaks to her social media followers directly. "Not only is it highly poisonous, the *ricinus communis* is merciless at suffocating and stealing resources from its native counterparts."

She kneels on the cool, damp earth beside the potted shrub. Behind her, thorned bougainvillea blossoms creep up a wooden fence and a row of blue polyethylene barrels store rainwater. A gust sweeps through and makes music of a windchime hanging from a jacaranda tree.

Elyse's long, dark hair whips around her face as she ends her broadcast, leaving her hidden audience with a meditative closing thought. "Nature is brutal, isn't it? It's impolite. It takes what it wants, and it doesn't ask permission. Given the option to shrink or thrive, it will choose to thrive no matter the cost."

Rising from the ground, she pats the dirt off her grass-stained overalls. Muddy rings wrap around her wrists. A light pulses in her periphery—her phone, the screen brightened with a call. She hesitates before yanking it off the stand to answer.

"Stella," Elyse says, trying to keep the guilt out of her voice.

"Where are you? You said you'd be here an hour ago." Stella's voice is barely audible over the sounds of chatter and laughter in the background.

"I lost track of time. I don't think I can make it. It's like a two-hour bus ride."

"I'm calling you an Uber."

Elyse closes her eyes and quietly seethes. "I can't let you do that. It's practically rush hour...surge pricing—"

"Shane in a blue Honda Accord is on his way," Stella interrupts. "He'll be there in twenty minutes."

Stella's tactics crack like a whip, the sting of urgency jolting Elyse into motion. Quickly gathering her equipment from the garden, she dashes inside the bungalow. She sheds her dirty boots and socks in haste. Her bare feet pound against the hardwood floors, thumps echoing against unadorned walls in the expanse of vacant space.

Running on panic, Elyse is halfway up the stairs before she has the wherewithal to object. "Cancel," she cries, rushing toward the bathroom. "I haven't even taken a shower, and I've been in the garden."

"Well, then you'd better hurry."

"I'm a mess right now. I don't even know what to wear."

"The black dress. It's fine, just wear that."

The last time Elyse wore it was at the funeral. In that stuffy parlor, Andrew's friends and family shared lighthearted anecdotes as the bruises he'd left still yellowed Stella's back. He wasn't someone worth remembering fondly and pretending in that dress felt like she was wearing a costume.

Memories and the frantic rush to get ready meld and her vision blurs. When it clears, all she can focus on are the suds bubbling in her nylon loofah, her world narrowing to this one, disorienting detail. The pads of her fingers have gone pruny. *Focus.* She takes deep breaths, steamy air filling her lungs steadily to slow her rapid heartbeat, reconnecting her tether to reality.

Stella can be so pushy. Attending a social gathering where she won't know anyone is bad enough—tack on looking slipshod. An act of contortion zips her dress midway up her back, and a wire hanger finishes the job. The thought of faking her own death crosses her mind as she glides a boar-bristle brush through her hair, gathering it up from her nape and securing it with a black elastic to form a wet bun on top of her head. Her phone vibrates, alerting her the Uber is outside.

A pained groan escapes her as she grabs her bag and rushes out the door. He's in the driveway, and she opens the door to the back seat. Craning his neck, he confirms, "Elyse?"

"Mm-hmm." She forces a smile and slides in against the stained, gray cloth upholstery. Just as a click secures her seat belt, Shane's eyes flit up at her through the rearview mirror.

"Manhattan Beach, huh?"

"Yup."

His eyes linger on her a little too long, making her uneasy. Staring down at her phone, she jumps in and out of apps aimlessly. A few swipes of her thumb retrieve the Instagram app. Avoiding Shane's gaze, she reads the comments on her last video.

 3

You're gorgeous.
Amazing. 🖤
🔥🔥🔥
MONSTER
YOU KILLED MY SON

A bitter tang spreads across her mouth. Jaw clenched, she forces down a quiet scream and it settles, burning her gut like a swallowed ember. She deletes the comments and blocks the account that posted them.

Twenty-five hundred miles of distance and years of time separate her from that dark place, and yet the memory of George Ramos fills her with a familiar regret. Why had she ever let him in?

Chapter Two

Elyse was fourteen when she started seeing her therapist, Dr. Guillermo Delgado. Right away, he'd insisted she call him by his first name, as if that would place them on equal footing. Adults were always doing patronizing stuff like that. Skepticism kept a tight grip on her secrets, but eventually, he wore her down. While Child Protective Services had briefed him on some of the darker details of her story, Elyse opened up about where it all started.

George Ramos always smiled and waved as she walked home from school. Even if it felt a bit odd at first—an older boy like him, out of high school a few years, calling over a twelve-year-old girl to chat, it was kind of nice. Still dressed in his bright construction vest and boots, he'd always ask her about her day and seemed to care about hearing her answer. At first, she'd just wave shyly before crossing the street to her house. But each day he'd talk to her a little more, until he finally coaxed out some words.

"You're so pretty. Why don't you ever smile? You'd be even prettier if you smiled."

She shrugged at him and looked back at her house, where pastel pink strips of paint peeled off the crumbling stucco. "I'll smile when I have something to smile about." It was the most she'd ever said to him, and he was delighted, laughing hysterically with a mix of surprise and amusement. It made her want to smile too, but she held it back, instead pulling at her fingers.

"What happened to your hands?"

They were stained the color of saffron. "Oh. In chemistry we did an experiment to test carbohydrates. We were dipping potatoes in iodine and mine spilled."

George squinted at her hands and smirked. "I usually just dip my potatoes in ketchup."

She tried her best not to laugh, but his silly tone broke her, and she smiled, turning her face. "That's a bad joke."

"Ah, but I got you. Don't hide it, pretty girl. I knew I'd make you smile one day."

Most days after that, she'd stop and chat with him in his gravel driveway. Sometimes his mother would be out there with him, chain-smoking in her plastic patio chair. It went on like this for a few weeks, until one day he finally asked her, "Aren't you hot wearing all that?" He motioned toward her long sleeves and uniform khaki pants in the sweltering heat. Her eyes shamefully fell to her shoes, rubber soles worn down and tattered from constant use. "I can hear him yelling, you know. I thought maybe he was whooping your mom. But he probably hits you too, huh?"

The words hurt somehow. They embarrassed her. She'd done her best to hide the bruises, to keep her family's

dysfunction a secret. Without speaking, she turned and rushed home. He shouted for her, but she kept going until she was behind her front door.

Inside, her mother lay on the worn sofa, staring blankly at a daytime talk show, the volume turned up too loud. Elyse's fingers tightened around the doorknob as she took in the scene. The room was dim, the heavy curtains drawn, blocking out the afternoon sun. Bags of chips and candy littered the coffee table, bottles of nail polish and magazines strewn about. Her mother hauled her face around slowly. Her eyes, bloodshot and distant, met Elyse's for a brief moment before drifting back to the television screen. "What time is it?" she mumbled, her voice hoarse. The smell of stale cigarettes permeated the house.

"Four something." The blaring sound of the television was making it hard to think, so Elyse reached for the remote and turned the volume down a few notches. She sat beside her mother and gestured toward the junk food. "Is that all you ate today?"

"I don't have the energy to cook."

"I'll make something. You need to eat real food. That's why you don't have energy."

Venturing into the kitchen to scavenge a meal, her mind wandered back to that carbohydrate experiment, how the long chains of glucose molecules changed color under the iodine. Remembering George's dumb joke made her smile to herself. He'd meant well. Maybe she shouldn't have run away, she thought.

Then, she felt the pain. With a grip of her hair and a quick tug, her father forced her out of his way. A sharp sting on her scalp drew her attention to his hand, which he shook out, a bundle of long brown strands falling from his fist and landing on the floor. Giving her a disgusted look, he finished his stride to the fridge to retrieve a beer.

After dinner, she inspected her head in her bedroom mirror and found a white patch of scalp the size of an egg. Taking a brush, she shifted the hair in different directions, trying to come up with a hairstyle to wear for the rest of the school year. That's when she heard it for the first time—a light knock at her window. She ignored it at first, thinking it was a squirrel or some other wildlife. But when it continued, she turned to find a man's silhouette behind the glass. Panicked, she froze.

"Elyse, it's George," he whispered.

Hearing his familiar voice was a relief, even if it was strange for him to be out there at this late hour. She wondered how he knew which room was hers. With a grunt, she lifted the window just enough to talk. He'd already removed the screen.

"What are you doing here?"

"Can I come in? The mosquitos are eating me."

She turned toward her door, hurrying over to lock it. If her father knew she'd let a boy into her room, he'd kill her, especially an older boy like George. By the time she turned around, George had already hoisted his upper body onto the window ledge, using the strength of his arms to pull himself forward. His boots momentarily caught on the edge, but with a little wiggle and a groan, he managed to free himself, sliding onto the brown carpeting. Once inside, he took a moment to brush off the bits of leaves and dirt from his clothes.

"You ran off earlier, and I didn't get to tell you," he said, keeping his voice hushed. "I'm sorry if I hurt your feelings. We're friends, aren't we?"

He stepped closer and she could smell the familiar scent of liquor on his breath. She nodded because she was afraid not to.

"Everybody needs a friend sometimes. Can I give you a hug?"

She didn't want to, but before she could say no, he'd already pulled her into an embrace. Her body tensed at first, but then he squeezed, and something shifted. Heat rose to her face,

her eyes. Her chest tightened and she started to sob. It was like a levee broke and the floodwaters escaped, drowning everything in their path.

Stroking her hair, he soothed her. "Shhh, it's okay. Let it out."

Despite her apprehension there was something oddly comforting about it. Over time, she'd learned to trust him, to let her guard down. So when he pulled her into bed and held her there, wrapped up in his arms, she didn't protest.

That first night was innocent. She lay with him until the tears stopped, then he kissed her forehead and whispered, "Goodnight," before climbing back outside and disappearing into the dark.

The sound of a white noise machine *whooshed* in the background of Guillermo's office as Elyse eyed a rainbow-colored emotions wheel on the table between them. A shelf behind him held rows of books and vibrant binders. He nodded at her, his eyebrows drawn together. "Do you know why you kept letting George in, even after the abuse started?"

Elyse sat on the edge of the plush, gray sofa, squeezing a balled-up tissue in her fist, wondering how she could have been so stupid. "I guess I was scared of what might happen if I didn't."

"When it stopped, was that because at some point you refused to let him in?"

Knees drawn up to her chest, she hugged her arms tight around them, curling herself into a protective shell. The heels of her feet, covered by white cotton socks, rested at the sofa's edge. She dropped her head, pressing her cheek against the worn denim fabric of her jeans.

"You're safe here, Elyse," he said softly. "I'm here to help you."

The words were desperate to escape, even as her tongue threatened to choke them back. "It stopped because I killed

him," she said. It was the first time she'd ever told anybody, and a strange sense of calm came over her.

Guillermo remained measured, seeming to diffuse his alarm by tightening his grip on his yellow legal pad and adjusting in his seat. "Did you plan to kill him?"

"Mm-hmm."

"How?"

"My class went to the History Miami Museum. They were talking about how the natives used fruit from the manchineel trees to kill Ponce de León." Even at fourteen, the irony was not lost on her that it was George who forged her father's signature on her permission slip. He'd even given her the twenty dollars she needed to attend.

The thought of the permission slip in her backpack burned a hole in her stomach the entire bus ride and walk home. Money was tight. Asking for a signature and twenty dollars meant she'd have to speak up and let the burden of her existence be acknowledged. Being noticed was always a roll of the dice, a decision she made voluntarily only under the most extreme circumstances.

That night when George visited, he asked her why she looked so worried. "I'll take care of it," he promised after she explained. "Lay back."

By then she'd stopped fighting him off, having resigned herself to the pain of it. After, he caught his breath and pulled her into an embrace. "Let me see the paper."

On the bus to the museum, thinking of the way she earned her spot on the trip made her sick. George and her, their disgusting act. He was ever present in her mind that day. Sitting in a dim theatre, the image on the screen a row of ashen trees with bright green leaves lining a South Florida shoreline. A male voice narrated.

While it might look harmless, every part of this tree is toxic. Indigenous peoples of this land knew its dangers well and harnessed its lethal properties. Legend has it, in 1521 during his second expedition to Florida, Ponce de León was struck by an arrow poisoned with manchineel sap. He retreated to Cuba, where he later died from his wounds.

The image of the fruit on the screen looked like nothing more than a green apple. The mangroves behind her house were full of them. She'd been warned to avoid touching them, especially in the rain, but she'd never known why. The idea that something so innocent could hide such a dark secret resonated with something deep within her.

"And that gave you the idea?" Guillermo asked.

"Mm-hmm."

Guillermo nudged the emotions chart across the table toward her. The room was filled with soft, natural light that filtered through beige curtains and cast a warm glow on the sterile walls adorned with framed diplomas. "How did it make you feel?"

Elyse unfolded herself, reluctantly picked up the wheel and studied it for a moment. Before George died, she had felt sad, angry, and heartbroken. But after he was gone, she felt something else. "Free."

Toxic sap from the manchineel was known to form nasty blisters on the skin, so she was sure to wear gloves that day when plucking the fruit from the tree in her backyard, cutting it up in her kitchen, blending it into a paste to stir in with peanut butter. She invited George over for lunch.

"My parents aren't home," she said.

A predatory smile spread across his lips. Watching his excitement grow, looking into his eyes as he took the first bites, watching him struggle minutes later—it all made her feel so powerful.

"Are you okay?" she asked him, feigning innocence.

He wasn't feeling well, he said. Maybe he was coming down with something. He went home to get some rest. He never woke up, killed by a mix of the toxic effects—swelling in his mouth and throat, then aspirating on his own vomit.

Guillermo nodded and scribbled a thought. Afterward, he lectured her on the value of human life. How in society there are laws made to protect all kinds of people, even bad people, and she shouldn't take matters into her own hands unless she has no other choice.

Blah blah blah.

It didn't have to be that way. Someone could have helped her, but no one did. Maybe if they had, George would be in a prison cell and not in an urn on his mother's mantle.

She challenged him. "So, some Spanish guy like Ponce de León showed up and told all the natives, '*These are the rules now, follow them or else.*' Well, who put him in charge? Now you lecture me on how we're all supposed to follow the rules, how they help people. But they never helped me, and they didn't help the natives either."

His eyes lit up with a hint of amusement and he calmly smiled at her. "Everything you've been through with George and your time in foster care, I know it's been a lot. You're trying to make sense of your experiences. But there's another way. What if I can help you?"

"Good luck."

"You don't think you can be helped?"

"Maybe I'm too broken."

"May I tell you a story?"

Crossing her arms over her chest, she stared at him with a blank, indifferent gaze. "Yeah, alright," she mumbled.

He leaned forward and rested his elbows on his knees. "A group of scientists made a recreation of Earth inside a dome with all kinds of plant species. Purified water. Fertile soil. The ideal amount of light to make everything grow. Everything was perfect, except the trees would only get so tall before they would fall over. The scientists couldn't understand what was wrong. Eventually, they realized they'd forgotten to provide wind. The trees needed the wind to challenge them to make their roots dig in deeper so they could grow taller. The things that are challenging you haven't broken you, Elyse. They're making you stronger."

"If you say so."

Later, she couldn't stop thinking about what Guillermo said. What if what happened with George could make her stronger? She wanted to believe it was possible.

Chapter Three

Elyse makes her way through a narrow concrete alleyway that opens to the Pacific Ocean, finally reaching Stella's front porch. The glass doors reveal a house teeming with party guests. Laughter and the rhythmic beats of soulful music spill onto the beach, causing every fiber of her being to tense.

Before she can suppress it, she hears George's voice in her mind. *Nice of Stella to let you do her dirty work then disappear. Now you're all alone again. You're so afraid, aren't you? Afraid the next kind smile hides another monster. But we both know the only monster is the one you see every time you look in the mirror.*

"It's only a few hours," she murmurs to herself, trying to stoke her courage. With a deep breath, she pushes George's words out of her mind. She takes down her hair, now only just damp, and gives it a shake, allowing the air-dried waves to fall haphazardly. The glass pane gives her a quick look at her reflection. It's not exactly sophisticated, but it'll have to do. Then, despite the sweat pooling beneath her dress and the desire to retreat, Elyse gathers herself and opens the door.

The party roars at her.

She ascends a steel wire and birchwood staircase to the second floor, where she spots Stella, platinum-haired and radiating old Hollywood glamour, engaging with a crowd of chic strangers. A man in a sleek, black outfit offers a tray of champagne flutes; she takes one and quickly shoots it back. The fizzing bubbles expand in her chest, and she suppresses a burp, expelling it softly through her nose. Scanning the room, she locates an unoccupied section of oceanfront balcony and claims it as her own, snagging a glass of white wine from a passing tray.

The sun dips below the horizon, casting a warm, golden glow over the Pacific and everything it touches. Elyse cradles her wineglass and focuses on her breathing. Her moment of serenity is interrupted by Stella's voice, approaching from behind. "Elyse, honey, I want you to meet Ben Deluca. He's a manager at King. I told him a little bit about you."

A rush of anxiety fills her, and the thought of a forced introduction briefly tempts her to leap over the railing. Turning, she lifts her chin to find his face, her gaze traveling upward over the broad expanse of his torso.

"Oh." A note of surprise escapes her, and his formidable stature causes her to instinctively step back for safety.

"Nice to finally meet you. Stella won't stop bragging about you." His heavy brows knit together, thick yet well-groomed. He extends his hand and Elyse's hand disappears within it.

"What, um, what do you do?" she asks.

Joining her on the balcony, he says, "I'm an attorney. I handle all aspects of my client's careers—contracts, negotiation,

promoting talents, major life decisions. Maybe I could take you to lunch. We could talk." It rolls off his tongue like he says it a hundred times a day, and yet, it doesn't sound rehearsed. She notices his voice carries a hint of a New York accent.

Right after he gives her his card, and before she can politely decline his offer, a petite blonde woman emerges from the crowd to cling onto his arm.

"Excuse me," he says as he's swiftly ushered away.

Elyse tucks his card into her bra and returns her gaze toward the ocean. *This sucks.* The sunset's hues and the sea blur together as tears threaten to spill. She doesn't want to be here, not at a farewell party. Not for her only friend in LA.

Once the party dies down inside, Stella finds her and pulls her onto a couch.

"So?" Stella's hands are clasped with excitement. "Did you meet anyone fun?"

"Just that one guy you introduced me to," she says. "Who was that blonde?"

"Ana King. His wife. Isn't she beautiful?"

"I don't know, she was kind of a blur. Everyone was." Elyse sinks into a white leather sectional, letting out a deep listless puff of air.

Stella rests her head on hers. "It's not forever."

"I know."

"Promise me you'll call Ben."

Elyse sighs. She doesn't want to fight with Stella on their last night together, but she won't make a promise she doesn't intend to keep. "I'm not an actress or an influencer or whatever. I just need income. Steady, reliable income."

Stella shakes her head. "I don't understand why you won't let me help you."

The subject exhausts Elyse. She's not a hired gun. Money had nothing to do with her choosing to help Stella, and she's already taken enough of Stella's goodwill. If she hadn't been on

the verge of homelessness, she never would have let herself be talked into moving into one of Stella's rental properties. She'd tried to start paying rent once she could, but Stella refused to cash a single check and every Venmo payment Elyse sent was promptly returned.

Since Elyse was fired from the health club, a stack of overdue utility bills has begun to pile up on her kitchen counter. Her fridge is nearly barren, and the lone credit card she's been surviving on is dangerously close to its limit. She needs something that pays yesterday. But she can't keep running from one debt to another, one favor to the next.

"Please," Elyse begs. "You've done enough. Just let me figure this out on my own. I can get a normal job."

Stella waves her hand dismissively. "Oh, you don't want a normal job. When you left Miami, you could have moved anywhere but you chose LA."

It wasn't exactly a choice. Standing at the bus station counter at Miami International Airport with only her clothes and life savings in her backpack, she asked the ticket agent, "What's the furthest away from here I can get with $250?"

He'd looked her up and down warily before clicking through screens on his computer. "Los Angeles," he replied after a pause, tapping a few keys. "It's a long ride."

Elyse nodded. "When's the next bus?"

As she'd boarded, she felt less like she was making a conscious decision and more like she was a dandelion seed, carried and blown in by the winds of fate. Watching the only city she'd ever known recede behind her, she clung to the hope of a fresh start.

Snapping back to the present, she meets Stella's smirking gaze and pushes back. "You're saying everyone in LA wants to be famous?"

"Yes. And if you don't, why do you have so many followers?"

Throwing her head back, she scoffs. "It's a gardening account."

"I've read the comments. It's a thirst trap and you know it."

While it would be nice to earn money making inspirational nature videos instead of being groped by jerks for tips as a server or selling Chad's stupid water machines at the health club, it's risky. She already finds herself policing the comment section for echoes of her past. The thought of amplifying her voice against that threat makes her a bit lightheaded. Even the best mask reveals its seams under the glare of a spotlight.

Stella takes Elyse's hands in hers. "The investigation is closed. You're free to live your life. I don't want you isolating yourself while I'm gone. I owe you so much and—"

"You don't owe me anything."

"But I *do*." She squeezes Elyse's hands. "I love you. Please. Call Ben."

"Okay," she concedes. "I'll call."

As she walks away from Stella's house, a daunting emptiness consumes her. The ride home stretches on, longer than usual tonight. Darkness envelops the surroundings, with the lights of Los Angeles strobing her distorted reflection in the car window. Each flash gives a transient glimpse of her own melancholy.

One afternoon a few days after Stella's party, Elyse spots Ben's business card on her bedroom floor between a standing mirror and a pile of laundry. It must have fallen there when she undressed after the party. A cold sweat breaks out on her neck, and she averts her eyes, determined to focus on editing a new video for her followers.

She sits on her mattress, which rests directly on the floor, and opens her MacBook in her lap. Her editing lasts all of two minutes before the curiosity of Ben's card starts drawing her eye to it again and again. Tension builds with each glance, until she

finally pries it off the hardwood with a fingernail and scowls at it.

Maybe some due diligence would put this curiosity to rest. With a few stilted taps of her keyboard, the King Management website loads in her browser. It looks fancy, featuring a photo of their massive office building near Beverly Hills encased in mirrored glass. She scrolls through the page to their list of services—modeling, film, television, musicians, social influencers, and photography.

Nope. None of those. Why did she make such a ridiculous promise to Stella? She plugs in his number and agonizes over the call button until she can't stand it anymore. *Just get it over with.* Moments after pushing send, a man's voice answers.

"King Management, how may I direct your call?"

"Ben Deluca, please."

Chapter Four

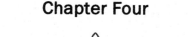

A small glass vase with a bundle of wildflowers inside—purple iris and orange poppy—sits on the center of a white tablecloth. The walls are lined with modern, minimalist art. Elyse took the bus here to meet Ben for lunch at this swanky Italian restaurant in Century City.

Soft Italian music plays, and the aroma of freshly baked bread makes her mouth water. Her empty stomach groans like a haunted house as he stands to greet her enthusiastically in a crisp suit. Somehow, she'd forgotten how physically imposing he is in person and yet every inch of him has an underlying aura of refinement.

The cotton tank dress she chose for the occasion came off the clearance rack at Target, but it's pretty—the color of honeycomb—and it hugs her in the right places.

"Stella tells me you might be in need of a little guidance." He straightens in his seat and smooths out his tie.

"I'm in need of a job."

A wry smile slowly spreads across his face, and his dark downturned eyes glitter at her with amusement. "Maybe you can start by telling me what kind of work you're interested in."

Wringing her clammy hands, she blurts, "I worked at a couple of restaurants. I was a hostess at one, server at another, but the hours were bad. So, then I worked at a SoCal Sculpt, it's a health—"

"In the entertainment industry, I mean," he says, cutting her off. "I checked out your content. It's very sweet."

"Sweet?" It wasn't meant to be *sweet*. It was meant to be educational, inspirational. It was supposed to teach humanity valuable lessons about life. The waiter interrupts before Ben can elaborate.

Elyse hurriedly scans her options, her anxiety mounting at the prices. *Geez.* "Uh, the um...chicken skewers, please." It's the least expensive thing on the menu. "Just water to drink."

Ben chooses a wine with a posh-sounding name, likely paired to his sophisticated dish. The waiter nods, retrieving their menus.

"I didn't mean any disrespect. You're obviously very beautiful. I'm just not sure about the content. There's no clear mission, no clear brand. What are your followers there to see?"

"Well, the science behind the garden, meditations, life lessons."

Before she can even finish her sentence, he's shaking his head in disagreement. "They're there to see you. The posts with the highest engagement are of you in your garden. No matter what subject you're talking about, if you're in the post they're

liking it, commenting. The engagement with posts is drastically lower when you're not in them."

"That's disappointing."

The odd look he gives her suggests he can't understand why she'd feel that way. He rubs his palms against his pant legs, seeming to carefully consider what he'll say next. The brief silence lasts just long enough to magnify her self-doubt.

"I've worked with some incredibly talented people who lack a certain aesthetic and have trouble booking consistently. That's disappointing. With your bone structure, your eyes, your body... I could book you yesterday doing almost anything. Have you ever acted? Do you sing? Dance? Model?"

"No. I don't really have any talents."

He laughs slightly as a finger scratches his temple.

Surely, he's wondering what he's doing here. Pushing her empty bread plate aside, she decides to put this poor man out of his misery and go. "I'm really sorry to waste your time. Stella insisted I meet with you. Honestly, I just need income to keep the lights on and eat. I can't even afford lunch at this place."

"Hold on." He gestures to stop her. "Lunch is on me." Taking a beat to study her, he asks, "Your last name. Santiago. Where's your family from?"

"Cuba originally."

Perking up again with a bright look, he presses his hands to his chest. "Me too. Well, half. My mother's side. Do you speak Spanish?"

"No." Her answer sounds like an apology. "Do you?"

"Yeah." He studies her like he's trying to decipher something. "You know, I moved to LA ten years ago with nothing. I know what it's like to feel like you're just trying to survive. But if you don't let yourself dream bigger than that, that's all you're ever going to do. Look, you've got over a hundred thousand followers all on your own. That's not easy. You've got something.

I can help you pump those numbers up, but it'll mean switching up the content a bit."

"Switch up the content like how?" It comes out sounding more defensive than she'd intended.

"Well, for one thing, I think the way you shoot your videos could benefit from a little artistic guidance. You're in a garden, you're beautiful, the garden is beautiful, you're on a visual platform, and yet the content doesn't inspire the way it could."

Hmm. That's actually good feedback. Alright. Maybe she could use his help. "Anything else?" She looks at him, but his eyes are focused on a server approaching their table with their meals. The aroma of garlic yanks at her gut. Her stomach gurgles, and she hastily presses a hand to her belly hoping Ben hadn't caught the sound. Once his eyes meet hers again, they're filled with humor.

"For revenue, we can look at sponsored content and booking you wherever makes sense so you don't starve to death. I'd recommend taking acting classes so we can broaden your options. Work on your confidence."

Work on my confidence? Geez. Is it that obvious? She considers acting classes for a millisecond, and the image it illustrates in her mind makes her heart speed up and jump into her throat. Her appetite fades. The charred wooden skewer twists between her fingers on her plate. "I can't afford acting classes."

Pausing mid-chew, he wipes his mouth with his napkin, then reaches into his jacket. He pulls out a black leather checkbook and a fancy-looking pen. It scribbles back and forth for a moment before he tears out the check and offers it to her. She accepts it purely out of curiosity.

It's written from his business account—a simple white background with a logo of a crowned lion. King Management is printed in bold letters. Payable to Elyse Santiago in the amount of twelve hundred dollars.

"I can't accept this."

"It isn't a gift. Consider it an advance."

"You don't even know me. I could skip town and you'd never see me again."

His brows lift slightly, and she can't tell if he's surprised or entertained by her candor, but a hint of a smile appears on his lips. "Sweetheart, I'm not sure if you understand how this works, but all of this is a gamble. If I didn't think you have potential and could make us both a lot of money, I wouldn't be sitting here with you."

Each sentence is animated by a hand gesture, mirroring the New York-tinged rhythm of his voice. "Cash the check. Go to the Lila Donovan acting studio on Sunset. She's a friend of mine. That will cover the tuition for her six-week program."

An advance? This isn't just a lunch anymore—it's a leap, and she's not sure she can stick the landing. Heat rises in her cheeks. He's being generous and sincerely trying to help her. It's not something that happens every day. It's not something that happens *ever*. "Why are you helping me?"

Ben sits back with an earnest look. "Stella had a lot of great things to say about you. Not just about your potential but about who you are as a person. I've known her a long time, and I trust her judgment. Do you have headshots?"

"No," she says regretfully.

"Good headshots will run you between five and twelve hundred. I could refer you to someone, but because I know you're strapped for cash right now, I'm thinking we get creative. One of my clients is Kieran Hines. Brilliant photographer. Maybe he'd be open to an exchange. Work for work. I'll talk to him." Holding her in an intent gaze, he casually motions toward her dress with his fork. "That dress you're wearing is perfect. Eyes are important in headshots. Yours are so unique, wide set and a lovely gold color. I don't think I've ever seen that color before. You'll want them to stand out."

"Oh." Caught off guard, she folds her arms in front of herself. Her fair skin is quick to blush, and her chest and cheeks must be painted pink. "Okay."

He's undeniably handsome, but it doesn't matter. He has a ring on his finger. She tries to brush the momentary surge of attraction aside and fumbles with the napkin in her lap.

"Buen provecho," he says. The corners of his mouth turn up and his fork goes to work on a sun-dried tomato. The aroma of basil emanates from his plate.

"Buon appetito."

He nods through his swallow, like he plans to say something but his mouth is full. "You know the other half is Italian."

"Other half of what?"

He laughs through a chew and covers his mouth. "Me. I probably should have said that."

She remembers what he said about being half Cuban and laughs with him. Strong jawline, high cheekbones, prominent brow—she can see it.

The waiter returns, probably having noticed Ben's empty wineglass.

"You don't drink?" Ben asks, casting a quick look at Elyse's water.

"Oh, I do."

"Would you like a glass?"

"Sure."

He holds up two fingers to the waiter. "Two, please."

She likes him more already. When it arrives, she savors the faint sweetness that tingles her mouth and warms all the way down to her belly. Sip by sip, it wears down the anxious edge of making small talk.

"I was surprised Stella left the business," he says, leaning back in his chair. "She's a fantastic publicist. She could put a cardigan on Michael Corleone and convince anyone he was Mr.

Rogers. She could spin anything." There's a hint of nostalgia in his tone.

Stella doesn't have to spin anything anymore. She inherited a fortune. Enough money to do all the things she's ever wanted to do but was too afraid to try on her own. Elyse did a good thing, she reminds herself, even if it did take Stella away.

It's only been a few nights without her, listening to the hum of the refrigerator, alone and fretting about George Ramos instead of enjoying the pleasant distraction of her best friend's company.

The thoughts threaten her composure, and she tries to collect herself but it's too late. The tears start to burn. Reaching into her lap to grab her napkin, she presses the delicate fabric into her tear duct with her index finger. A soft Italian ballad plays in a faint whisper in the background as conversations thrum all around them.

Ben leans forward, his eyebrows pulled together. "I didn't mean to upset you."

"No, it's okay. I'm sorry," she says. "I just miss her."

"I can tell she really cares about you."

"She's my best friend. I don't— It can be lonely out here sometimes." Stopping herself, she sets down her empty glass. The wine is making her talk too much. She doesn't know this man.

Ben's hand drifts in her direction as if to offer comfort, but hesitates short of actually touching her. He shifts uncomfortably in his seat, seeming to grapple with how to help.

Taking a moment, she rests back in her chair, then disperses the emotional weight at the table with an embarrassed smile and wave of her hand. Her stomach stretches uncomfortably, stuffed with grilled chicken and table bread. A satisfied *oof* slips out and she pats her belly. "Guess I overdid it with the bread," she says, trying to lighten the mood.

He gives her a warm look. "Did you get enough to eat?"

"Mm-hmm."

"You want to order something to go? For dinner?"

The question makes her skip a breath. Opening her mouth to decline, she loses her words. Her expression must cause him to second-guess himself.

"I'm sorry. I hope I didn't offend you," he says softly.

"No, I appreciate it. But you really don't have to do that."

"I want to. Order whatever you want." He shrugs it off like it's no big deal, but if he'd seen the state of her fridge, he'd understand how much this gesture means to her.

"That's really sweet. Thank you."

"Don't mention it."

* * *

After lunch, Ben walks her out. The buzz from the wine numbs her just enough to make her feel buoyant and coaxes out a smile. A warm breeze brushes her skin. The smell of coffee from a nearby cafe carries in the air and mixes with the faint odor of gasoline and burnt rubber from the street.

Pulling a ticket from his pocket, he asks, "Did you valet?"

"Oh, I don't drive."

He gives her the same look everyone in Los Angeles gives her when she tells them she doesn't drive. The look says, "*How is that possible?*" It's not a city designed for pedestrians, but she once had a panic attack on the freeway and never went back.

"You're headed back to Highland Park?"

Oh no, he's about to offer me a ride. Please don't. "Mm-hmm."

"Can I give you a lift?"

She waves off the suggestion. "I don't want to put you out."

"It's no trouble. I have time."

"Okay. Thanks."

The valet pulls up in a black Range Rover that's surprisingly low-key. It's nice, but it's not the kind of thing she expected from a flashy guy like him—the suit, the expensive-looking watch, writing out $1,200 checks on a whim.

Once he opens the door, the mix of smells outside is replaced with the scent of leather. There isn't a fleck of dust to be found and everything looks freshly cleaned and moisturized. Ben might be the most put together person she's ever met. Even Stella's car was a mess—magazines and makeup bags strewn about, a metal water bottle in the backseat that rolled and clunked around each time she jerked the wheel.

When he gets in, she notices he's taken off his jacket and rolled up his sleeves. Starting up the car, the music he'd been listening to before resumes. It's soulful mood music, but she only catches a few seconds before he turns it down.

He taps the buttons on the navigation system as she recites her address. Light shoots through the windshield when they emerge from the shade of a tree, and they squint under the brightness for a moment before he grabs a pair of slick sunglasses off the dash and slides them on. She can't help but steal a quick glance at him as he does, marveling at how effortlessly cool he looks in the moment.

Passing the time with polite conversation, she finds herself drawn to the timbre of his voice. It's rich and deep. If he whispered in her ear, she'd probably die.

"So, how'd you get into science?" he asks.

"I always loved science in school. Thinking about how everything—the universe, a flower, a cloud—it's all just atoms and molecules, bonding and reacting according to natural laws." As the word *laws* leaves her mouth, she remembers his profession and jumps on the connection by excitedly adding, "Hey, you studied man's law and I studied nature's law."

Hearing herself, she cringes. *Ugh. I'm such a dork.*

He turns his head to glance at her, a small smirk on his lips. "You studied it in college?"

"Mm-hmm." Clearing her throat, the excitement in her tone wanes. "University of Miami. I didn't graduate though. Just had a few semesters of biochemistry."

As he nods at the road, she wonders if he's curious why she didn't finish her major but is too polite to pry. "I needed to work. So, I took some time off," she lies.

They talk about how difficult it is to work and go to school simultaneously, how Ben juggled law school and a full-time job.

When they pull up to her house, it's after two-thirty. He slides off his shades and hooks them on his shirt. His sturdy, olive-toned hand shifts the car into park, then slides off the gearshift. A thick finger idly teases the edge of a cupholder. His nails are clean and manicured. A light blanket of hair starts at his wrist and disappears under the roll of his shirt folded up around his burly forearms.

Their eyes finally meet, and he's grinning at her with a twinkle in his eye. Realizing she'd just not so subtly checked him out, her face burns and she reaches for the door.

"Thank you," she says, slowly backing out of the vehicle with a brown paper take-out bag hooked on her arm. "For the ride."

"You're very welcome."

Embarrassment weighs down her limbs as she trudges to her front porch. Unlocking the door, she notices he's waiting for her to get inside before he drives away. She waves at him, and he waves back.

Phew. Assignment complete. Elyse sends Stella a text as she climbs the stairs to her bedroom, her footsteps echoing in the empty space.

Had lunch with Ben.

Her phone vibrates with Stella's response.

Isn't he great?

Of course he is, Elyse scoffs. Stella thinks she's so clever. She's up to something, Elyse just hasn't figured out what.

He's alright.

Imagining Stella's annoyed pinched expression gives Elyse a small thrill as she discards her dress. She slips into a pair of worn-in jeans and a soft shirt. Her heels are swapped for sturdy boots, and she ventures outside into her garden with a tripod tucked under her arm.

Sitting in a patch of lush green, her phone records as she offers lessons and meditations on life's delicate balance. Turning over a broad leaf, she exposes small crawling insects to the camera. Plants sway in the breeze behind her. "Every organism plays a part in an ecosystem. Insects will eat this leaf, birds will eat the insects and become prey to snakes and foxes. Everything is part of a cycle of being the eater...or the eaten. Introduce something new, or take something vital away, and the entire system could be thrown into chaos."

Ending the recording, Elyse sits in contemplation for a moment, breathing in the fresh air. The natural world around her hums and chirps. Her phone vibrates.

I'm so proud of you for taking a risk. This could be a new beginning.

Elyse reads Stella's message and lets out a slow breath, hoping to release the cynicism from her body. Maybe she's right.

Chapter Five

Ben returns to the King Management building after dropping off Elyse. High heels click and clack in a rhythmic pattern against the polished marble floors, keeping time behind a low murmur of voices that fill the lobby.

The elevator takes Ben to the twentieth floor, where his large office overlooks Los Angeles. The glass walls provide unobstructed views of the building's interior. Plush loungers are lined up in perfect symmetry. Modern, glass pendant lights hang overhead in a row down the long corridor between offices and cubicles.

The only wall not made of glass in Ben's office is adorned with a row of framed movie posters, each featuring one of Ben's clients. *Bloodoath. Bloodoath: Reckoning. Bloodoath: Redemption.*

As he eases into his chair, one of the assistants from legal sticks his head through the glass doorway. "Is Mr. King in a meeting?"

Being the son-in-law of the firm's founding partner and having the office next door has its perks, but it also means everyone treats Ben like Chuck's keeper. Instead of voicing his frustration, Ben rests his elbows on the polished mahogany surface of his desk, pressing his fingers to his temples to emphasize his headache. "Is he not in his office?"

The assistant nods and points next door. "His blinds are closed and the door is shut."

Ben shrugs. "Okay, then he's in a meeting." Considering the discussion complete, he returns to work on his laptop. Eventually, the assistant disappears from his doorway. Except now Ben can't remember what he was about to do. *Where the fuck is Janine?*

"Janine!" His pulse throbs in his temples. There's a good reason her desk is right outside his door. Squinting against the glare of sunlight reflecting on the glass wall, he can make out the outline of her empty chair.

Muttering to himself, he turns back to his laptop. The afternoon is spent on the phone making call after scheduled call. Those finally complete, he opens a contract he needs to review before the end of the day on his laptop and scans it with his cheek sinking onto his fist. *Parties, consideration, exclusivity, indemnity, yada yada, etc. etc.*

What an odd young woman, he thinks, his mind wandering back to lunch. Her beauty was irrefutable, but she was strange. Something in her gorgeous eyes had an untamed intensity, an almost feral look akin to a threatened animal. It was puzzling because she had such a gentle demeanor. He can't seem to shake her from his thoughts.

Opening a new email message, he starts to write.

From: Ben Deluca, Esq.
Subject: Follow-Up
Date: June 18, 2017 16:09
To: Elyse Santiago

Elyse,

I enjoyed our lunch today and appreciate you taking the time out of your busy schedule. It was lovely getting to know you better. In follow-up to our conversation regarding representation, here's a link to the agreement we discussed. Look it over and let me know if you have any questions.

Looking forward to seeing you again.

Best,
Ben

He scans it again and again. *Looking forward to seeing you again.* It's personal but professional. As he hits send, his phone is buzzing. It's Ana.

"Are you on your way home yet?"

Checking the time, he decides he probably should head home although he hadn't planned to until her call. "I'm walking out of my office now."

The sun is low enough in the sky that it shines a blinding light horizontally through the windows of Ben's floor.

"Is Daddy there?"

"Hold on, give me a second." He pokes his head out of his office. Charles's blinds are open and his chair is empty. "He's not there, why?"

"I just wanted to make sure you weren't leaving before he was."

"Did he say something about what time I leave? I'm here all the time."

"I just don't want him to think you're lazy."

Jaw clenched, he bites back harsh words as he strides toward the elevator. How can he be an asshole for working late all the time *and* an asshole for leaving early? "I'm getting in the elevator, going to lose you." The doors close and he hangs up before she can answer.

Janine is walking into the building as he approaches the exit, and Ben's fists clench at the sight of her. With swift steps, he closes in on her, intent on letting her have it. "Where've you been all day?"

The light dims behind her pale eyes and her freckled face slacks. "You told me to deliver scripts."

"You're FedEx now? I told you to *have the scripts delivered.*" He speaks slowly and clearly so she can understand. "Send a courier. Use your head for once. I haven't been able to get shit done all day."

"I'm sorry, Mr. Deluca."

"Don't be sorry. Just be at your desk."

***

At home, Ben finds Ana on the couch in their living room with the glow of her cell phone illuminating her face. Her finger flicks up slowly as she swipes again and again. "Hey," she says flatly without looking up, still wearing her workout clothes from yoga.

"Hey." He loosens his tie and slips out of his jacket, hanging it over the back of an armchair. Their housekeeper, Flora, hustles toward him with a warm smile marked with deep lines in the corners of her eyes.

"Good evening, Mr. Deluca," she says sweetly, emphasizing every syllable against her accent. She reminds him of his mother before she got sick, only instead of Ben taking care of her, Flora takes care of him.

If Ana wasn't home, Flora would give him a warm hug and a kiss on the cheek, but instead she shoves her tan, wrinkled hands into the pockets of her apron and smiles at him before taking his jacket from the chair. "Would you like to sit for dinner?"

He looks to Ana. "Babe?"

"I already ate," Ana says, not bothering to lift her gaze.

Nodding to Flora, he heads toward the dining room and leaves Ana to continue her doom scroll. A place setting is waiting at one end of their long ebony dining table, where Ben sits and waits to be served. The room is dim, lit only from the warm light of a crystal chandelier. Flora closes the long, silk curtains.

"¿Cómo te fue hoy, mijo?" she whispers to him in Spanish. *How was your day, my son?*

Ana doesn't like it when they speak to each other in Spanish. She says it feels like they are plotting against her or something. Usually, Flora is just checking in on him. They keep their voices low as she sets his plate in front of him.

"Sí, todo bien, Doña Flora. ¿ Y tú, cómo te fue?" *Yes, everything's fine, Ms. Flora. How was your day?*

"Tranquilo." *Quiet.*

Watching with anticipation, she affectionately brushes her hand against his back and awaits his reaction with a broad smile and held breath. Not wanting to make her wait, he brings the silver utensil to his mouth and gets a full bite. "Mmm, muy rico." *Very good.*

Flora lets out a content sigh and pats him on the back before leaving him alone to eat.

Later that night, he walks down a long hallway to their private gym. On the mat, he crouches and bends so his arms

hang down like an ape. Gripping a metal bar with three-hundred-pounds of iron, he raises his hips and digs in his heels, then straightens himself with a guttural grunt. The bar quivers slightly with each rep, demanding a steady grip that challenges his hands and forearms.

He repeats his lifts until his legs threaten to give out. After, he looks at himself in the mirror. For a moment, the skinny kid in second-hand clothes looks back and a familiar ache radiates within him. Grabbing his shirt by its collar, he pulls it over his head. His deltoids, pectorals, and biceps twitch and contract as he flexes. *Hmm.* Patting his stomach, he thinks it could use a little more definition.

Elyse seemed to like what he was working with. He made her blush. It's been a while since he'd done that. Maybe it's been a while since he'd noticed.

It's late. With a sore back, he trots up the stairs to the master bathroom, peeling off his workout clothes and letting them land on the floor. The glass and stone shower quickly fills with steam as he stands under the warm jets, pressure washing off the day.

One of his good friends in New York is a creative director at First Robin marketing agency, and he remembers him saying something about an organic cosmetics brand they signed recently. Organics. Plants. Elyse would make a great brand ambassador. It could set her up with some recurring revenue. But he can't justify flying her out to New York for a job that will pay next to nothing. Plus, she's green and kind of a nervous wreck. Sending her out there alone could be a disaster. Unless...

Eddie Sanz. One of his big earners in New York. Maybe call it a client visit and expense it. Go with her. That could work. He stops himself. *You're not even sure you'll ever hear from her again.* Thinking about what she said—skipping town—makes him smile.

Ben turns off the water and steps out onto a plush Egyptian cotton bathmat. He reaches for a fluffy white towel hanging beside the stall, drying off before wrapping it around his waist. Walking into the bedroom, he finds Ana in bed, engrossed in her phone.

With her thick, black glasses perched on her nose, she scrolls intently, her blonde hair pulled back. "That woman you met at Stella's party, what's her name again?"

"Elyse Santiago. Why?" he asks, a hint of suspicion in his voice. He remembers Ana asking who he was talking to that day and now he regrets telling her.

Ana's curiosity seems piqued. "She's strange, don't you think?" She already has Elyse's YouTube pulled up and shows Ben a video of her, hands buried in the soil. Her sweet, ethereal voice plays as he steps into his pajama pants, casually hoisting them up around his waist and tying the drawstring.

"Invasive plants like these are the lonely wanderers of the botanical world," Elyse says. A gloved hand holds up a complex root system. "They're swept into new environments from distant places, driven by their quest to survive."

Listening to her, Ben can't help but smile. He quickly hides it before Ana can see. "She's unique," he admits.

"I wonder why Stella begged you to help her."

He doesn't remember her begging per se. "Apparently, they're very close. I think Stella might have been it for her out here. Now that she's gone, I kinda feel bad for the girl. Maybe you can take her to yoga with you or something. She seemed like she could use a friend."

Ana wrinkles her nose, and a small burst of laughter escapes her lips. "Yoga? With her? You can't be serious."

"Don't be like that." He slips into bed and punches a pillow before resting into it. His body relaxes and he hums into his down feather comforter's soft embrace.

Ana's glasses click against the end table, and she turns off her light. "As much as you complain about depending on Daddy, if it wasn't for his money, you wouldn't have the luxury of wasting your time doing free favors for everyone."

Hearing the words *Daddy* and *money* in the same sentence makes him grind his teeth and his muscles tense. It's not unusual for Ben to develop new talent. Although Elyse claims she doesn't have any, Stella insisted she does. Maybe she's just shy. Lacking in self-confidence. Either way, he promised to try and that's what he intends to do. Charles King is plenty rich. If some of the financial comfort Ben and Ana enjoy can subsidize a little help for those in need from time to time, so what?

He makes his voice diplomatic. "Fine. I'm a hypocrite. Is that what you want to hear?"

"Yes. Thank you."

"Goodnight," Ben says, reaching over to pull her toward him, but she pushes him away. He breathes hard in frustration. "What's wrong?"

Turning over theatrically, she glares at him. "You disappear all night and suddenly decide to notice me now?"

"Are you kidding? You were glued to your phone. You could have had dinner with me, but you chose not to."

Sitting up, she turns on the light. "You always come home late. Should I starve waiting for you?"

"That's not what I'm saying. It's just that when I leave early you worry I'm not working hard enough."

Ana's laugh drips with condescension. "Your paycheck? It's hardly a drop in our bucket. If you quit tomorrow, we'd be just fine."

There it is. He doesn't matter. He's insignificant. She knows all the right buttons to push, all his insecurities. The things he wants to say are unkind so he bites his tongue. "Fine. Sorry I asked."

Rolling over, he settles onto his back. Just as he closes his eyes and starts to relax, her fist crashes into his gut like a hammer. His breath is driven out, a pained gasp escaping his lips. Eyes wide in a mix of pain and surprise, he struggles to draw a full breath.

"What the fuck's the matter with you?" He jumps out of bed and tucks a pillow under his arm. "Jesus, Ana. Control yourself."

"Where do you think you're going?"

"I'm sleeping in my office. Don't follow me."

Chapter Six

There's something satisfying about pushing the entrance doors to the King office and being met with the resistance of a lock. It's Wednesday morning and Ben is the first one in. He'd left home early, hoping to avoid Ana. She'd either be remorseful and apologize, or be so worked up about him sleeping in his office, they'd get into a fight and she'd take another swing at him. He wasn't going to stick around to find out which it was.

The rising sun casts a golden glow over the horizon as he makes his way to his desk. He checks his emails. There's an eSignature confirmation. Elyse signed. A rush of excitement surges through him. He's never been so eager to make exactly no money at all.

What time is it in New York? Glancing at his watch, he adds three hours—nine-thirty. He picks up the handset of his desk phone and dials his buddy Mateus.

"*¿Asere, que bola?*" Mateus answers. *What's up, dude?* His voice booms with enthusiasm.

"Hey, listen, you were telling me about that organic cosmetics brand?"

"EcoFX?"

"Yeah. I have someone who would be perfect. I'm texting you her Instagram. She's beautiful, she's got over a hundred thousand followers, and we've got projects on deck to lift those numbers quickly. Her whole brand is focused on the earth and nature. She was made for this campaign." As he speaks, he pulls up Elyse on his phone and sends her profile to Mateus.

When he gets it, Mateus lets out a long, low whistle—he's impressed. "Your timing is perfect because they ordered some work, and they want to focus on social media. We haven't scheduled a shoot date. When's she available?"

He takes a shot in the dark. "Whenever you need her."

"She's in New York?"

"LA."

"You know this is going to pay like three thousand, tops. Right?"

Ben rubs his face. Why is he doing this again? "I have to insist on six. But I guarantee once your client sees her, they'll want her as a brand ambassador. There's a lot we can do on social media from LA afterward. Plus, I'll probably see a few clients while I'm out there."

"Oh," Mateus says with a mix of surprise and playful suspicion. "You're coming too, *papi chulo*?" *Loverboy.*

Ben chuckles. "Fuck off. It's just business."

"If you say so. Should I expect a visit?"

"Yeah, we'll grab a drink or something."

After they hang up, Ben is energized. He hopes she's ready for this. A simple photo shoot. She'll be fine.

Hmm.

Staring at his phone, a sinking feeling sets in. It is a long way to go for very little money. Does he truly want to help her, or is this about him too? He can't ignore the exhilarating prospect of putting thousands of miles between himself and Ana, even if just for a few days. Is he doing this to help Elyse, or is he using her as an excuse to escape?

It can be both, he decides. An Ana detox to restore a bit of his spirit in a familiar place, while doing a good deed along the way.

The sound of Janine dropping her bag on her desk steals his attention. "Janine."

"Coming, Mr. Deluca."

Her sensible loafers shuffle across the gray and charcoal commercial carpeting in his office. Notebook in hand, she stands at the ready. At his desk, eyes closed, he presses his fingers to his temple like he's suffering a migraine or trying to communicate with a spirit in the afterlife.

"Tell Kieran Hines to send over some dates for a shoot. Elyse is going to model for him, but not for pay, for headshots. Find out if he's good with that, then schedule the session with Elyse. Also, First Robin is going to be in touch with dates on a New York shoot for her, and I'll need you to book travel and hotel for us. While I'm there, I want to see Eddie Sanz if possible, so call him once we get the dates and see if he's free for dinner."

She's scribbling fast as he whips through his demands. "Yes, sir. Got it. I'll circle back with the dates once I've updated your calendar."

"Good." As she scurries to her desk, he has another thought. "Janine."

Returning to his desk, she waits. His voice softens. "Don't tell anyone I'm flying out with Elyse. It's not anything untoward,

it's just that we're not making any money doing this. It's kind of a personal favor for a friend, and I don't want to have to explain to anyone. Okay?"

She shrugs like she couldn't care less. "Yeah, okay. I won't say anything."

"Good. Close the door on your way out."

The morning is spent on the phone pimping out clients and massaging egos. At lunch, a Caesar salad sits mostly untouched amidst a barrage of emails. A knock disrupts his focus. Red hair appears above the frosted strip on his office door. "Come in."

"Sorry to bother you. Kieran is fine with doing headshots, but he's working out of Mojave for the body paint series so she'd have to meet him out there."

"Mojave? Like the desert?" Ben asks incredulously.

"Yes, sir. It's about four hours from here."

"Jesus Christ." Pausing, he looks out the window, scanning the view of the city skyline. "Elyse doesn't drive, so clear my schedule that day."

"He said he's free next Wednesday the twenty-sixth," she says, scanning his calendar. "You have a dinner reservation with your wife at Providence at seven that night. Do you want me to cancel it?"

"No, hold on a second."

Considering the unpredictable duration of shoots, he works out the logistics. If he leaves at three a.m. and gets there by seven, maybe he can make it back in time. It doesn't make sense, but he can't resist the urge to help her, even if it means going against his better judgment.

"See if he can do another day. If he can't, move the dinner to eight and tell Kieran we'll be there early as fuck."

"You got it. Also, you asked me to remind you about your two o'clock tee time with Mr. King."

Checking his watch—1:42—he nods. "Thank you." Standing up, he checks his pockets and takes a mental inventory. Pausing, he looks at Janine. "Did you say the body paint series?"

"Yes, sir."

Wonderful. They just met and already he's asking Elyse to do nudity. She's going to think he's a scumbag. "Alright." He starts toward the door. "Warn her she won't be wearing much. Make sure she's okay with it. Just...be gentle about it."

***

The Beverly Oaks Country Club's hilly greens stretch through canyons dotted with mansions under a cloudless sky. Chuck drives a golf cart down the fairway toward the tenth hole, wind mussing up his fluffy white hair that frames his abundant forehead. The motor whirs and he makes a sharp turn. Ben grips on to the grab handle and holds his breath to brace for impact, but it never comes.

Chuck is telling Ben about the projects his production company are working on. "This woman needs to be beautiful, feminine. The character is some kind of Latina. You know." Glancing at the tan skin of Ben's arms and the downy of dark hair exposed by the short sleeves of his black golf polo he asks, "You're Puerto Rican or Mexican or something, right?"

"Cuban," Ben says dryly. He's only been married to Chuck's daughter for five years. Why bother to remember a detail like that?

"Yes, that too."

The brakes squeal and the cart jerks to a stop. Ben is already reaching for his phone. "I know someone who would be perfect." Finding his favorite video of Elyse, he passes the phone to Chuck, who lifts his glasses from where they hang around his neck to get a better look.

Peering over Chuck's shoulder, Ben watches Elyse in her garden. The sun is hitting her cheekbones just right. "These delicate flowers have a sweet scent but contain a deadly poison." Her nose grazes the petals of a flower. Taking a deep breath, she closes her eyes, a serene smile spreading across her face. When she turns to face the camera, her amber eyes catch the light and they glitter. "Isn't it fascinating how something so beautiful can also be so dangerous?"

If she extended her hand, surely a bluebird would be compelled to perch on her finger. Chuck's expression briefly softens as he watches the video, before fading back into his usual gruff demeanor. "Is she a botanist or something?"

Ben chuckles, his gaze lingering on the video for a moment longer, a subtle smile tugging at the corners of his mouth. "It's a gardening account. She teaches life lessons or whatever, but just look at the comments."

Pressing the little speech bubble, Chuck scans the responses filled with fire emojis, kissy faces and hearts. *You are so beautiful. Wow. Are you real? Bellisima! Very pretty intelligent girl. You have a beautiful smile.*

"She's beautiful, but can she act?"

"She's an excellent actress." There isn't a hint of doubt in his voice. Expanding on client talents comes with the territory. It's not lying, it's advocacy. "She's got a real talent for making the ordinary seem magical."

Chuck snorts at Ben's response. "Magical, huh?" A lawnmower buzzes faintly in the distance as he steps to the tee. The smell of freshly cut grass wafts in the air. He seems to think it over before turning to Ben. "Alright. Set up a meeting." His phone starts to buzz. "Hold on a sec."

"You can't take that," Ben says, but it's too late.

Chuck is already shouting into his phone. Ben looks around. It's empty enough to avoid an awkward confrontation with the

45

club staff, though it's doubtful anyone would have the balls to tell Chuck to get off his phone anyway.

"Sorry about that. Ana's planning my retirement party, and she can't make a single decision without calling me first."

Taken aback, Ben pauses and repeats Chuck's words in his head to make sure he heard correctly. "You're retiring?"

"Yes. At the end of the year. I thought I told you."

Tugging on his gloves, Ben shakes his head. "No, this is the first I've heard." Settling into position, he swings. The club slices through the air with a *whush* and his eyes follow the ball. It cuts through the warm air and hits a tree with a hollow *tock* before landing in the brown mulch below. *Shit.* "Where will that leave things at King?"

Chuck leans over to him and squeezes his shoulder. "Don't start licking your chops yet, son. Partnerships are earned not given."

Asshole. That's not what he meant. Any dream he had of becoming a partner was crushed years ago. Deep down he knew he lacked the upbringing and cultural capital they wanted.

The old guard spoke in a language that a younger Ben was desperate to master. Despite his meticulous efforts—his polished words, tailored attire, club memberships, and presence at every key event—he still caught that lingering glance from them, that split-second too long reminder of his otherness. Ana insisted it was just his imagination, but Ben had long since resigned himself to the reality.

"I don't expect you to give me anything, Chuck."

Chuck takes a few practice swings and stares off into the distance, lost in a thought, then turns to Ben. "How'd you find this girl?"

"Stella introduced us."

Chuck's face turns sour. "I don't know about that one. One day Andrew is doing triathlons as a hobby, the next he dies of a heart attack. Suddenly, Stella is a wealthy widow."

What is he suggesting? Stella is a good person. Sure, her tactics were a little dubious at times, but that's what it takes to succeed in this town. It doesn't make her a killer. "Come on. You really think Stella had something to do with that?"

Chuck smirks and nods, satisfied with himself. "I'm never wrong about these things."

Chapter Seven

"Nude?" Elyse echoes back.

"Technically, you'll be covered in paint." Janine clears her throat. "It's artistic."

With a sardonic laugh, Elyse paces the room, cell phone in hand. Anxiety wears down the skin inside her mouth where she's been chewing, thinking about the men in her comments who ask her if she's starting an OnlyFans when she posts fully clothed. If she poses nude, she can only imagine the things her followers would say.

"The sessions are private—there's no audience, just you and him. Maybe an assistant." The drone of the King office chatter bustles in the background. "Oh," Janine remembers, "and Mr. Deluca will be there."

I bet he will. "Can you tell him I want to talk about this, please?"

After hanging up, George's venomous voice slithers into her ear. *Did you think you were more than just a piece of prime rib for those men to feed on? When you're exposed out there, do you think they'll finally see the darkness in you? It's only a matter of time until the whole world knows what you really are.*

Distraught, Elyse tries to shake off the haunting words, but her breath becomes erratic. *Ben seems so caring and trustworthy. You trusted me once too, didn't you? Boy, Ben moves fast. It was months before I had you out of your clothes.*

Taking deep breaths, she reminds herself Stella wouldn't introduce her to a creep. She must be overreacting, she tells herself. But she can't seem to relax. A thick nausea beleaguers her, consuming every thought.

That night, Elyse lies in bed envisioning herself out in the desert, naked, with strange men leering. Come morning, she finds her nightshirt drenched in sweat. There's no way she can go through with this.

Elyse waits at Little Havana, a Cuban cafe with comfort food she hopes will soften the blow of her impending breakup with Ben's services. Sweaty palms crumple the ochre paper of an envelope in her lap. She plans to return the cash inside to Ben instead of paying her past-due power bill with it, which is what she really wants to do.

It's crowded. Walls painted in avocado and mango hues showcase illustrations of Cuba. Palm trees in big plastic pots divide the small dining room from the bar. Upon Ben's arrival, his jacket finds its place on the back of his chair, and he rolls his shirt sleeves up neatly. A swift peck on her cheek serves as his greeting. Settling down opposite her, he catches the unease in her eyes and a flash of concern crosses his face. "What's wrong?"

Taking a moment to gather her courage, she recites her prepared remarks. "Thank you for meeting with me. I asked you here to let you know that I'm sorry, but I can't do this." Her hands tremble as she slides the manilla envelope across the table.

"What's this?"

"The money for acting classes. I'm sorry. I just don't think this is for me."

Ben leans back and a deep audible sigh escapes him. The slight clearing of his throat and twitch of his jaw suggest he's displeased. Elyse can't be sure if he's upset with her, with Janine or himself, but watching him contain his frustration makes her want to fold into herself, burrow deep into the earth.

With a measured voice, he finally says, "It's okay." Drawing closer, he assures her. "I'm not going to force you to do anything you don't want to do, but I think you should keep an open mind here. Kieran's a very talented artist. Have you seen the rest of the series?"

The truth is, once she heard the word *nude*, she'd written the whole thing off. "No."

Ben lifts his phone, thumbing through something briefly. "It's really something special. Here," he offers, passing her his iPhone.

Kieran's account features photographs, mostly of beautiful women wearing only elaborate and colorful body paint, taken in interesting locations—a warehouse, the red oak forest, on the water. They're not just tasteful, they're truly awe inspiring. The women's nakedness is the least interesting thing about the photos.

Returning his phone, she notices his eyes fixed on her, cautiously assessing her reaction. "If you don't want to be a part of this, we'll find another solution. But don't quit," he pleads. "You've got something special, Elyse."

Picking at her cuticle, the chatter of the room seems louder.

He presses on. "You know, I met with a film producer yesterday, and he fell in love with you after watching just one video."

"Really?"

"Yeah, really," Ben says, a glint in his eye. "He was so impressed, he said he wants to meet with you. I think you should give this a shot." As he says it, he slides the money back to her.

Looking at it, and then at him, she bites her lip. "I don't know."

"Do you know the kind of money these guys would pay someone like you, someone with a built-in following?"

The word *money* draws her attention, and she can't help but feel a surge of excitement. Material possessions don't really do it for her. The fewer things that anchor her to a place, the better. But choosing what bills to pay every month, surviving off the generosity of others, it's soul sucking. All Elyse wants is to stand on her own. Not just survive, but thrive.

A spark lights up Ben's eyes, clearly catching the intrigue in her expression. Closing the gap between them, the weight of the moment deepens his gaze. His voice drops to a conspiratorial whisper. "I promise you, Elyse. You do this shoot, you're doubling your followers. No doubt in my mind. With that much clout, do you know how much money we could get you for one sponsored post? Brands are going to beg you to promote them. And that's only the beginning. We keep up that momentum, and you could launch your own lines—gardening supplies, workshops, books. You name it." Softening, his dark eyes gleam at her through thick lashes black as midnight. "You'll make so much money, you'll need to hire someone to count it all."

Taking a pause for effect, he leans back and lets his words sink in, gives her space to consider. But his eyes, deep and persuasive, never let her go. An unexpected jolt of confidence rushes through her. Maybe she should give it another try. She nods, covering the envelope with her hand. "Okay."

A grin slowly spreads across his face. "This is where it starts. Just you wait."

***

An old man approaches and speaks to them in Spanish. Ben talks to the man in a rapid-fire exchange, and Elyse recognizes just enough to understand he's ordered them shots of *aguardiente* to celebrate.

When they arrive, he raises his glass. "To making you rich."

The sound of mambo loudly pours in from the patio as they throw the shots back together, and the nostalgic taste of spicy licorice coats her tongue. Ben squints a little as the sharpness hits him, rubbing his chest. "I just remembered why I stopped drinking this shit."

Couples are dancing outside. Looking around the restaurant, Ben seems at ease. "Nice choice."

"I love this place. Makes me miss Miami."

"What do you miss about it?"

Hmm. Now that she's challenged to come up with an explanation, there aren't many reasons she can recall. Nothing that's easy to articulate at least. It'd be so easy to say friends or family, but that wasn't it. Maybe she'd romanticized it, but no matter how many strange places she found herself shuffled in and out of with a garbage bag filled with her things, her city was always a constant.

"It just felt like home, I guess. I could go anywhere and think of a memory or a story attached to something— streets, houses. Everything out here is just...empty. It feels kind of lonely."

"I know what you mean. I felt like that a lot when I left New York. I still do, sometimes."

"Lonely?"

"Yeah."

"Well, you have Ana."

A moment of surprise flits across his face and a crease forms in his brow at the sound of her name. "I do have Ana," he says as he straightens out a napkin. "What about you? Do you have anyone special in your life?"

She pushes a glistening piece of *platano maduro* back and forth with a fork. It catches a few black grains of rice as it goes. "No," she says with a laugh. "I'm bad at dating. I gave up."

"Well how do you expect to meet someone?"

"I dunno." She shrugs. "How'd you meet your wife?"

"Her father was kind of a mentor. I ended up at King right out of law school. Ana and I met at an event." Trailing off, his finger absentmindedly traces the rim of his glass.

Sunlight through a window casts long shadows on the terracotta floor, bathing him in light as he loses himself in a wistful memory. They're close enough that she can smell his cologne, something citrusy mixed with something that's just him. Inhaling it, a warm effervescence rises in her, and she can't be sure if it's the drinks or Ben's company that makes her giddy.

"For me, it was easy. She was beautiful, smart," he continues. "I figure maybe there was some novelty in dating a guy like me, Bronx-bred, growing up sheltered like she did." His fingers brush the back of his neck and he takes a deep breath. "It was different back then." The murmur of people speaking Spanish in the background fill Ben's long, distant pause. A blink breaks his trance, and he looks a little embarrassed for oversharing.

Elyse tries to lighten the mood. "Maybe I'll meet a handsome Uber driver."

With a playful tilt of his beer, he suggests, "You could meet a guy in your acting class."

"Maybe."

Winking, he motions to the waiter. The sounds of congas and piano join forces with the liquor, and Elyse starts to sway to the music. Ben orders another round.

Staring at the patio, he taps the table to the drum's beat, then turns to her with a sly smile. "You know how to dance?"

The question makes her nerves flare, and she shakes her head. "Do you?"

Rising from the table, he offers her his hand in response.

"No way. This was supposed to be a business lunch," she protests.

Tilting his head, he gives her a pouting look and joins his hands in a prayer pose. "Just one song. I need a dance partner."

Panic sets in instantly. Though she's not nearly drunk enough for this, she can't resist his adorable pleading expression. Quickly finishing her beer, she follows him to the patio. Standing up, the weight of her intoxication becomes evident, causing her balance to falter slightly.

They navigate through the doors to a spot just for them. As Ben prepares to lead her into position, she hesitates. "I don't remember what to do."

Gently, he raises her hand to rest on his brawny shoulder. Their fingers interlock, his hand engulfing hers, while his other hand finds a spot on the small of her back. Watching his footwork, Elyse struggles with the timing, either lagging behind or moving too soon with each step.

"Relax. Hear that?" he asks, patting her back to the beat. "That's the conga." His rich, deep voice is at her ear. The heat of his mouth grazes the hair follicles near her temple and every cell in her body stands at attention.

Focus. The beat is hidden between layers of trumpets and the syncopated rhythm of the piano, but she finds it. Letting each fall of his hand guide her, she takes a deep breath and nods in confirmation. They start to dance in step.

"See. You remember."

With confidence, he moves to the rhythm of the music. Somehow, his strong hands are surprising in their gentleness, sliding down her waist and hips. As he directs her movements,

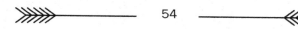

sparks of sensation shoot through her. In his arms, she's fragile, and yet, she's never felt more safe. It's as if nothing could harm her as long as she's near him.

The clang of the cowbell and tempo of the piano come to a crescendo. Then, it's over. Elyse takes a bow and Ben playfully hoots and claps for her.

The song changes, and he pulls her back into starting position before they find the rhythm again. They dance and drink, their table filling with empty glasses and bottles until the afternoon light begins to fade. On their last break, she orders shots of tequila.

"I can't. I need to sober up," Ben insists, but the shots arrive quickly, and Elyse downs them both without a moment of hesitation. Soon, everything becomes a haze. One moment they're talking and the next, he's shaking her awake where she'd passed out on her barstool. "Hey, Elyse. Look at me. Can you walk?"

"Walk?" Planting her feet proves difficult, as they seem encased in lead. The room spins into a blur. Offering his shoulders for support, he encourages her to hold on. Clinging to him, her fingers tighten around the fabric of his shirt, relying on his sturdiness to stay upright.

"Looks like we found your limit." As he crouches, his left forearm slides under her knees, ready to lift her.

Pressing her face against the crook of his neck, she mumbles, "Mmm, you smell so good."

His chuckle, rich and resonant, vibrates against her. "That's the second time you've said that."

"It is?"

The cool air whips around her until she hears the low *thunk* of a car door unlocking and takes in the familiar scent of leather. After he tucks her into the passenger seat, silence surrounds her, interrupted only when he leans over to fasten her seat belt.

A gentle shake from Ben's hand on her arm awakens her. "You're home," he says softly.

Outside, the world appears as a whirlwind, reminiscent of a ship tossed in a storm. Nausea overtakes her just before the gate, resulting in her stomach contents spilling onto the grass by the porch.

Crouching beside her, he asks, "You okay?"

"Mmm...'m okay, 'm okay."

Using Ben for support, they shuffle toward the door. "Where are your keys?"

She gags. "Dunno."

After a bit of cursing and rummaging in her purse, the sound of jangling keys and a grunt precedes the embrace of cool air-conditioning against her skin.

Looking around the empty space, he asks, "You just move in?" Before she can answer, she rushes to the downstairs bathroom, heaving into the toilet.

"Jesus, Elyse," he says from beside her, his voice filled with concern. As he strokes her back for comfort, he asks, "Do you have any water, juice, anything? You're gonna dehydrate yourself."

Before she can respond, another bout of nausea overtakes her and Ben disappears outside.

From the kitchen, the fridge door opens. "Alright." His voice carries from the other room. "We have every condiment known to man, a bottle of wine, and a jar of coffee. This is the saddest fridge I've ever seen in my life." The door clicks shut. "Stay put. I'm going to the store."

As the bathroom tile cools her, the distant sound of the door shutting reaches her ears. Eyes heavy, she closes them only for a moment, then stirs when a gentle shake interrupts her. The sight of a plastic shopping bag at Ben's feet, replete with snacks and sports drinks, welcomes her as she opens her eyes.

"Mm," she murmurs, noticing the numbness in her arm from resting on it. As she sits up, dizziness overwhelms her.

"Drink this," he advises, offering an open bottle of electrolyte drink. "It'll help."

The salty cherry flavor of the drink is off-putting. After a few reluctant swallows, she finds the room shifting.

"Let's get you to bed." He helps her up, then guides her upstairs with a supporting arm around her waist. Upon reaching her room, a brief pause ensues as Ben's gaze settles on the mattress, followed by a pensive hum. He then gently lays her down, removing her shoes in the process. Crawling beside her, he asks, "How do you feel?"

A playful tug on his shirt brings him closer, their faces inches apart, close enough to feel each other's breath.

"You're very drunk," he notes, eliciting a round of giggles from her.

"Stay the night," she pleads softly.

A restrained chuckle and a groan reserved for suffering painful temptations escapes him. "I can't."

"Don't you think I'm pretty?"

"I think you're beautiful." With a gentle touch, he brushes a stray strand of hair off her face and presses a kiss on her forehead. "Goodnight, Elyse."

Darkness engulfs her as her eyes close.

When she wakes, her room is an intolerable temperature and the sun is offensively bright. A pain radiates from deep in her brain and throbs with each heartbeat. A trash can from the bathroom sits beside her mattress on the floor. Ben must have left it there. Memories from the night flood back and weigh on her, pulsing with an unbearable ache.

Thinking of the way she flirted with him makes her want to suffocate herself with a pillow. All night, any time he'd say something cute or smile a gorgeous smile that made her heart swell ten sizes, she'd zero in on his wedding ring and bite the inside of her lip. It was a crude form of psychological conditioning, like knocking a dog on the nose with a rolled-up newspaper. It didn't work.

He could have left her there at the restaurant or dropped her off at her doorstep, but he stayed and worried about her hydration before tucking her into bed.

Phone held overhead, she lies on her back and pulls up a Google search. *Ana King*. Numerous articles appear.

Hollywood Heiress Ana King Net Worth; A-List Agency Head's Daughter Celebrates 28th Birthday. There's a photo of Ana and Ben at an event, her on his arm and him laughing. *Gosh*. She's so beautiful. Like an honest-to-goodness princess. They look so happy together. Everything she reads paints an idyllic picture of Ben's life.

Elyse clicks on the article about net worth and reads the paragraphs set between photos of the Kings' sprawling house in Los Angeles.

The King family fortune is enormous —around $2.5 billion, according to Reuters. Ana's grandfather, Bertrand King, was an American film producer and co-founder of King Pictures, which sold to Picturesque in 2003 for $1 billion. When King died at age 88 from congestive heart failure, his estate was divided equally between his two sons, Charles and Joseph. The brothers founded King Management in Los Angeles, estimated to be worth $5 billion.

It's so much money, she laughs out loud. The laughter fades to stinging regret thinking how she'd made such a fool of herself. *Oh God*. She puts her phone aside, deliberately placing it on the floor face down.

Only a cruel universe would dangle Ben in front of her yet make him Ana's. The world is merciless. Predators only eat what they kill. Plants suffocate their competition. Survival of the

fittest demands that only the traits best suited to their environment survive. This is Los Angeles. Ana is gorgeous, connected and filthy rich. Elyse never stood a chance.

And yet, happily married men don't dance all afternoon with women they just met. They certainly don't carry them out of a bar like a fireman carries someone out of a burning building and plant a gentle kiss on their forehead.

It was different back then, he said. What did that mean?

Chapter Eight

A flying object makes contact with Ben's forehead. It's hard and heavy. He's barely made it through the front door when it ricochets off and explodes with a high-pitched, brittle sound against the floor.

"*Fuck*! What was that?" He presses his hand against the pain and looks at the mess on the ground. The remnants of a gold label and shattered glass sit in a puddle of dark liquid. The sharp smell of alcohol fills the air.

Ana gets in his face. "Where were you?"

Mustering all his strength not to retaliate, he touches the tender lump on his forehead and winces in pain. Blood wets his fingers. *Goddamit, Ana.*

"You can't just throw shit at me whenever you get angry." Retreating, he falls into an overstuffed armchair.

She sits across from him. "Explain yourself."

Pulling a monogrammed handkerchief from his pocket, he dabs at the blood. "I was out with a client. Drank a little too much. I needed to sober up. I didn't do anything wrong."

"A female client?"

"No."

"I don't believe you."

"Fuck this," he says and bolts to their bedroom. Familiar with the motions, he pulls out a suitcase and starts packing.

"Oh, here we go again. Ben is pretending to leave. What ever will I do?"

"Fuck you."

As soon as he says it, a slap cracks across his mouth like a whip. Grabbing her arms, he pins her against the wall. "Is this what you want? You want me to hurt you?" Bits of spit spray from his mouth. A vein throbs in his neck.

This might be the day he finally kills her and goes to prison for the rest of his life. With nothing left to live for, he'd march straight into the police station and confess. Everything, even his career, is hers, wrapped around her bony little finger. Though hurting her isn't truly within him, in moments like these, he wishes it were.

Her laughter begins softly, then escalates into a maniacal cackle, echoing around their bedroom. It's a familiar taunt, her way of stoking the flames. But he refuses to take the bait, turning away from her to continue packing. She grabs a fistful of hair on the back of his head and yanks.

Twisting around, he frees himself and grabs her. Rather than throw her against the wall, he shoves her onto the bed and walks away, leaving his suitcase unpacked. "Just keep it all."

In the garage, his key fob hangs on a hook. Grabbing it quickly, he slides into his car. There's no destination in mind. No

close friends in LA to confide in. Driving aimlessly, the thought of hurling himself off a cliff crosses his mind. He doesn't cry, not since the first dozen times he's done this. He's numb to it now.

Gazing at the gash on his forehead in the rearview mirror, a sharp pain makes him wince. A crust has formed, but the wound remains tender. "Fuck."

Ana's name flashes on the car stereo, and his display lights up.

"What?" he answers.

"Come home." Her voice quivers, sounding tearful.

Ben sighs at the exhausting predictability of it all. "Have you calmed down?"

"Yes. Please just come home."

"On my way."

Turning the car, a sense of defeat settles within him. This is how it goes time after time. What else can he do? She's one-hundred-twenty pounds soaking wet, and he's a man. It doesn't matter if Ana's attacks were wrong, illegal, immoral or unethical. Fights are won in court, and the King family resources know no limits. Ben would spend the rest of his life fighting a battle while struggling to survive.

When he gets inside, she's waiting for him, her face raw and swollen from crying. His clothes are put away and his suitcase is back in the closet. She strokes his forehead where the bottle left its mark and studies it with glossy eyes filled with remorse. "I'm so sorry."

"Please, Ana. I'm begging you. We can't keep doing this."

"I know. I was just so angry you didn't call."

"Come here." He pulls her into his arms. "I'm sorry."

***

Later that morning, the office buzzes with activity, and Ben tries not to look as shitty as he feels as he lumbers toward his office. Janine is at her desk and stands to follow him in.

This already. "What's up?"

"Kieran Hines can only do the twenty-sixth."

With a weary sigh, he falls into his chair and drags a hand down his face. "Whatever. Set it up. And I need you to have Carrie schedule time for Elyse and Chuck to meet on Seth's project."

"Okay. First Robin sent over dates. Do you want to schedule with Mr. King after you get back from New York?"

Shooting her a confused look, his fingers massage his temples in small circular motions. "I thought they wanted headshots?"

"I guess they didn't. They sent over the contract yesterday afternoon, but you never came back from lunch."

If she's judging him, she's doing a good job hiding it. "How much?"

She consults her notes. "Six thousand?" Her tone suggests it can't be right.

He nods emphatically, knowing full well she must think he's insane. "Good. Call Elyse and give her the info."

"Got it." She offers a playful salute before spinning back to her desk.

He's painted himself into a fine corner. A calendar full of unpaid quality time with his favorite wackadoo. Thinking of her sends a rush of warmth through him. It was a high price he paid, but last night was more fun than he'd had in a long time. If Elyse could hold her booze, it would have been a perfect night.

"Mr. King," Janine calls, rushing from her desk to intercept Chuck's stride to Ben's door. She's too slow. Her voice pulls him out of his daydream just as Chuck strolls inside. Though she hurries behind him, the door shuts, leaving her standing outside with only a halo of red curls visible through the strip of frosted glass.

Chuck yanks a chair in front of Ben's desk so hard it bounces on two legs. Once it settles, he sits down with a tense exhale and glares at Ben, letting him suffer for a moment in silence. "I trust you enjoyed yourself last night."

"Chuck," Ben says, palms out. "It was innocent. I was with a client." Before he can continue, Chuck interrupts.

"You realize I can see your calendar when you lie to my daughter about where you've been, don't you?"

"It wasn't a lie. She *is* a client. And nothing happened. She drank too much and—"

Chuck closes his eyes and holds up a hand as if he doesn't care to hear any more. "Perception, Ben. What you did, what you didn't do..." He shakes his head as if he's not interested in knowing either. "Ana called me beside herself."

Ben's shoulders slump and he winces, his chin falling into his hand. "I'm sorry. I should have called and let her know I was going to be late, but—"

"I built this firm with integrity and family values. If you're making a habit of being out with women into the early hours, it would be such a pity if people started to talk. And if they did, who would want to work with the man who betrayed my family's trust?"

Shifting uncomfortably in his seat, Ben's stomach twists tightly and a cold sweat breaks over his brow.

Chuck stands and hovers over his desk. "You know better than to harm what's mine. Don't you?"

"Yes, sir."

Chuck shoots Ben a chilling look, the kind a snake gives a rat before devouring it whole. "Good." He pats the surface of Ben's desk, dismissing himself, and leaves the office.

Alone inside the silent room, it's as if a bomb has gone off and Ben is stunned, suspended in the moment of detonation.

Rubbing his face, he takes a deep breath, feeling the tension leave his shoulders as he settles into his seat.

Through the intercom he calls a defeated, "Janine."

"Coming."

Creeping inside with a strained smile and her notebook, her gaze flits from his eyes to the gash on his forehead. "Yes?"

He clears his throat. "I need you to update my calendar."

"Sure thing. What should I update?"

"The appointments with Elyse," he says, his voice casual. Inside, his anxious mind rushes through images of the million ways this doesn't end well, and yet, he presses on.

Janine nods, a hint of a smile playing on her lips. "The ones we just talked about?"

"Yeah, those." Looking away, his attention falls to the surface of his desk, where he drags a finger across the glossy edge. "Could you rename them? Just call them...external meeting."

"Of course," she replies softly. There's a pause, filled only with the hum of the air conditioner and the low murmur of office chatter. "Is there anything else you'd like me to do?"

The morning's disastrous events replay in his memory for a moment. Ben hesitates, his throat dry. "I think that'll be it for now."

The way she lingers, it's as if she wants to say something more but she doesn't. When he's alone again, he stares out of his office window at the radiant skyline and takes an inventory of what's at stake.

All those people down there and their worries, shuffling from place to place. Fretting about money and success. Belonging. It's the life he led before Ana. Although he often feels like an imposter in this life, it's a far more manageable sensation while looking down from the twentieth floor.

He spends his days with people the world idolizes and goes home to a mansion in the hills. It's more than anything he ever imagined was attainable. To have a home, a career, a family, all once seemed so out of reach. It's not perfect, but even with Ana's volatile temper, his life is better than most. He's being an idiot spending time with Elyse.

That evening, he returns home intent on making things right. The house is quiet and he finds Ana in the den, AirPods tucked into her ears as she lies under a blanket. When she sees him, her eyes widen and she sits up. "My goodness, look who managed to find his way home at a reasonable hour."

A dull ache of self-loathing tightens around him as he settles next to her with a weary exhale. "I'm sorry."

Pressing her lips into a thin line, she extends an expectant hand. "Phone."

The mistrust in her demand is obvious. *Whatever*. Truly, he has nothing to hide. Maybe if he hadn't been out all night, she wouldn't have a reason not to trust him. Retrieving the phone from his pocket, he offers it to her. With expert precision, her thumb swiftly enters his password, pulling up his call and text history and searching for signs of a secret family or God only knows what.

Once her inspection ends, the phone is calmly placed on the coffee table in front of him. Taking it, he returns it to his pocket. She then plugs her AirPods back in and settles into the sofa. Ben's fingers tentatively touch her thigh, then brush the edge of the blanket she's draped in. He attempts to draw it back to come closer, but she evades his reach, wrapping the blanket tighter. With narrowed eyes pointed at him, she seemingly wills him to be struck dead.

"Alright, I'll leave you alone."

Rising, he ambles to his office, a sanctuary in this house. A space distinctly his. Rich woods and leather give the room a masculine ambiance. Behind a custom-made mahogany desk is a monochromatic print of the New York skyline at night. Glass shelves nearby showcase his treasured Yankees memorabilia—

a baseball autographed by Mickey Mantle and Yogi Berra; a framed Jorge Posada jersey; and the pride of his collection, a 2000 World Series bat signed by Derek Jeter and Doc Gooden.

That World Series marked the first ever showdown between the Yankees and Mets. The city pulsated with anticipation. Fresh from a fallout with his cousins in Queens, Ben had relocated to his aunt's place in the Bronx, right in the core of Yankees territory.

With his shitty luck, she only had one small television and the games were televised at the same time she watched her telenovelas. The last thing he wanted was to get kicked out of another house, so he swallowed his disappointment and did his chores dutifully while excited shouts and chants of neighbors vibrated through the apartment walls. He could have cried. Buying that piece of history felt like he'd recovered a stolen piece of his adolescence.

Now, he looks at these trinkets through the soft light and wonders when the fleeting joy of acquiring these things began to take the place of real happiness, of warmth and human connection. Lying there alone on his office sofa, his yearning for it tightens his throat and an ache spreads through him. It doesn't feel like a choice he made consciously, but rather, several small missteps led him astray until he found himself lost, far off the path he started on.

Feeling Elyse's gentle affection, the way she looked at him, he hadn't realized how long it'd been since he's felt desired, how much he'd missed it. He loads her YouTube channel on his phone, and when her face appears on the screen, his heart beats harder.

"This one sprouted up so tall almost overnight. Do you notice anything?" she says, focusing the camera on a patch of low, leafy plants hidden in the shadow of a tall stalk and broad leaves. "These little guys are fighting for sun." A garden glove is tugged off her hand and she touches the earth with her bare fingers. "It's cool here. Dark. If I don't do something, they'll wither away. On the outside, it might seem like nature is being cruel. But aren't we all fighting for a place in the light?"

Chapter Nine

"Un-fucking-believable," Ben mutters, glancing at his watch. It's pitch black and silent outside on Elyse's front porch. All his calls have gone to voicemail, and they're already running late. He bangs on the door, forcefully this time, and jabs the bell again.

Several minutes later, the bolt clicks and Elyse appears in the doorway. With her legs crossed and strands of messy hair breaking free from a ponytail, she looks a sight.

"I overslept," she groans, bouncing. "Hold on, I'm gonna pee my pants." Without another word, she rushes off and leaves the door ajar.

Stepping inside with a sigh of exasperation, Ben calls out, "Come on, Elyse. You knew about this." It resonates in the dark living room. Feeling the wall for a switch, he finds one and flips it. Nothing. "Did you lose power?" he shouts to her through the door, trying another switch.

From the bathroom, Elyse emerges, lighting a candle on the counter. The warm light illuminates her figure, dressed only in a T-shirt and panties. It's a side of her he's never seen before, and his eyes are momentarily drawn to the soft curve of her hip.

"I mixed up the due dates on the bill. I thought I had more time. My phone died and my alarm didn't go off."

A moment ago, he was ready to lash out. Yet as he steps closer, his agitation ebbs and a wave of pity swells. "Hey," he says, brushing a gentle touch against her arm. "Why didn't you use the money I gave you?"

Elyse looks up at him, her gold eyes shining in the candlelight. "Because I promised I'd use it for classes." Her voice is small and defeated.

It flattens him. In fact, she may have actually broken his heart. He takes a deep breath and reaches out to smooth her messy hair. "Don't worry," he says, trying to offer her some reassurance. "We'll figure something out, okay?"

"Okay."

In a rush, she prepares herself, and soon they're on the road, facing a four-hour journey. Elyse succumbs to sleep shortly after they begin.

The sun rises but a haze of clouds thinly veil the sky and leave it drab. Everything around them blends into a wash of gray—dusty concrete, faded asphalt and piles of sand heaped beside the road. Low mountains peek through random strip malls in the distance as they whip past construction and clutches of palm trees.

When she wakes, Elyse seems different. Withdrawn. She looks out the window, lost in the world outside. Treading gently, he broaches the subject he suspects she's trying to avoid.

"What are you doing for money these days?"

"Just this. I'm looking for jobs but it's tough." Hesitating for a moment, she fidgets with her fingers. "I got fired from my last job."

He's afraid to ask, but he has to know. "For what?"

"Just some misunderstandings." A glint of humor fills her eyes, mouth twitching like she's trying to hold back a smile. Her mood seems to lighten. "You know those water machines that make water more alkaline?"

He nods.

Leaning back, she draws a deep breath. "Well, my boss wanted me to sell them. I'm pretty sure they were just filtered water fountains. Total scam." As she goes on, her sweet, ethereal voice takes on an unexpected edge. "Anyway, he'd give members this phony pH test and tell them their bodies were too acidic, which is complete nonsense. I told him he was an idiot and I wasn't selling his stupid machines."

Biting his lip, he suppresses a laugh. As adorable as her rant is, he can't encourage her flying off the handle on a client just because she disagrees with them. "You'll meet plenty of idiots in this business. You're going to have to learn to pick your battles."

Before she can reply, his phone starts to go off and Ana's name flashes on his display. A surge of panic hits him as he struggles to transfer the call to his phone, only for it to connect automatically through the car's handsfree system. "Shit," he mutters under his breath. The thought of Ana letting loose with Elyse listening makes his stomach sink. Raising a finger to his lips, he gestures for Elyse to stay silent. "Hey," he answers, trying to sound casual.

As they drive north, the outline of a mountain ridge grows more distinct. "You're in Lancaster?" Ana asks, though her tone suggests she's already aware. After making him activate location services on his phone, he knows she's watching.

"Uh, maybe. I don't know. Just following the GPS."

"Are you alone?"

Casting an apologetic glance at Elyse, he answers, "Yeah."

Elyse raises an eyebrow and fixes him with a curious expression. He shrugs and shakes his head slightly to let her know he'll explain later. There's a long pause, and he can hear Ana breathing on the other end.

"You left without saying goodbye."

"I know, I'm sorry. I didn't want to wake you. It's just a long drive and I was trying to beat traffic. I'll call you when I get there, okay? I need to focus on driving right now."

A hiss of irritation teems through the speakers. "Be careful."

"I will."

After the call ends, Ben shoots Elyse a sheepish glance. "Sorry about that." Rubbing the back of his neck, a tense sigh escapes him. "I didn't want to lie, but I didn't want her to get upset."

Nodding slowly, Elyse's tawny eyes widen slightly as if she's just learned something interesting. He already knows what she's thinking—Ana must have a good reason not to trust him around other women.

"Don't get me wrong," he preempts, taking his eyes off the road to gauge her expression. "I've always been faithful." The word brings an unexpected heat to his face, yet he can't seem to stop his confession. "She's just possessive, you know? Tracks me. Reads my texts," he adds, briefly lifting his phone for Elyse to see, emphasizing his point.

Elyse shifts in her seat and turns her body toward him. "You must have gotten into some trouble the other night, huh?"

He hesitates before managing a clipped, "Yeah."

"I'm sorry."

"Don't worry about it."

They're surrounded by clay-colored hills with patches of low green shrubs clotted together like cotton balls. She relaxes back

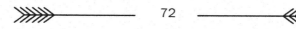

and frowns at them. "I've never been out here before. It's strange being in a place that looks so desperate for water like this. In Florida, it's either rainy or sunny. Sometimes both at the same time. You get sick of the green. The vegetation just grows and grows wild. Out here, it's just dust."

Grateful she's changed the subject, he goes along with it. "This is Death Valley, sweetheart. We're in the desert."

"Why would anyone live where nothing grows?"

"I don't know. I grew up in the city, so I guess it's kind of the same. It's just a different kind of life, I guess."

Letting her head roll back against the seat, she rests an elbow on the center console. "If the world was ending, I'd want to be somewhere I could survive on my own. In the desert, you'd starve or run out of water. In the city, people would tear each other to pieces. At least in the swamp you'd stand a chance."

"Mosquitos. Gators. None of that sounds bad to you?"

"You can burn sage and rosemary to keep mosquitos away. Gators don't bother you unless you're in their space. And they taste just like chicken."

Turning to her, he laughs. "You've eaten alligator?"

"It's a South Florida delicacy," she says, beaming.

"Are you some kind of a swamp person?"

"I'd like to think so. Didn't you learn any survival stuff as a kid?"

"Yeah, don't make eye contact with anyone on the train."

Picturing this ethereal creature growing right from the earth and emerging from the swamp with mystical powers to hypnotize perfectly intelligent men into behaving like total morons, he chuckles to himself. Looking over at her, he watches her gaze out at the barren landscape. The delicate contours of her face bathe in the soft light that filters through the car windows. In that moment, the tension that had clung to him since their rushed departure melts away and he finds an unexpected comfort in her presence.

Chapter Ten

They pull up to an RV parked off a long dirt road in the middle of nowhere. It's the first time Ben has visited Kieran out here. He's not sure this is a legal setup or who owns this stretch of land, but there's no one around for miles.

Elyse climbs up the stairs first. He watches her body move and how Kieran's face lights up when he sees her. Kieran is younger than Ben, maybe by ten years. Elyse's age. His arms, visible in his shabby black T-shirt, are covered in tattoos. The RV is at least forty feet long, and the black pearlescent exterior gleams in the sunlight. Ben is struck by the skunky smell that mixes with the stink of dirty laundry and cigarettes.

"Kieran, this is Elyse."

"I know," he says, leaning into a hug. "I started following you, girl. Got me learning about plants and shit."

Elyse's laugh is muffled against his shoulder. "I followed you too. Your work is amazing."

Pulling apart, Kieran stretches up to some overhead storage, retrieving some sketches done in colored pencil. Addressing Elyse, he explains the colorful design. "This might change a little based on the curves of your body." When he mentions her curves, Kieran places a hand on her hip and studies her for a moment before turning and pulling open a drawer. Reaching inside, he retrieves a sealed plastic package. "My models will sometimes wear these if they're not comfortable being fully nude."

Taking the flesh-toned silicon discs roughly three inches in diameter and stick-on, strapless panties in her hands, Elyse seems to hold her breath.

"You good?" Ben asks.

"Mm-hmm."

"Good. We'll give you some privacy to change then." He stands and waves at Kieran for him to follow.

There's no shade outside in the heat, and the sun beats down on them ruthlessly. Ben squints at Kieran and his greasy hair pulled up into a stupid bun. "She's not gonna fuck you, so maybe you should pump the brakes a little."

Kieran holds up his hands defensively with a cocky smile. "Hey, man. I'm just being friendly."

"Be less friendly."

Just then, Elyse calls out in distress from inside. "Ben!"

Oh no. Rushing inside, he finds her curled up on the upholstered bench seat like a pill bug, naked but for her silicon patches, her knees pressed to her shoulders with her arms wrapped tight around them. Her head is tucked down and she's trembling. Sitting beside her, he tries to make his voice sweet.

"Hey, what's the matter?"

When she looks at him, tears stream down her cheeks. "I'm sorry. I'm freaking out."

Wanting to comfort her, he hesitates, unsure of where to put his hands. Eventually, he gently strokes her hair, whispering, "There's no pressure here. If you want to go home, it's okay. You don't have to do this."

The words sound foreign to him as they leave his mouth. His pep talks don't usually offer quitting as the first available option, but she seems so fragile. Memories from Little Havana resurface—the slight tremor in Elyse's hands, the hesitation in her eyes, the subtle shifts in her body language. Each telling him more about her state of mind than her words ever could. All these silent cues spoke volumes about her unease, revealing her underlying fear.

Yet, Ben had bided his time, watching Elyse's every move, calculating, predicting. And when he'd sensed vulnerability, he went in for the kill. When she'd finally agreed, the thrill of victory had surged through him, stronger than any drug. But in its wake, guilt rises, sharp and unwelcome. He never should have made her do this.

The corners of her mouth turn down and her bottom lip quivers. "Are you going to be here the whole time?" With wide, tear-filled eyes and a voice tinged with desperation, she seeks reassurance.

God, she's so pretty like this. The longing in her eyes—a plea for comfort, for safety—does something to him.

"Yes, sweetheart, I'm not going anywhere."

"Hey, have some water," Kieran says and hands her a bottle. Ben hadn't noticed him come back in.

Elyse looks up at Kieran through wet lashes. "I'm so sorry."

"No, don't apologize. You're naked in the desert with some stranger who wants to paint all over your body. Sounds pretty weird to me too." He makes her laugh and she relaxes.

"Ready?" Kieran asks her.

"Yeah," she says. "I think so."

The bright sun shines through the RV's skylight, and when she stands, Ben can see all of her aside from the few inches covered with nude-colored patches. His gaze falls down her body and up again—her breasts, waist, hips and thighs form a lovely hourglass. Her sand-toned skin is radiant and flawless. For a moment, he forgets how to breathe, fighting every visceral instinct urging him to touch her.

Looking away, his thumbs pretend to be at work on his phone. *It's not anything you haven't seen before. Quit staring. You're going to make her uncomfortable, asshole.*

She stands very still as Kieran canvasses her body with a metal airbrush tool connected to a small tank of pigment. Painting goes on for hours, and when Kieran's done, she's a work of art. Ben's eyes follow the trails of paint that wind like climbing vines up and down her body, flaring into extravagant untamed blooms in vibrant shades.

Outside, the sun is high. An expanse of sand is littered with low, wheat-colored tufts and desert grass in pale-green hues. The camera drone lifts off the ground and remains suspended at points Kieran directs, as he clicks shot by shot. Elyse follows his commands—bending, turning, and arching her back across the terrain. Ben can't take his eyes off her. She's actually doing well.

After, Kieran shows Ben a few of the shots. "I'm planning on editing, but look how great these are." He pulls up a photo on his laptop. The light hits her bone structure just right and brightens the honeyed shades of her eyes, which somehow bear both tenderness and ferocity. His chest aches.

"Wow, Elyse. Look at you."

Kieran clicks through the photos. "These are good, but I'd like to try again when the sun is lower."

Looking at his watch, Ben confirms, "What's that, like another two-three hours?"

"Prolly more."

Well, shit. This whole day was ill conceived. It was obvious every step of the way, even as he was planning it, but he just kept going.

Elyse is sitting in the dinette booth and staring out the window. There is something about her that makes him want to do stupid things. Like standing here looking at her painted up like a goddess instead of getting in his car and driving southwest to Los Angeles.

After her vulnerable moment, he made her feel safe, promised he'd stay. And now he's thinking of leaving her alone in the desert with a man she doesn't know. The thought is untenable, and he expels it with a deep pained breath as he dials Ana. Pushing the call button, he closes his eyes and braces himself.

"I'm sorry. I'm not going to be home in time for dinner."

Ana's sighs into the phone, cold and weary. "I knew you'd disappoint me."

"I'm stuck in Mojave. I can't just leave. You know how this works."

"Stay there, then. Don't come home." The line goes dead.

Chapter Eleven

Elyse used to have a friend in high school named Celia whose dad was a cocaine cowboy and lived in a mansion on the canal. In their driveway, they had an RV just like this that made the perfect hook-up hideout—Celia with her boyfriend and Elyse with whoever Celia's boyfriend brought with him. Now, being in an RV just makes her think about sex.

Staring out into the desert through the dinette window, eating a granola bar, her tongue fights with bits of chewy dried cranberries that stick between her molars. Ben is in and out every few minutes on the phone. Kieran sits across from her and picks the label off a green glass beer bottle with his paint-stained fingernail.

"Ben seems very protective of you," he says.

"Mm-hmm."

"Have you met his wife?"

Elyse had been focusing on the wrapper of her granola bar crinkling between her knuckles. The word *wife* causes her to look up at him.

"No."

He leans in and whispers to her. "She's fucking psycho."

Her eyes widen with intrigue. "Really?"

"I went to one of their parties once. Really swank, full of fancy folks. I catch Ana absolutely losing it on some catering dude. Like, full-on meltdown. She chucked an entire tray of food at the poor guy. But the crazy bit? She's out in the main room, like five minutes later, flashing that big plastic smile and acting like nothing happened."

"Oh, wow." Ben said she was bad, but she had no idea.

He leans closer with a smirk and raises an eyebrow. "I'm pretty sure she beats him."

Beats him? She fights back the urge to laugh. Ben's like a brick wall. Thinking of Ana pushing him around is such a bizarre image, she wonders how it's even possible. "How do you know?"

"I don't. Not for sure. But I've heard things. People talk."

Does Stella know about this? Now that she thinks of it, she had noticed a cut on his forehead today but didn't think anything of it. Maybe that's the trouble she got him into.

"The whole family is fucked. Have you met Charles?"

"No, who's that?"

"Ana's father. He owns King. Biggest creep on the planet." Kieran pops open a window and pulls out a yellow box of American Spirit cigarettes. "I went out with Janine a couple of times, and she told me he takes meetings at hotels and spends his days getting jerked off by girls who want a part in a movie."

"Gross." She remembers Charles's photo on the King website— thinning white hair, gray skin like crepe paper and a

self-satisfied expression—and recoils at the thought. She heard that kind of thing happened sometimes, but Ben never made her feel anything less than safe.

Ben's return is announced by the squeal of the RV door. Kieran quickly perks up as Ben climbs up the steps.

"It's hot as hell out there," he says, crumpling into the beige, leather co-pilot seat that pivots toward the living space.

Kieran stands and opens a large stainless-steel fridge. "You want a cold beer?"

"Yes," Ben says, like he's never been more sure of anything in his life.

Kieran looks at her. "Elyse?"

"No, thanks."

If it wasn't for her prior bad behavior, she wouldn't be making a point to stay sober. Leaning behind the stainless-steel door, Kieran passes her a water. With a sly wink to Elyse, he marches up to Ben, handing him a beer. "What happened to your forehead?"

Looking away, Ben brings his fingers to the scab. A twinge of sympathy rises in her. It wasn't nice for Kieran to put him on the spot like that.

"A uh…" He covers the mouth of the beer with his hand and pries off the cap with his wedding ring. "I was pulling down a storage trunk from the attic and it slipped."

Kieran looks at Elyse with confirmation, but she averts her focus to the plastic bottle cap on the table. It slides back and forth, sticking slightly to the surface. Could the blonde blurry woman she saw at the party have done that to Ben? She's the same size as Elyse. Isn't she afraid of him? Elyse wouldn't be stupid enough to take a swing at a grizzly bear. If Ana really gave him that gash and she's still breathing, then he has biblical levels of restraint.

Later, they take another round of photos. Kieran is right. It's so much more beautiful at sunset. The rich, warm colors blend around a red orb of light disappearing behind a ridge of slate.

After living in latex skin all day, she's desperate for a shower and clothing. The RV's bathroom is surprisingly spacious but not as clean as she'd like. Clumps of hair and remnants of other paint projects in bright colors litter the floor and stick into corners and crevices. The warm water and her hands do the work of peeling every square inch of latex off her body. It washes down the drain and sticks to the grate, where her toe breaks it into digestible bits.

Quickly drying and dressing, she slides the door open, where she finds Kieran at the dinette table blowing cigarette smoke out of the open window. Ben is in the co-pilot seat typing furiously on his cell phone. Once the typing stops, he lets out a heavy sigh and looks at her with tired eyes. "You ready?"

Ambling toward him through the kitchen, bits of grit from the tile floor stick to the soles of her feet. She nods. "Mm-hmm."

Kieran is watching *Rick & Morty* on a flatscreen mounted on the opposite wall surrounded by dark walnut storage cabinets. "Stay a while. I have a couple frozen pizzas and plenty of beer." His gaze doesn't leave the screen.

Standing, Ben slips his phone into his dress pant pocket. "As tempting as that sounds, we've got a long drive ahead of us."

"It's about to be pitch black out there. I wouldn't recommend it. Why not go in the morning? The couch has a pull-out bed."

The idea lights up her brain. "It is a long drive," she says and bores into him to send a psychic message. *I want you.*

A look of anguish crosses his face as he seems to struggle with the idea. "Ahhh...I don't know."

She takes a step closer, her eyes wide and imploring. "By the time we get back, it'll be after midnight. You'll have been

awake almost twenty-four hours. That's not safe." Reaching out, she lightly touches his arm. "Please, Ben," she asks, her voice a sweet hush.

Kieran claps his hands in victory before Ben can protest. "I'm preheating the oven."

Ben's shoulders sink and he rubs his neck, letting out a quiet, strained sigh. "Alright." He turns toward the stairs. "I guess we'll stay."

***

They're sitting around the dinette booth playing Trivial Pursuit. Ben is slumped against the upholstered seat, looking every bit the part of a weary soldier in a POW camp. Drawing a card, Elyse announces, "She was an American film actress who became the Princess of Monaco."

"Grace Kelly," Ben answers. He swipes a hand over his exhausted face, then props his cheek up on his fist.

"You know who looks like Grace Kelly?" Kieran draws deeply from a joint and shoots Ben a teasing look. Putting his arm around Elyse, he ushers her closer. "Ana. How's she doing?"

As it gets later, Kieran's passive aggressive jabs at Ben have grown more obvious. *She does look a bit like Grace Kelly*, Elyse thinks. A real-life princess. Of course she does. Elyse rips into her slice of frozen pizza, then flings the card onto the pile, glowering at it.

The mention of Ana's name seems to be the last straw in a long string of irritating things Ben suffered that day. "She's good," he says, abruptly rising from the booth. "I'm gonna go get ready for bed." Snatching up his gym bag from a leather couch, he disappears into Kieran's room behind the sliding door.

Waiting for the door to close, Kieran raises his eyebrows at Elyse. "Somebody's grumpy."

"He's had a long day." She draws back, freeing herself from his embrace. "We both have. I think we just need to get some sleep."

"Well, there's the pull-out couch," he says, motioning toward it. "The cushions are pretty big, you can set 'em on the floor. And then, you know, the bedroom." A roguish glint forms in his eyes. "Of course, you're welcome to join me."

Heat creeps up her neck at the bold invitation. He's just the kind of guy she'd go for if Ben wasn't around. An easy, low-stakes good time. Sure, he's a slob and a horrible gossip who spilled every scandalous detail about the King family within hours of meeting her. But she wouldn't be giving him her secrets. He probably wouldn't even try to get to know her at all. Just the way she likes it.

Just then, Ben exits Kieran's bedroom wearing clothes from his gym bag—a white UCLA Law T-shirt that clings to the ridges of his chest and hugs the bulk of his biceps, and gray cotton joggers. The sight of him makes her bite the inside of her lip.

"Thanks, but I'll sleep out here."

Ben must have heard her because he raises his brows.

"Take the bed."

"I'd prefer the floor. Really." It's a lie, but the cushions aren't large enough to accommodate Ben's stature, and it's bad enough he's staying the night against his will.

Before bed, Ben sets up the sofa bed, revealing a plastic-covered mattress and rakes his fingers through his hair. "Fuck my life."

It makes her laugh, but all humor fades once she considers what she's sleeping on tonight. She'd bet real money Kieran doesn't own a mop, and she's afraid of what might be living on that floor.

It's dark, shades cover all the windows, and Elyse curls up on the sofa cushions set on the floor of the kitchen. With all the lights off, she takes in an infinite sea of stars through the

skylight. Amid the hushed silence, Kieran's snoring emanates from the RV's far end. The erratic spurts and snorts punctuate the quiet, reminiscent of a misfiring moped engine. This was not the best idea she's ever had.

Ben groans and turns, grumbling to himself. The metal frame of the pull-out bed creaks under him. Getting up, Elyse walks to the door that separates the bedroom from the rest of the RV and slides it closed. It dampens the sound to a dull roar.

"Thanks," Ben says.

"You're welcome." She returns to the cushions and covers herself with the blanket. It's not long before she hears the bed's metal frame squeak and sees Ben's head peek out from over the edge. "If we ran a blacklight over those cushions you're lying on, you'd run for the hills," he whispers. He props his head up on his arm. "If you want to come up, we can share."

Just as the thing she wants to happen most begins to happen, her fight or flight activates. All at once, she can't speak, her mind goes blank, and her heart hammers against her ribs like a scared bird flapping its wings against the bars of a cage.

Years ago, George hijacked her dopamine and imbued each molecule of her pleasure with a tinge of dread. Even now, his ghost can reach through time from the depths of hell to steal her joy, trapping her in a dichotomy of desire and fear. According to Guillermo, it's her brain's way of saying, "Be careful. I remember something like this, and it hurt us." In the past, she's managed to dull this reaction with glasses of wine and shots of tequila, but tonight she's stone sober and in a panic.

Ben's deep, gentle voice interrupts her moment of crisis. "I promise to keep my hands to myself."

"Okay."

Scooting over to the far side of the bed, Ben makes room for her. She slips in beside him, adrenaline surging. Even at the very edge, she's close enough to feel the heat radiating off his body. The limited space makes it impossible not to touch. Each inhale through her nose receives his slightly sweet scent and fills her with a sense of calm and safety. Androstenone, androstenol, and carbonyl—the biochemical compounds that give humans their unique musk. If his could be captured in a bottle, she'd never have trouble falling asleep again.

"Goodnight, Elyse," Ben whispers, and an electrical current pulses through her.

"Goodnight."

It's quiet except for Kieran's muffled snores. As she gazes at the stars, time seems to blur. Fatigue weighs down her eyelids, and a gnawing unease knots up her stomach. She's filled with the ache of wanting, and the anxiety of being so close to getting what she wants.

"You asleep?" Ben whispers.

"No."

Shifting with a slight squirm, the bed emits a soft creak beneath him. "I'm sorry for not listening when you said you weren't comfortable with the shoot." Genuine remorse colors his voice, making her wonder if he's been searching for the perfect moment to apologize since her panic attack. "But you really stepped out of your comfort zone. You were incredible."

She holds his gaze, her face a mask, revealing nothing. But inside, she's confronted with a confusing blend of gratitude and resentment—gratitude for being pulled out of her comfort zone and for him staying nearby all day to ensure her safety, but resentment for being gently pushed off a cliff. "Thanks."

Elyse's gaze drifts upward to the vast expanse above. The pinholes of light in the night sky shimmer and pulse with distant energy. After a moment, Ben's voice breaks the silence. "This bed is really uncomfortable."

"Mm," she says. "And you're used to sleeping on mattresses stuffed with golden goose feathers." Her words carry an unintentional bite of snark.

A gentle rumble of laughter emanates from him. "Hey," he counters, a teasing note in his voice. "I've spent plenty of nights on sofa beds. Didn't get my own bed until I came out here. It was one of those twin-size dorm beds everyone complains about. I was over the moon."

Imagining Ben's broad frame filling a small mattress, his feet dangling off the edge is an interesting thought. "Why didn't you have a bed?"

The rise and fall of his chest draws her eye as he stares quietly at the stars. "After my mom died, I bounced around a lot. Aunts, cousins. They did what they could, but no one ever kept me long."

Heat spreads across her face. "I'm sorry, I didn't know." Going from one home to the next, never having stability or any real place of her own, she knows too well how painful that is. Memories of her past flood her mind, and George's ghost lurks, threatening to reveal dark truths. Ben could ask questions, dig deeper, and she's not ready to expose that raw nerve. "That must have been hard."

"It could have been worse. I had her until I was thirteen, so I'm grateful for that."

"What was her name?"

"Liliana."

Like the lily flower. "What a beautiful name," she says. Beautiful and dangerous. Elyse has extracted calcium oxalate crystals from lily flowers before. Microscopic needles, invisible to the naked eye. Ingesting them is a good way to ruin your day.

"Yeah, she was beautiful."

The lightness in his voice contrasts with an undercurrent of sadness. A pang of regret turns her belly, wondering why she had to go and make a stupid sarcastic joke. He must sense her discomfort because he graciously puts her out of her misery and fills the lull.

"It's actually stuffed with horsehair. My mattress."

"Horsehair?"

"The hair of a horse," he says, chuckling. "It sounds nuts, but it's really comfortable."

It takes her by surprise and she laughs. They both do. She smiles so big for so long, it's a conscious effort to stop. They say goodnight again and time stretches on forever, all the while her telepathic efforts to will his body onto hers reap no results.

In the clarity of the night, the Milky Way reveals itself in a smoky band, a sight she had never witnessed with her naked eye. The celestial panorama overhead serves as a stark reminder of the universe's indifference to her desires.

Nature is impolite. It's not trapped by the constraints of society or morality or the laws of man. It's free in the truest sense. She preaches this to her followers all the time. Now it's late, they're in bed together, and she can't even muster the courage to kiss him. What a hypocrite. But she tells herself it has to be his choice, he has so much more to lose. Their silent inaction gnaws at her until she eventually falls asleep.

By morning, the RV fills with light. It pours in through the skylight and seeps through every seam in the shades to reveal thousands of floating particles of dust giving the space a dreamy haze. She reaches for Ben, but he isn't there.

"Good morning."

Turning toward the sound of his voice, she notices his bag is on the dinette table and his gym clothes are folded beside it. He's wearing his dress pants and shirt from the day before. "Did you sleep okay?"

Wiping the crust from her eyes, she mumbles, "Not too bad," then cups her hand to her mouth, to sniff her breath. It isn't the freshest, but it's not bad enough to send him packing. Her fingers comb her hair, then she massages her face back to life.

"Kieran's still asleep, but I don't think we should wait until noon when he wakes up to leave so I wrote him a note. What can I do to help you get ready?"

"Uh..." She looks around. Everything she needs is already in her canvas shoulder bag. "Nothing really. I'm good."

She gets up to use the bathroom and looks at herself in the mirror. The woven pattern of the blanket is imprinted on her puffy cheek. Pulling her hair back in an elastic she kept around her wrist, she wonders, *what does Princess Ana looks like in the morning?*

When she closes the bathroom door behind her, Ben is feeling his pockets. "Alright, I'm hitting the head, then we're hitting the road."

Tiptoeing toward his gym bag, she sees it's unzipped and the shirt he slept in is just sitting there. Pressing it to her nose, she inhales deeply and tiny fireworks explode across her skin. *It was in his trunk this whole time. He won't miss it. He won't even notice it's gone.* Snatching the shirt, she shoves it in her canvas purse and zips his bag shut right before the bathroom door opens.

"Ready?"

"Yup."

Chapter Twelve

The ride home is quiet except for the sounds of the wind whipping by. They ramble through the rugged terrain until it gives way to rolling hills of green. With the window rolled down, Elyse's hair dances through the air behind her like chocolate-colored waves.

Music plays in the background—a velvety love song full of longing and regret. He lowers the volume to a lingering hush. "Kieran will be in Malibu in a few days. He said he'd do the headshots there, so we don't have to drive all the way back."

Turning to him, she nods, then looks away again.

So much for small talk. Maybe she's upset. Does she feel rejected by him? How can he tell her it's complicated? That he wants her, but he can't have an affair because his wife has psychic abilities bordering on omniscience. Somehow, she always knows when he's up to something. He never should have spent the night, invited her to bed.

Once she rolls up the window, the silence becomes deafening. Even if sex was an option, he wouldn't want their first time together to be on some weird mattress covered in plastic anyway. Not with those creaky metal bars straining underneath and Kieran sawing logs ten feet away. He would want it to be private, comfortable. Somewhere he could take his time with her and make it special. Assuming sex were even on the table, which it's not. It can't be.

Their eyes meet and he gives her a weak smile. She smiles back, then turns away, letting her shoulders sink with a listless sigh.

She *is* upset. Tensing his grip on the steering wheel, he focuses forward and contemplates the silent miles of road that lie ahead.

The stillness is interrupted by Elyse's soft voice. "Can I ask you something?"

The caution in her tone sets his pulse racing. With a quick glance, he catches her tense expression before refocusing on the road. "Yeah, sure."

Pausing, she carefully forms her next words. "I don't want to pry, but... did a trunk really hit you?"

A sinking feeling overtakes him. "Yeah. Why?"

"No reason."

"Bullshit."

Facing him squarely, her expression taut, she responds. "Fine, if you really want to know, I don't believe a trunk hit you. I think Ana, who you said doesn't let you have any privacy... well, it just kind of sounds a little like..." she trails off.

"Like what?"

She clears her throat, a flush rising on her neck. "It seems abusive. And if she's like that, then maybe she's the one who did it. That's all."

Shame engulfs him. He has no words. No one has ever had the nerve to come out and ask before. The dysfunction of his marriage must be more obvious than he thought. Time seems to hold its breath, and for a while it's quiet except for the dull rush of passing cars.

"I'm sorry," she says softly. "It's none of my business. I shouldn't have said anything."

Ben straightens himself up in his seat, too stunned to speak. The thought of appearing weak, of letting a woman half his size maim him on a regular basis—track him, control him—is humiliating. He's a man, and when he's with Elyse, she makes him feel like one. That feeling is gone now.

"You've been so sweet, and I didn't even say thank you. Thank you. Really. For everything."

"Don't mention it."

"No, really. You're like the nicest person I've met in LA."

Sweet. Nice. The words sting like insults.

"Oh yeah? That's funny because everyone else says I'm an asshole." He narrows his eyes at her, his voice dripping with sarcasm. "You've been here, what? A year? What the fuck do you know? You don't know anything about me. Maybe instead of making up stories, you ought to mind your own business. Worry about how to pay your fucking power bill."

How's that for nice.

Blinking slowly, she seems to process his unprovoked attack. The atmosphere in the car thickens, weighed down by the tension between them. Taking a shaky breath, she turns her face toward the window and speaks to the cold landscape outside. "I'm sorry I asked you a personal question. It won't happen again." Her wounded voice a whisper.

Way to go, asshole. The regret is intense and immediate.

"You didn't just ask me a personal question. You made up this whole narrative about my marriage that you know nothing about."

Silence.

He continues. "You look at me with pity and go on about how I'm so *sweet* and so *nice* like I'm some kind of little bitch or something." Each whiny word makes him hate himself a little more as they leave his mouth, but he can't seem to stop himself. His aggravation rises, each sentence only digging his hole deeper. "It had to be Kieran. *Ese cabrón. Bochinchando todo el tiempo como una vieja.* He was just trying to get lucky, you know. He'd say anything." *That asshole. Gossiping all the time like an old woman.*

If he could disappear, he would, but there are hours left to go before they reach LA. *Calm down*, he tells himself. It's just her showing him she cares. That's a good thing. Not something to get all bent out of shape about. Silence hangs in the air, and he decides to let it go until he hears her whimper. He turns to her to find tears wetting her face. *Good job, idiot. You made her cry.*

Whatever he's triggered is more than just hurt feelings. She's clearly in pain, and he doesn't know what to do. It's a few miles of open road and listening to her weep before he can muster the words to say, "I'm sorry. Your heart was in the right place. I shouldn't have said those things."

Turning her head slightly, she opens her mouth as if to speak, then hesitates. He tries to read her with stolen glances taken off the road. When she finally says something, her voice is surprisingly steady, although she doesn't look at him.

"Sometimes things from my past make me see things differently. I've been wrong about people before." Gripping the edge of the seat, she casts the same fearful look at him she had in Kieran's RV. "Was I wrong about you?"

It guts him. Inside, he's grappling with a desire to reassure her while guarding this agonizing secret. Reflecting on his feelings for Elyse, he knows it's more than just a physical attraction. There's a fragility about her that awakens something protective within him. And yet, there's a strength in her. Life has knocked her down, but she persists even in fear. Now, she asked Ben a question out of genuine concern—a question no one has ever been brave enough to ask—and he punished her for it.

"No." Taking her hand, he kisses it. "You're not wrong about anything."

The steady pace of the tires hitting the road fills the cabin with a gentle whir. She looks at him, eyes rimmed with red and full of tears. "It doesn't make you weak, you know. I think you're very strong. I can't imagine why anyone would be dumb enough to raise a hand to you."

The thought of Elyse seeing him as a potential danger, leaves a bitter taste in his mouth. He's always known his formidable size could be intimidating, but he'd learned to balance it with gentleness to avoid making anyone feel unsafe around him. "I've never hit a woman in my life, and I never will."

"I didn't think you would. She knows you won't. That's why she thinks she can get away with it. But everyone has a limit. Even you."

"Look, it's not that big a deal. Alright? She's got a little temper, and I'm no angel myself. But I've got it under control. Thank you for your concern, it's very sweet, but...we don't need to get into it. I'm fine."

The tense atmosphere that permeated the car after their confrontation begins to wane as the miles go by. As embarrassed as he initially felt to be confronted with it, telling her is cathartic, as if he'd been held underwater all these years and only now came up for air, pulling in a deep life-sustaining breath.

If he added up all the time they've spent together it would barely fill a weekend, and yet he trusts her with it. Even more, somehow he knows she understands. The day they met, those gorgeous eyes drew him in with a recognition of something he can't define, but looking in them provides a warm and familiar comfort.

When they finally pull up to her house, he walks her to the door. The urge to kiss her is suppressed, and instead he stands, reaches for his wallet and counts out ten hundred-dollar bills.

"Turn your lights back on and make sure you pay your cell phone bill, otherwise I don't know how I'm going to stay in touch with you."

"I can't take your money."

"You did a full day's work in the desert. You earned this."

Elyse's shoulders slump and looks at the money in his hand for a while. "I thought you were supposed to be an a-hole."

He smiles, finding it cute she doesn't curse. "Yeah, well. Take the money and shut up about it. How's that?"

After a few reluctant moments, she accepts, then hugs him tight. They rock together for a moment, and he kisses the hollow of her temple.

As he drives away, the last few days replay in his mind, and he's left with an unexpected glimmer of hope.

Chapter Thirteen

The speakerphone trills as Elyse fishes Ben's UCLA Law shirt from her bag and presses it to her nose. A despairing ache radiates through her and her eyes well with tears. She hasn't let her guard down like this before, not since George. How could she let this happen?

"Elyse," Stella answers brightly.

"Did you set us up on purpose?"

"What?"

"Ben and me. Did you know about Ana? How she treats him?"

Stella goes silent, and the lull of voices in the background fade. A door squeals shut and Stella lowers her voice. "Everyone knows Ana King is an evil bitch, that's not a secret." She sighs. "Anyway, I've always liked Ben. I thought you'd have chemistry."

Tightening her fists, Elyse paces her room, incensed. "Don't you see how manipulative that is?"

"Oh, relax," she says. "So I meddled. I just thought if you could get to know him you two would hit it off."

"And I'd be moved to help him like I helped you?"

Elyse was working as a locker room attendant at SoCal Sculpt when she met Stella. They only shared friendly passing smiles on the gym floor, until one day Stella approached her and insisted Elyse should be modeling or acting.

"I'm too short to model and I've never acted before in my life."

Talking about plants on social media seemed harmless enough. Lots of people were making online content. Stella encouraged her, took her to lunch, dinner, and eventually invited her to her home. That's where she met Andrew. It's impossible to forget the cold intensity in the long, unflinching look he gave her, as if to let her know her influence was a threat and he wasn't someone to be trifled with, so don't get any ideas.

The welts on Stella's body had not gone unnoticed, and Elyse drew comparisons to her own beatings. Stella explained them away with an endless slew of plausible excuses, but Elyse knew better. She had bruises once too. They'd made her an easier target for George to groom.

A grown man like him, finding a young girl in long sleeves and pants in the middle of the sweltering Miami summer, smelled her distress like a predator sniffs out prey. Armed with promises of love and protection, she was a broad target. It felt good to have someone who seemed to care paying her a little attention after being so starved for affection.

For a while it was nice. Living in that house, she walked around with a pit of fear in her stomach. But then he knocked on her window, and she finally found a safe place in the world while in his arms. Looking back, that's exactly what he wanted her to feel. It made it easier for him to do what came next.

Watching Stella suffer that way dredged up all the things Elyse hoped to forget, and she couldn't stay silent. One night after they'd polished off two bottles of wine, Elyse told Stella about George. It seemed to shock her at first, scare her. But it wasn't long before her expression of fear turned to curiosity. "How did you get away with it?"

Elyse didn't want to talk about it, but she saw Stella's desperation. "The manchineel fruit, it caused an inflammatory response."

Stella nodded pensively for a moment, then leaned toward Elyse with big eyes and a bright idea. "Andrew has a heart condition."

Even better. Manchineel trees don't grow in southern California but oleander does. The glycosides in oleander create a reaction, an imbalance causing more calcium to bind to the proteins responsible for muscle contractions, leading to cardiac arrest.

"Is it undetectable?" Stella asked.

"If they look close enough, they'll find it. But when there's an explanation so obvious no one needs to look any closer, they usually won't."

And they didn't. Elyse delivered a glass vial to Stella at home. "They're very bitter. You'll need to mix this with something sweet." Stella did the rest.

But Ana isn't Andrew, and Elyse doesn't have the luxury of an underlying health issue to mimic. She has the added challenge of Ana's youth and notoriety. Even if she could pull it off, Ben doesn't want this. *Does he?*

"Did he put you up to this?" Elyse asks.

"Of course not," Stella says defensively. "He'd be horrified. That wasn't my intention at all."

Elyse doesn't know what to believe. She wants to scream but instead takes a deep, steadying breath. "Why didn't you just tell me? Why'd you have to be so underhanded about it?"

"Please, don't be upset. I know that because of the pain you've been through, you push people away. Ben puts on a tough guy act, but he's one of the kindest people I know. I wasn't trying to trick you or force anything. I honestly believed there could be something there, and I hoped that if you got to know him, you might see that too. You like him, don't you?"

"You knew I would," she mutters, falling back onto her mattress. She should have known Stella wouldn't give up pulling strings so easily. Even thousands of miles away, LA is alive and well in her heart. Stella always loved it when a story came together.

"Because I know you. Better than you think. You'll never admit it, but you want love. I know you do."

"Love?" Elyse laughs cynically. "He's never going to leave Ana in a million years. Sure, she's crazy. But this isn't you and Andrew. Ben isn't helpless. We spent the night together last night. He had every opportunity, and nothing happened. I even tried to talk to him about Ana and it just made him angry. I'm not getting involved."

"Why do you think I stayed with Andrew as long as I did? Where else was I going to go? Ben probably feels trapped. I'd bet that prenup is iron-clad, and the King family has a lot of influence in this business." She exhales quietly into the phone. "Forget it, okay? I'm not asking you to do anything. This isn't some elaborate scheme. I just overstepped a little, and I'm sorry."

Elyse clutches Ben's shirt, hugging it. "I don't know if I can. I mean...she's young. Well known. Healthy. It's too dangerous."

"You'll think of something."

***

Connected to a random open Wi-Fi network, Elyse launches an incognito search window on her MacBook. *Mortality rates and common causes of death in women aged 25-30.*

It's just research, she tells herself. Never a bad idea to stay up-to-date on the latest medical news. She's keeping things fresh. That's all.

Every morbid click inspires new scenarios. *Cardiovascular disease?* The woman looks like a fitness instructor. *Next.*

Autoimmune diseases. "Lupus," she whispers, letting the name roll off her tongue. A smirk creeps across her face. "Symptoms include severe inflammation. Hmm."

She closes out of the browser and shuts her laptop. A girl can dream. Some people take virtual tours of mansions they'll never afford on Zillow. Elyse fantasizes about interesting ways to kill Ben's wife. Everyone is different.

Maybe if Ana posed an actual threat to Ben, it wouldn't just be a daydream. But he told her himself—he's got everything under control. He probably still loves the evil hag. The fact is, he had a chance—many chances—to take Elyse any way he wanted her and he didn't. He's not that into her. Time to move on. She forces herself out of bed and into her overalls.

Outside, the sun blazes down hot and insistent as Elyse looks at the uniform green of her lawn. It's a symbol of ecological ignorance that has irritated her since she moved in—watching the neighbors water and mow, obsessing over their small plots of conformity. She wanted something wild.

Grabbing a spade, she begins to dig up the grass, each clump she uproots a release of her pent-up emotions. Her sweat becomes a baptism of sorts—a cleansing. By dusk, Elyse's yard is a mess of overturned soil.

Pretty flowers won't change the ugliness inside you. Ben saw it, you know. That's why he doesn't want you, George taunts.

She lies down on a cleared patch of earth, feeling the cool dirt against her flushed skin. Closing her eyes, she can sense the life beneath. She whispers to the tiny organisms, "Come on microbes. Give momma that serotonin."

You're still that scared little girl, looking for attention in all the wrong places. Ben's probably laughing about you with Ana right now.

"Go away," she says, roughly tearing open a packet labeled *California Native Wildflower Mix*. She begins to sprinkle the seeds, envisioning a stunning, drought-resistant meadow of native flowers to attract bees and butterflies. It's not the best time of year for this, but there are over a hundred gallons of rainwater in barrels lined up in her backyard ready to help these little babies germinate.

By nightfall, the physical exertion takes its toll, and Elyse is spent. Sitting on her porch, dirt smeared on her face and arms, she surveys her handiwork. A moment of stillness draws a sting to her eyes.

That night, after her bath, she curls up in bed with Ben's T-shirt, hoping to soothe herself a little. Every touch, every look exchanged, every whispered word, all come flooding back, and George appears to make a final jab. *At least you have a momento to remember what you'll never have.*

"You should know better by now not to underestimate me."

Chapter Fourteen

It's early afternoon when Ben slips into the house. Sun filters in through the curtains, filling the towering space with natural light. It's eerily quiet, the only sound the dull thud of his footsteps as he creeps inside.

Reaching the living room, he freezes, finding Ana watching him from the hall. As she closes the distance between them, he quickly assesses her facial expression—it's relaxed, her posture is loose and she's not rushing toward him. His nerves ease.

"Hey." The sweetness in her voice catches him off guard. She strokes his cheek, sporting a saccharine smile while examining his face. Unease stirs within him, making his heart race.

"Hey. I'm sorry I wasn't here."

"I'm sorry I gave you such a hard time yesterday, baby."

"We can go out tonight if you want."

"Let's stay home. We can binge a show. Get in our pajamas. Order out."

He's surprised at the laid-back suggestion. This isn't like her. It hasn't been like her in years. "Really?"

A gentle kiss from her causes the hairs on the back of his neck to stand up. Suspicion stirs within him: what might she be planning?

A large flatscreen television hangs above their fireplace and its carved white, wooden mantle. Together on the couch, Ben and Ana find comfort beneath a cashmere blanket. Ana's warmth spreads while her head finds a spot in his lap, cushioned underneath. While he caresses her hair, they watch Michael Scott propose to Holly Flax on *The Office*.

Ana looks up at him. "Do you remember when you proposed, and Aunt Mel dropped that bottle of perfume on the floor?"

"Of course I do. It smashed and the whole room smelled like Shalimar. The wheezing. Holy shit. I thought I was gonna die that day."

Her laugh is warm and wistful. It wasn't all bad, not always.

When the food arrives, they move to the floor to be closer to the waxy brown paper boxes of red and green Thai curries resting on the teak coffee table. They're popped open with beads of condensation clinging to the glossy inner walls and emit the aroma of spices and coconut. Ben hovers over them. "I don't think I've had the red before."

Taking a bite of the savory chicken and rice, he shifts his focus back to the television. Out of his peripheral vision, he detects a sudden movement toward his mouth. Recoiling sharply, a surprised expression crosses his face. Upon closer inspection, Ana sits poised, offering him a forkful of food.

Relaxing his shoulders, he lets his mouth fall open so she can feed him a bite. "Mmm, that's good."

She rubs his thigh. "Do you want to switch?"

"Oh, no. Thank you." Her offer is sweet and it makes him uneasy. "Where's Flora?"

"I gave her the night off."

Distraction fills his eyes as he fixates on the television. A nagging thought persists. This is a ruse to lull him into a false sense of safety. Of course, he should be skeptical. She doesn't love him. When was the last time she just wanted to *hang out*? "Why are you being so nice to me?"

With a scoff, she replies, "Am I really that bad?"

Now she's suspicious and attempting to figure out why he's so nervous. Under her icy gaze, every move he makes seems fraught with implications. He should have just shut up and eaten his food.

"You look guilty."

Responding defensively, he asks, "Guilty of what?"

"That's what I'm trying to figure out. Who were you really with last night?"

"I told you. I was with Kieran."

With a quickened breath and darkened eyes, she sweeps the Thai curry off the table. It splatters onto the floor and his lap. The fabric of his gray cotton joggers is stained disgusting shades of green and brown. "Wow, very nice." Climbing off the floor to clean himself up, he mutters under his breath, "You stupid fucking bitch."

As he tries to distance himself, a sudden blow from a glass vase to the back of his head halts his escape. It shatters upon impact, fragments scattering across the floor. Ana's aim is getting better with practice. Reaching up, his fingers find the wet stickiness of blood. The warmth of it trickles slowly down his neck. *Don't strangle her. She could have your head on a pike, and no one would believe it was self-defense.*

"Oh no, you're bleeding," Racing toward him with bare feet, Ana seems to ignore the broken glass scattered in her path.

"Hey, stop!" Alarmed, he moves quickly to intercept her. "You're going to hurt yourself. Just stay there until I can clean this up."

Rushing to the closet, he retrieves a broom and dustpan. By the time he's back, she's collapsed in tears beside the scattered shards. Swiftly, he lifts her from the dangerous mess and carries her to the living room. Once there, he's startled to see her hands smeared with blood. Frantically, he checks them for cuts.

"It's your blood," she says.

Touching the back of his head, he finds his hair soaked. *Oh fuck.* The adrenaline rush subsides and pains shows up in full force.

"Let me look," she says. Bending forward, he lets her separate his hair with her fingers. Each touch burns on his injured scalp. She really got him good.

"Oh no. I think you need stitches. Oh my God, babe. I'm so sorry."

This was a first. Their spats have never required medical attention before. The distinct coppery scent of his blood, reminiscent of fresh pennies, becomes overwhelming and his vision starts to narrow. Stumbling toward the wall for support, he reaches out, unintentionally smearing blood onto the pristine white wainscoting. There's so much of it.

Ana reaches for him. "Come on, I'll drive you to urgent care."

She fetches him fresh clothes and swiftly collects his keys. In the garage, their paths converge and, with a weary gait, he settles into the passenger seat.

Sitting in the urgent care waiting room, Ben props his head up on his fist and stares off into space as Ana gently strokes her palm across his back. What will he say? Not, *My insane wife threw a heavy glass object at my head.* If they report it, it won't matter if he doesn't want to press charges. She'll be arrested, Chuck will lose his mind, and Ben will be out on his ass.

"I slipped and fell backward into a sconce."

"The glass just shattered," Ana adds.

The nurse releases Ben's head and clicks her tongue. She fiddles with her pockets, then types on a laptop on wheels. "Yup, you're gonna need to have that closed up."

With precision, the doctor applies a numbing agent to the wound before securing it with two staples. Ben is grateful to learn he doesn't have to shave a patch out of the back of his head, saving him the trouble of explaining to everyone how he's just so clumsy.

Waiting for the discharge paperwork, they're alone together in the small exam room. Ana leans against a counter full of swabs and disposable gloves. A poster of a depressed-looking overweight man wearing a blood pressure cuff hangs on the wall. Illustrations of hearts and kidneys float around him.

"I can't do this anymore."

"I'm sorry. I lost my temper."

"It's getting worse, Ana."

She starts to cry. "I know. I need help."

"You blew off therapy. You don't want help. You want a punching bag, and I'm not doing that anymore."

There's a knock at the door, then a nurse is pushing her way through. "Here are your aftercare instructions," she sings and hands him a sheet of paper. On the top it reads *Wound Care and Staple Removal*. She hands him a little plastic packet with a sterile staple remover and white sheet of gauze. "You can either come back or remove them at home in about two weeks. Okay?"

"Thanks."

They check out, and Ana hands him his keys. When he starts the car, the music from his phone starts to play and

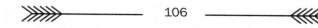

makes Elyse appear in his mind. A pulse of regret shoots through him and he quickly turns it off.

Encased in silence, the lights of oncoming cars whip past them as they drive home. Amidst the quiet, a soft sob breaks through. Glancing her way, he sees tears streaking her face. *Jesus. Gimme a break.* He's the one with staples in his head, and she's crying.

Dabbing her eyes with the hem of her shirt, she snivels, "You know, I was trying to have a good night tonight. Why'd you have to pick a fight?"

Yeah, you're the victim here. This is all my fault. "I don't want to fight."

They reach home, parking in the garage. Climbing the stairs, he picks up a pillow and blanket from their bed, intending to retreat to his office.

"Don't go."

"Ana, I can't tonight. Not tonight."

Meeting his gaze with a dead, unwavering stare, she says, "I wasn't asking."

"I don't want to fight, I just want to go."

"You don't get to go."

Before he can exit, she intercepts him, snatching a ceramic jar from a side table and brandishing it as if she intends to throw it at him.

"Are you fucking kidding me?" he screams. The stink of antiseptic is still on him, and she's ready to injure him again. Squeezing all the power of his restraint in his fists, he clenches his jaw and prays not to lose control. Tonight might be the night. *If you start hitting her, you won't stop until you kill her.* He storms to the closet to get his bags.

"Oh, here comes the theatre."

Ignoring her, he gathers a pile of shirts. But she jumps in, blocking his way and scattering his clothes. "Hold on a second."

"I'm tired of your shit. We're done, you and me."

Picking his things up off the floor, he continues to pack. His gym bag is missing something—his shirt is gone. He loved that shirt. He must have left it in Kieran's RV. *Goddamnit.*

"Did you fuck her?"

"No."

"Liar."

Ben shakes his head and shrugs. "I should have fucked her. It doesn't even make a difference to you. I wanted to, trust me, and I could have."

"Of course you do. You found a trainwreck like your mother so you can swoop in and save the day."

"Fuck you. I don't love you anymore."

Without a moment of hesitation, Ana swings and her fist lands with a forceful thud against Ben's cheek.

Fuck. It stings. He grabs her wrist and they struggle to the ground. "Why can't you fucking control yourself?"

"You're hurting me!"

As the pressure mounts, he fears his brain might implode. His breath comes short and ragged. "I asked you to let me go!" He screams. Pleads. "Why won't you just let me go?" Vision becoming a blur, he suddenly becomes aware of the force in his hands as a sharp cry escapes her. Recoiling, he falls back, distancing himself from the scene. *Oh fuck.* He really hurt her. She'll probably have bruises on her arms.

Her stifled sobs go on and on. "I'm telling Daddy."

Of course she will. He doesn't have an ounce of fight left in him. "Tell him. I don't care anymore. Take it all, Ana. Take everything I've ever worked for. Do what you need to do. You've ruined my life. I fucking wish I'd never met you."

Climbing to his feet, he continues to pack.

"You think I ruined your life? You don't know what it means to have your life ruined yet. I haven't even gotten started." She heckles him from the edge of the bed. "You will pray for the piece of shit life you had before you met me."

Ignoring her, he fills his bags until they can't hold any more. Three trips take him up and down the stairs and into the garage, where he loads up the Range Rover. Where will he even go?

On his last trip to their bedroom, Ana sits on the edge of the bed and stares daggers at him. "I'm firing Flora first thing in the morning."

It stops him in his tracks. "Why would you do that? This has nothing to do with her."

She shrugs as if to say, *oh well*. "Things keep going missing around here. I'd have to let the neighborhood know. It's my responsibility as a member of the community to warn others, right?"

Ben's eyes widen in shock, realizing the depth of her manipulation. "You're lying. You'd ruin an innocent woman's life just to get back at me?"

Ana tilts her head, feigning innocence. "I'm just doing what I think is right. Protecting our neighbors."

Poor Flora took care of him for years. In many ways, she was like a second mother to him. No wonder Ana kept her around. Disbelief washes over him, quickly replaced by anger. But he knows he needs to stay calm.

"Ana, please. You and I both know that's not true. Don't do that."

Ana leans back, a satisfied smile on her face. "Then come to bed. I'll have Flora help you unpack in the morning."

He wants to cry. Scream. Punch a hole in the wall. Tears don't usually come so quickly, but he's been driven to them. If he appeases her now, maybe he can set Flora up somewhere else while he figures things out.

"Are you going to try to hurt me?"

"No. I promise."

"Fine."

***

All weekend, Ana watched Ben closely, never leaving him alone. Flora went about her business oblivious to Ana's threat, and Ben couldn't find a moment to warn her.

It's now Monday morning, and they sit at the kitchen counter. Ben, dressed in a gray bespoke suit and sipping his morning coffee, looks ready for work. Sunlight pours in through the floor-to-ceiling windows, casting a warm glow on the polished wooden floors. Yet, the mood is dark, heavy with the looming threat of violence.

Flora bends to lift a stack of water bottles that arrived that morning from Hawaii. Something about a volcano and alkaline pH that Ana was convinced would keep her young and beautiful forever. Meanwhile, he secretly hopes it gives her some kind of rare parasite that eats her insides.

As Ben scans the labels promoting the benefits of alkaline water, he remembers Elyse's adorable scientific rant and it gives him a small glimmer of joy in an otherwise painful morning. He slides off the stool to help Flora.

"Let me."

"No, I've got it." She squats and picks up a stack of three boxes that is almost as tall as she is.

Ben's eyes widen. *Jesus.* For a tiny woman, Flora has farmer strength. Grabbing a box from the top, he follows her into the pantry. Once he sets them down, he becomes aware of a moment of privacy behind the door and the weight of the humiliation he's endured that weekend and all the days before come crashing down on him.

Tears fill his eyes, blurring his vision. Grief coils around him and tightens, squeezing until he can't breathe. He leans against the marble countertop to steady himself. The vast expanse of the pantry, larger than his first apartment, only serves to heighten his sense of isolation. Surrounded by meticulously arranged gourmet provisions and ornate displays, the room is

more like an art installation inspired by a pantry than a place to store food.

"*Mijo,*" Flora whispers. *My son.* Her voice is soft and comforting. Bending to her, she embraces him. Affectionate brushes of her hand against his back comfort him as she holds him, then reaches up to touch his face, stroking her manicured thumb over the sore spot where Ana's fist left her mark.

"*Voy a dejarla,*" he says. *I'm going to leave her.*

"*Bueno,*" she says. *Good.*

"*Me preocupa que te vaya a botar. Ella dirá mentiras sobre ti. No quiero que tengas problemas por mi culpa,*" he finally tells her. *I'm worried she's going to fire you. That she will lie about you. I don't want you to have problems because of me.*

"*Que haga lo que le dé la gana. Esa no me asusta y yo voy a estar bien,*" Flora says with a smile, waving toward the door dismissively. *She can do whatever she wants. I'm not scared of her, and I will be fine.*

"*No quiero perderte,*" he confesses. *I don't want to lose you.*

"*Pase lo que pase, ahora somos familia. No me perderás,*" she reassures him. *No matter what happens, we're family now. You won't lose me.*

Flora smiles tenderly and offers a loving look that loosens the knots in his stomach. Taking a deep, steadying breath, Ben steps back, running a hand through his hair and attempting to regain a semblance of composure.

"*Te quiero,*" he says, kissing her cheek. *I love you.*

Taking another deep breath, he knows he has to face what's beyond the door. Ana is there, scrolling through her phone, oblivious to everything around her. She doesn't look up as they enter. A surge of defiance rises up in him. *This is the beginning of the end.*

Chapter Fifteen

"Well, well, well. Look who's ready on time." Ben shows up looking dapper, his broad shoulders and muscular build hinting at the strength beneath his tailored suit. Hugging her, he presses his lips to her cheek and sends goosebumps over her skin. He looks around at her yard. "What happened to your grass?"

"I ripped it all up. Pretty soon this will all be wildflowers."

"Huh," he says, surveying the soil. "I can't wait to see it."

As he bends to pick up her carry-on, a purple mark on his cheekbone becomes obvious under the bright morning light. Tracing her index finger over it, she asks, "Did Ana do this?"

"I don't wanna talk about it. It's just gonna piss me off."

The thought of Ana's audacity makes her heart beat faster and anger bubbles inside her. No scenario Elyse can fathom is a fate cruel enough for Ana. She deserves to suffer.

As he loads her bag into the Range Rover, she climbs inside, and for the first time, she notices it's in a disarray. A leather toiletry bag is on the dashboard, men's dress shoes rest on the floor of the passenger side. A rolled-up magazine is wedged between her seat and the center console.

"Sorry," he says, reaching over to take the shoes. "I was in a rush this morning, and I grabbed a few things on the way out." Opening the rear passenger door, he unzips his luggage. She untucks the magazine from the seat and rolls it flat against her lap. It curves up on the sides from where the pages were bent. It's *Variety*. On the cover is a beautiful blonde woman in a black jumpsuit. Elyse's eyes are instantly drawn to a mailing label on the bottom of the cover. *Ben Deluca, 1994 Tower Grove Drive, Beverly Hills, CA 90210.*

1994 Tower Grove Drive. She repeats it to herself in her mind, picturing a grassy patch of earth with collections of tall buildings, the Leaning Tower, the Eiffel Tower, Rapunzel in her tower letting down her hair. The numbers and images settle into the corners of her mind, tucked away for a time it might prove useful.

"*Atomic Blonde*," Ben says, disrupting her reverie as he settles back into the driver's seat.

"Hmm?"

Nodding toward the magazine cover, he fires up the engine. "Charlize Theron. I saw it at the *South By* festival. She's a badass in that movie."

"Oh."

He smoothly reverses out of her driveway. Elyse can't stay silent a moment longer. "You don't deserve that, you know. She has no right to hit you."

His eyes don't leave the road. "I know."

***

Once the plane touches down at LaGuardia, Elyse notices a shift in Ben's energy. He walks with a lively stride, like a coiled spring released. They settle into a sleek black Town Car bound toward Fifth Avenue.

Every passing mile intensifies the ache in her gut, and her fingers twitch in restless anticipation. She tries calming herself with slow breaths, a ritual Ben picks up on. "You okay?" He moves subtly, reducing the distance between them, their arms now sharing a leather armrest.

"Just a little nervous."

His fingers find hers, entwining them together, warm and reassuring, his touch and their proximity intoxicating. "The shoot with Kieran? That was the big leagues. This? This is just a warm-up. You got this."

His confidence is infectious, and she tries to absorb it.

In the quiet dim cabin, she notices something else. The ever-present voice of George's ghost, usually haunting whispers in the back of her mind, has fallen silent. With Ben, there's always a remarkable stillness. The adrenaline is still there, the fear lingers like a shadow, but George's voice? Gone.

The city's skyline comes into view. "I can't believe you've never been here," he says, a hint of nostalgia in his tone. Looking out the window, his expression softens taking in the vastness of it all. He seems utterly at peace being home.

"I can't believe I get to go on an adventure with you."

At her words, he turns to her and there's a change in his demeanor. A spark lights up in his eyes, the corners of his mouth curving up, clearly affected by her sentiment. Regarding her lips, he lets out a soft, yearning hum. It carries the richness of someone resisting a bite of the most tempting chocolate cake.

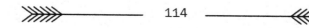

A flush rises to her cheeks, the implication of that sound resonating between them.

"Speaking of adventures," he says with a wink, letting the charged moment linger just a bit longer. "I'm having dinner with some old friends tonight if you'd care to join us."

"I get to meet your friends?"

As she looks up at him, his dark eyes glint with charm. He grins, playful, teasing. "You do. And they get to meet you."

***

Emerging from their Uber that night, they stand before a Brooklyn duplex humbly situated behind a chain-link fence. The summer heat has cooled after sunset. "Where are we?" she asks.

"This is my friend Vinny's place."

Ben is dressed in a casual ensemble—jeans, a simple white T-shirt, and a Yankees hat. Glancing over at him as they walk side by side, her eyes trace the breadth of his shoulders.

When he opens the door, Vinny greets Ben with a hearty, "Hollywood!" Vinny is a big guy, tall with round rosy cheeks and bedroom eyes.

Ben is pulled into a half embrace. "It's been a minute," he says, patting Vinny firmly on his broad back. "How the hell are you?" Before he can answer, Ben's hooked his hand onto Elyse's hip, corralling her inside. "This is Elyse. Elyse, this is Vinny."

She notices the smell of lemon-scented cleaner mixed with smoked hickory. Another man emerges from a narrow hallway and Ben throws up his arms to greet him. "Mateus!"

Mateus is short but has the swagger of a man twice his size. His eyes are fixed in a smile that seems like he's always in on a joke. Vinny and Mateus each hug Elyse as if they're old friends.

They meander through the living room on creaky wood floors.

"You see the Yankees?" Vinny asks. "Judge is carrying the whole thing."

"Classic cleanup hitter," Ben replies. "Unbelievable plate discipline."

Before long, the men are engrossed in a technical analysis of the game. Averages. Historical data. "Something smells good," she says, feeling out of place in the baseball conversation. Vinny announces he's been smoking meats on his deck all day.

The oval-shaped dining table where they gather to eat looks like it's from the 1970s with its wooden top and metallic rim. Green floral wallpaper in the kitchen looks like it's from the same era. They're eating the best barbecue Elyse has ever had when Vinny perks up like he's remembered something important. Rushing to another room, he returns with a yearbook—a shiny hardcover with a cougar emblazoned on it—and places it on the table. Ben nearly chokes on his brisket and looks at Vinny with a betrayed expression.

Elyse eagerly flips through the glossy pages of black and white photos. *Deluca*. The name makes her heart explode. There he is, at the periphery of a group shot. His slightly long hair curls around his ears. A polo swallows his thin frame, and pants are hitched up high on his lanky legs, revealing too much of his socks. All signs she recognizes of a kid not being well cared for—ill-fitting clothes, hair that needed a cut. If it wasn't for his eyebrows and smile, she wouldn't recognize him. An involuntary gasp escapes her lips.

Ben shakes his head. "We're going to Miami and pulling out your yearbooks."

"So, Elyse. What brings you to the city?" Vinny asks.

She looks up from flipping through yearbook pages. "I'm pretending to be a model."

Ben sucks his teeth. "Elyse," he says scoldingly, "you're not pretending to be anything. You were fantastic today."

Of course, he doesn't mention how the photographer cussed at her for not finding her light. Being scolded in front of an audience flustered her, a flash of warmth overtook her face. Ben had rushed over as soon as the F-bomb landed, closing the distance between him and the photographer in a few strides. The low hum of activity on set fell tensely silent. "You have an issue with her work, you talk to me. But you won't speak to her like that again. Now apologize."

The photographer, taken aback by Ben's forceful presence, hesitated for a moment. "Look, I... I'm sorry," he finally muttered, not meeting Elyse's eyes.

Watching the photographer's arrogance leave his body as he shrank in the shadow of Ben's towering frame, she had the urge to drag Ben into the nearest dressing room to show him just how grateful she felt.

"Santiago?" Mateus asks, pulling her out of her steamy fantasy. He seems to be confirming her last name.

"Mm-hmm."

"I was just saying it's about time Benny brings home a nice *Cubana*," he says. Ben clears his throat and throws Mateus a warning look. He shrugs in response with a cheeky smile. "What'd I say?"

"You went to the University of Miami for science, right?" Vinny asks.

"Yeah. Biochemistry," she says quizzically, then glances at Ben, who looks like he's in pain. She doesn't remember bringing it up here, although she'd mentioned it to Ben before.

By now, it's clear to Elyse they're enjoying Ben's discomfort, and in her own way, she's enjoying it too. From their dinner conversation, Elyse gathered that Ben's friends aren't fond of Ana. But their jovial ribbing has switched into a blatant effort to nurture something they suspect has sprouted between her and Ben.

"Beautiful and smart. She's checking all the boxes, Benny," Vinny says playfully.

"Alright," Ben says, holding up a hand for Vinny and Mateus to stop, a hint of irritation in his voice.

Elyse waits until Vinny and Mateus are talking to each other about the intricacies of their fantasy baseball league, then finds an ounce of bravery to lean in close to Ben's ear and whisper in the most sensual voice she can muster, "What else did you tell them about me?"

When he smiles and briefly looks away, she discovers he's even more handsome when he's a little flustered. Once their eyes meet, they become locked into a heated gaze that's as tangible as a touch. It unravels her composure.

"Well," he leans in closer, his voice dropping to a low hush. "I may have let it slip that I can't stop finding excuses to spend time with you even though you make exactly no money for me." He chuckles softly, and a hint of a smile plays on his lips. Shifting slightly in his seat to face her directly, he continues. "I find myself looking forward to our meetings, not because of work, but because I genuinely enjoy your company."

The room fades into the background and it's just them. His eyes hold a vulnerable sincerity he's never shown her before. Beneath the table, he subtly nudges her leg with his. "And not just because you're beautiful, but because you're gentle and sweet. You trust me. Let me take care of you, comfort you. I haven't known you long, but I've let you see sides of me that most people don't even know exist."

It's such a heartfelt declaration that her emotions don't know where to go. Her fingers curl around the edge of her chair, anchoring herself. She's not sure how much time passes before she realizes she's been holding her breath. Then, like clockwork, her adrenaline spikes and her stomach turns. George's ghost

isn't far away after all. *Please don't ruin this*, she wants to plead with it. He's taken enough from her.

"I'm making coffee," Vinny announces.

Ben turns to look at him, and just like that, the spell is broken. The room comes rushing back with a blast of color and sound, and her eyes adjust to the light. Looking at him too long was like staring into the sun.

Elyse stands in front of where Ben is sitting in a dining chair. He puts his hands on her hips as if he plans to hoist her up into the air, but instead rubs his hands up and down her thighs affectionately as if she were his. Lifting his Yankees cap, she musses up his thick locks, marveling at the plush feel of it between her fingers.

"Ready to go?"

She nods and he stands, letting his firm body glide against hers when he rises from his seat.

In the Uber, Elyse rests her head on Ben's shoulder, and he wraps his arm around her, drawing her closer. Being alone with him is different this time. Everything is charged with possibility. There's an unspoken comfort between them, an intimacy. She can feel Ben's breath on her hair, and it takes all her self-control not to lift her face and close the distance between them. Instead, she closes her eyes and savors the feeling of being held by him, of being near him for a small, cozy moment.

The car arrives to the hotel, and he helps her out by extending his hand. Once her hand is in his, he doesn't let go. They walk together to the elevators, and she clings to his arm.

"I like your friends."

"They like you too. I'm glad you got to meet them." Hooking his arm around her waist, he draws her near.

She brushes imaginary crumbs off his shirt. "Food was good," she says.

"Mmm. Yeah, it was." Ben's thumb gently grazes her cheek before he tucks a stray lock of hair behind her ear. The elevator chimes on the twelfth floor. "Goodnight," he says, his gaze lingering on her lips. Sensing a shift in his energy, she panics and instinctively steps back.

"Goodnight," she echoes, hastening out of the elevator without glancing back at the closing doors.

Quickening her pace toward her room, she berates herself. That was it. He was going to kiss her, she's sure of it. *Dang it.* She wanted it so badly she panicked. The keycard light blinks green, and she pushes through her door.

They have a late flight tomorrow. There's always morning.

Chapter Sixteen

Her suitcase is open on the floor as she digs inside to find something to sleep in—Ben's UCLA Law shirt. The scents of citrus, tobacco flower and his pheromones fire off each and every happy synapse in her brain. She'll never wash it.

Slipping her arms through the sleeves, she carefully guides her long hair through the collar, letting it cascade onto her shoulders. Those things he said. The way he'd looked at her. It wasn't her imagination; it was real and being so close to it was terrifying. It was the difference between holding a pistol in her hands and firing it. Withstanding the kickback takes strength she's not sure she has.

It's probably for the best they didn't kiss. She's already half in love with him. If she would have let him kiss her, she'd be done for. Brushing her teeth, she fights with a persistent ache. He's probably a good kisser. Even the pecks that landed on her cheek were so soft and warm it made her tingle just thinking about it. She rinses and spits, flips the light switch and heads to bed.

There's a knock on the door. *Oh, shoot.* A sudden wave of anxiety washes over her. She peers through the peephole. *Oh God.* There he is.

"Elyse?" he calls, his voice muffled through the door. He raps three more times. "It's Ben. Can I come in for a sec?"

Her palms grow clammy, and her knees wobble underneath her.

Sweet Ben, so gentle, so kind. Just like I was in the beginning, George hisses. *Remember what happened next? I do. Do you think he'd still want you if he knew the truth? You can't control the darkness inside you. The moment you let him in, he becomes your next victim.*

The metallic tang of fear coats her tongue. Shaking out her hands, she takes a deep breath before gripping the handle, then guides it open slowly, shutting out the threats of doom George's ghost screams at her in her mind.

"Hey," Ben starts, a hint of urgency in his eyes. A dimmed lamp provides a soft glow as he walks purposefully through the shadowy threshold into her room, his hands noticeably restless. Stopping, he exhales sharply through his nose and shakes his head. "I'm really sorry," he says. The door shuts behind him. "About earlier, I would never—"

The stitch of concern in his brow relaxes and his expression flashes with a glint of amused realization. Closing the distance between them, they lock eyes as he draws nearer. "You adorable little thief," he says, his voice low. "I was looking everywhere for that shirt."

122

"Oh," she says, glancing down. A flash of heat engulfs her cheeks. "Is this yours?"

She barely has time to lift her gaze before his hand firmly captures the back of her neck, pulling her into a kiss. All the lingering looks and flirtatious cues cannot prepare her for the lush warmth of his mouth on hers. It stuns her. A desperate sound escapes him as his arms envelope her, tightening and pulling her close until not a whisper of space exists between their bodies.

Matching his intensity, she glides against the solid ridges of his chest and shoulders, wrapping around him like the night they danced. They find a fervent ebb and flow. His fingers weave through her hair, and for a moment, she's lost in the realization this is the kiss she craved from the moment they met.

He shifts back, leaving her gasping and weakened by the dark look in his eyes. With a gentle tug, he exposes the curve of her neck and draws a line of kisses from beneath her ear to her collar bone. Every soft breath, every sound he makes sends shivers of desire coursing through her.

They plunge into a hungry kiss. His tongue tastes hers and he holds her face with both hands, as if she were the most precious thing in the world. Parting for a moment, he lifts his white T-shirt up and over his head. When they're drawn back together, it's magnetic, frantic. He tugs the hem of her shirt upward, removing it. It falls to the floor and she's bare before him, but for a pair of panties. He studies her as if to memorize every detail, and her skin tingles under his scrutiny.

"Jesus, just look at you," he says softly, stepping closer. Bending, he lifts her and she wraps her legs around him as he carries her to bed.

He sets her at the edge. As he undresses, she takes in the details of his physique. Ben in a tailored suit is a lovely sight, but unclothed, he is a colossus—tall and broad shouldered, an impressive expanse of chest that tapers to a sculpted core, arms muscular and defined, legs powerful and solid. The sight of him is a testament to masculine beauty.

The smooth skin of his lips graze and kiss her breasts, belly, and hips. Kneeling at her feet, he caresses her legs with his fingertips before parting them. He casts warm breath up her thighs and through the fabric of her panties. Kissing her, then inhaling deeply and kissing again, over and over until she aches for him to pull them off or push them to the side or anything to feel the unfiltered sensation of his mouth.

His fingers hook and inch them down, then he swiftly tugs her by her thighs to the edge of the bed. It's overwhelming to her senses—the sound of his delight, the heat of his mouth, the flick of his tongue. The feeling passes like tingling laps of electricity across her skin. She can't stay still; she writhes, grinds, arches, and stretches as the pleasure becomes unbearable. Her fingers comb through his hair. She's falling and she wails, clutching at sheets.

When she unseals her eyes, he towers over her, presenting himself and stroking slowly. "Is this what you want?" His iron-like voice sends a chill through her.

"Please."

In a heartbeat, he's over her, positioning himself between her thighs. She wraps her arms around him, bracing as he buries himself in her, a low groan escaping his lips. The sensation of being so deliciously full makes her whimper into his shoulder. Her fingers play across the bristle of hair at the nape of his neck and trail down his back. He feels so good.

"Ben," she whispers.

His hips flex in a deliberate and rhythmic motion and it's all too much. The way his arms cocoon her, the texture of his tongue in her mouth, how his scent is inhaled and converted into signals of adulation that pull at her heart. "Ben."

Until now, she's been a seedling buried in the cold earth, yearning, reaching out for more. Under his touch, she's being

drawn out, beginning to breach the surface. "Ben!" she cries. An eruption, emerging out into the stunning sunrise. It's her liberation. She unfurls with profound release into the nourishing warmth of his light. His thrusts accelerate until he stiffens, releasing a primal sound that resonates against her mouth.

After, she tenderly traces her fingers across his shoulders and down his arms. They lie on their sides and exchange looks of disbelief. "You're real," she says, resting her palm gently on his face.

His warm hand comes to rest on her cheek. With a gentle smile, he responds. "I am real. Are you?"

"I'm not sure." She laughs.

It's not long before their kisses deepen once more. Straddling his hips, her hair cascades over him. His hands run down her sides, down her hips and thighs. "You don't know how many times I've imagined you just like this." The desire in his voice steals her breath.

She loves the way he gazes up at her, how his expressions morph from anguish to ecstasy. It goes on this way—he takes her every way he can, and they make love, kiss and stare until they're compelled to go again and again. He hovers over her and catches his breath. Gentle kisses find her mouth, her nose, her chin.

"I think if we don't stop soon, one of us is going to break," he whispers against her neck.

They lie together on damp sheets. He looks at her with adoring and exhausted eyes, but then it's as if a thought passes him and his expression fades to sadness. He strokes her cheek, his eyes glossy.

"What's wrong?" she asks.

"Things have been so bad for so long, I'd forgotten what it was like to have this. Being here with you, I don't know how to go back. I wish we didn't have to."

Her hand traces a line up and down his torso along the soft blanket of hair. "Let's stay," she whispers. "Never go back."

He hums in agreement. "Where would we live?"

"We can stay with Vinny until we get on our feet."

His body shakes against hers with laughter. "I thought you didn't like the city," he teases. "You wanted to live somewhere you can survive Armageddon."

"Mmm, you're right. Are you sure you'd want to live in the swamp?"

"If that's where you are," he says and kisses the top of her head.

The moment is so perfect. Thinking of getting on a plane tomorrow and watching him drive away from her makes a lump grow in her throat.

They whisper to each other in the dark.

"What was it like to start over?" he asks, his voice mumbling against her forehead.

"Scary."

"Yeah, but you did it."

"Oh yeah." She laughs. "I'm killing it in LA. Pretty soon, I'll be able to afford a couch."

He lets out a tense sigh. "I've worked so hard my entire life, and when I leave, she'll take everything."

"You can start over. Start your own firm."

"I know Ana. She'll make it her mission to destroy my reputation. The King family and their money versus me. No one will believe me. Even if they do, they're better off taking her side. That's where all the money is. They have all the power."

"You said her father is your mentor, like a father to you, right?"

"Oh, I'm not kidding myself." He lets out a long, weary sigh. "She's his little princess. He knows what goes on. He just doesn't give a shit. He's the big gun. When she really wants to hurt me, she cries to Daddy. Ana always gets what she wants."

Lifting her gaze, she finds his eyes brimming with unshed tears. He's been carrying this hopelessness around with him, hiding it inside, and now he's trusting her to see how it's weighed on him. She can see the hurt in his face, the stitch of outrage in his brow that this unfair reality has trapped him.

He takes her hand and brings it to the back of his head, leading her fingers through his hair to feel a patch where his scalp dips and puckers.

"What is that?"

"Staples. We got into a fight, and she threw a vase at me when I was trying to leave."

Her heart races, threatening to beat out of her chest. The situation is far more perilous than she'd realized. "I want to help you."

"I know you do, sweetheart, but I don't think this can be helped. I just need to cut my losses and go."

"You don't deserve to lose everything. It's not fair."

Gently, he lifts her hand to his lips and presses a tender kiss there. "It's not, but you've already helped me. You gave me hope. You make me happy. Ana can't take that away."

Of course she can. "She could kill you."

With a resigned expression, one that suggests he's considered the possibility more than once, he says, "Let's not talk about this right now."

Rolling on her side, he wraps around her and tucks her body close against him. "In the morning," he says, punctuating his words with kisses against her neck, "we'll get breakfast before my meeting." His mouth slides down her shoulder, across her back. "And when I get back, we could make it a lazy day, stay in bed until our flight, order room service. How does that sound?"

"That sounds perfect."

Chapter Seventeen

There's a knock at her window. Her mind runs through potential consequences of her non-compliance and she's powerless. The ceaseless drumming makes her belly burn with anxiety until she's compelled to open the window to make it stop. But it's not George standing there this time, it's Ana.

At least, she thinks it's her. The woman standing there is a combination of images she knows to be Ana. The woman in those photos online, Grace Kelly, the blurry woman yanking Ben's arm at Stella's party. Even now her face is a blur, and though the figure has no discernible eyes, Elyse gets the sense she's being watched. Her heart pounds fast and she's engulfed in frigid cold.

It's dark in her childhood bedroom in Miami, but outside the sun is rising. Ana turns to it, and it makes her porcelain skin radiate in impossible ways. It's as if Elyse can see the cells, molecules and atoms on their routes as they ripple through the atmosphere, see how they nourish the blurry woman and the white birds of paradise that sway and turn their leaves toward the light.

Elyse climbs out of the window and she's outside herself. Watching. Guillermo would say it's her mind's way of protecting her from the pain.

She crawls out and onto the grass, then creeps to the backyard, where the manchineel is cruelly situated between lemon and orange trees for an untrained eye to dine on a final meal. A green fruit gets plucked from an ashen branch and she returns to the window, but Ana is gone. Ominous clouds overhead are moving fast. An overpowering sense of dread washes over her. She's too late.

The bedside clock reads 6:41 a.m. when she springs up and catches her breath. The surreal images of the dream linger in her mind.

"I'm here," Ben whispers and encloses her in his arms. The panic slowly starts to fade as she becomes aware of the familiar surroundings of the hotel room. The soft muted glow of dawn bathes the room in faint light through a dense veil of sheer curtains.

The bare skin of Ben's arms is cold to the touch from where the air-conditioning had been hitting him all night. She glides her hands to the parts of him that are still warm from being under their blanket—down his flat belly, his hip, the trail of hair beneath his navel. For a moment, when he kisses her, she's self-conscious about her morning mouth, but then his tongue brushes hers and he hums with such longing that nothing else matters. He pulls back with her lower lip trapped between his teeth and it sets fire to something in her.

Pressing his chest until he's flat on his back, she bathes his neck in kisses. Soft breaths escape his throat and escalate to gentle moans as she sweeps her lips down his sculpted chest and his belly. She relishes in his scent, the smoothness of his skin against her mouth, how his body jerks when she's found a tender spot.

This is what he deserves, to be loved and lavished with affection. He's so clearly been starved of it. She was starved too, in her own way. They were both so desperate for the things they were missing they overindulged to exhaustion, and yet, they've woken up with fresh appetites. His body responds to her, his fingers lost in her hair. Taking him into her mouth, he inhales sharply and lets out a low hum of approval.

Her lips sweep across the velvety texture of his skin. It's never been like this before. Not just an act, but a means of communicating. What she hopes to say is that he's become everything and there is no end to the depth of her devotion. Eyes half-closed, fluttering shut occasionally, he watches her. She hopes he can see the sincerity in her every movement.

Then, with urgency, Ben raises her up. His mouth finds her neck, her breasts, his broad palms slide down her waist, her hips. He lifts her effortlessly and she surrenders to her own fragility against his strength. He slides her onto him so they're connected face-to-face, and she's lost again.

They're lost in each other until his phone starts to vibrate and glow on the end table. His muscles tense against her.

"Fuck."

His mind is elsewhere now. He's panicked.

Easing out of his lap, she brushes his stubbled cheek with her thumb. "Do you need to answer it?"

He rubs his face, then rises from bed, clearly distressed. "No." He shakes his head. "Shit, I'm sorry."

Perched at the bed's edge, she sulks. Just being reminded of Ana threw his mind into a frenzy. Seeing him in this anxious

state over that horrible woman unsettles her stomach. He moves to sit beside her, head bowed. Drawing a deep breath, he lifts his gaze, eyes almost pleading. "I don't love her anymore."

"You're afraid of her."

He scoffs, but he doesn't deny it.

She strokes his cheekbone where Ana left the bruise. "I understand why you're afraid. She's hurt you, manipulated you. It's normal to feel this way when someone treats you like that."

His phone is still vibrating. Just listening to the endless buzzing makes her want to answer the phone and scream into it. He lunges at it and squeezes the power button to turn it off. Once the screen turns black, he tosses it aside.

Elyse gets up to open the curtains. The room has a park view, and the tops of trees in Central Park stretch out in varied hues of green laid out like a rug before the distant skyline. The people below are walking fast, jogging, busy on their devices. Even up here, the harmony of city sounds bounce against the glass.

His warmth is behind her and he kisses her shoulder. "Come back to bed. It's early still." She turns to face him, and he's even better in the light of day. Muscles ripple beneath his taut olive skin, lightly shaded with a downy of fine dark hair. His eyes glitter at her, soaking her in. Gently, with a single thick finger, he tilts her chin upward. He leans down, granting her a brief yet tender kiss, his lips grazing her cheek and then her neck.

"Do you know how badly I wanted you out there in that desert?" His words cast warm breath against her ear and his deep voice sends a chill through her. "How hard it was for me not to kiss you that night we danced?"

Any hurt she felt melts away. She takes his hand and leads him back to bed, where they make love under the soft, golden light of the early morning.

After, they lie intertwined, and he strokes her hair. They're lost in thought. She wonders about their recklessness and whether there's any kind of plan for what life will be like once they land in Los Angeles. But they don't talk about it. He simply cradles her in his arms, a silent understanding passing between them. Everything will work out the way it was meant to.

* * *

After breakfast, Elyse rides up to her floor and returns to her room, faced with the aftermath of their passionate morning. Sheets are bunched up at the foot of the bed. The room is filled with his scent. Her heart swells thinking about him—the heat of his mouth, the power in his arms when he gripped her, how he'd made her ache between her legs. It makes her dizzy.

In bed, she rests on her back and looks up at her screen as she swipes through comments and posts. There are thousands of them. Elyse forgot Janine had access to post to her social media accounts. She must have shared Kieran's photos last night. They already have over twenty thousand likes. She's gained twice as many followers, and the numbers keep growing. Ben was onto something after all.

She reads the comments.

Stunning
Queen 👑
💜💜💜
You'll pay for what you did to my son

With a swipe, she deletes the comment, then blocks the account. Eileen Ramos really needs to find a hobby. Elyse pictures her across the street, sitting in her open garage with her smartphone, a fat sweaty finger swiping for internet justice.

Elyse lets out a scornful groan. *Come on, lady, move on with your life.*

Elyse checks her email. Someone named Carrie sent her a meeting invite. *Untitled Seth Weidman Project Meeting - Charles King / Elyse Santiago - August 8, 2017 at 3pm, The Beverly, Room 325.*

A hotel room? Remembering how Kieran warned her about Charles King, a chill sweeps over her. Was he telling the truth? Her breath hitches and her throat goes dry.

No, this is good. She takes a deep breath and composes herself. It's a sign. An opportunity. Now is not the time to panic, now is the time to strategize. She dials Stella. The clatter of footsteps and the wind beating against the receiver when she answers lets Elyse know Stella must be on the move.

"It happened," Elyse says and bites her thumb, awaiting her reaction.

Stella squeals with excitement. "I knew it would. How was it?"

"Exceptional. Five out of five stars."

"How do you feel?"

"I'm scared. I want to tell him everything, but I know he'd just freak out." Elyse pinches the phone between her ear and shoulder while she packs up her suitcase.

Stella sighs. "Of course he'll freak out. Do not tell him."

The thought makes her ill. "I know. I won't. He just seemed so unhappy talking about her. You were right. He feels trapped."

"Well, if anyone could help him, it's you."

"I know." Elyse closes her suitcase and zips it shut. "But I don't think Ana is the right target. She's too young. Too healthy." She sits on the edge of her bed, remembering the things Ben said last night. "What do you know about Charles King?"

Chapter Eighteen

The drive to the airport is somber. Although she wants to reassure him everything will be okay, help is on the way, she knows he wouldn't approve of her true plans.

During the flight, he leans close, whispering, "I'm not letting you go, El. We'll make it work. I'll do whatever it takes." He accents his promises with gentle kisses.

As the plane taxis to the gate, he squeezes her hand, saying softly, "We're going to be okay."

She squeezes back. "We will. Just please be careful."

"I will."

"I mean it. No romantic texts or calls. We can't leave a paper trail."

He nods, unaware of the depth of her meaning. She's going to save him.

Once home, Elyse begins to research Charles King's habits and health, trying to find a way to make his passing seem natural and inevitable. She jumps back to her search history on Ana King.

Ana's grandfather, Bertrand King, was an American film producer and co-founder of King Pictures, which sold to Picturesque in 2003 for $1 billion. When King died at age 88 from congestive heart failure...

Heart failure. She types in *Charles King heart disease.*

She scans the search results but finds them irrelevant or unhelpful, consisting of general health advice or sensationalist headlines about celebrities and their health woes.

She searches for Joseph King.

Joseph King, co-founder of King Management and brother of Charles King, has passed away at the age of 63 from heart disease. The billionaire entrepreneur, who inherited his share of the King family fortune from his father Bertrand King, had a storied career in the entertainment industry, producing numerous films and television shows that captivated audiences around the world.

Interesting. If Ana's grandfather and uncle both died from heart-related issues, it's possible Charles could be predisposed to heart problems as well.

Elyse is filled with excitement over the implications of her hypothesis. She has everything she needs—a garden full of deadly plants, lab equipment, and an appointment with Charles

King. That pervert probably thinks he's getting lucky. He has no idea that being alone with her will be the deadliest mistake of his life.

Early on the morning of August 6th, Elyse slips on her green rubber gardening gloves and preps a ten-gallon bucket. It's overcast and the air is balmy and stagnant.

Children play in the yard behind her and let out joyful screams. The rare bit of moisture in the air has awakened the sweet scent of jasmine and honeysuckle in her garden. Long stems of white and pink oleander are snipped and bundled upright into a lethal bouquet.

She surveys her countertop, crowded with ingredients she'd picked up at Trader Joe's. They're swept tightly together. Sugar. Corn syrup. Sweetened condensed milk. Cream. Butter. Bourbon vanilla.

It's a new recipe, and she's not sure how much she'll need to achieve the fatal blood concentration of oleandrin. She snips off leaves into the bucket, layer after layer until the pile is several inches high. This can't be left to chance. The effects need to be powerful, and this many leaves could take down an elephant.

She slides on a respirator she kept on an unofficial long-term loan from the University of Miami's lab department. The silicon material grips her face, applying tight pressure against her cheeks and forehead, shielding her eyes, nose and mouth with plastic. The straps squeeze shut at the back of her head, and she takes a few labored breaths through the filtered valves.

The oven where she'll dry the leaves is preheated to four hundred degrees. They're spread out in thin, layered batches on cookie sheets. Her phone vibrates on the table. It's Ben. She holds her breath as her finger hesitates over the decline button, then sends his call to voicemail. He can't know what she's up to. The only way he'll be safe is if she keeps him out of this.

Once the leaves are dry, she yanks a fresh pair of purple latex gloves from a box. They stretch, grip and snap against her skin. It's time to go to work.

She pulverizes the leaves in a copper mortar. *Clank, clank, clank, clank.* The tool strikes against the metal, and she sways her hips to the rhythmic sound it creates in four-four time, like a cowbell keeping a steady beat.

Maybe she and Ben will cook together like this. She'd watch from the counter as he chops fresh herbs from her garden, the sleeves of his dress shirt rolled up to his elbows. After, they'd cuddle in front of a movie on a couch they'd own together. Maybe one of his client's movies. He'd press a warm kiss on her cheek, and they'd settle into the soft cushions and each other's bodies.

She fills an Erlenmeyer flask with the pulverized dust then covers it with ethanol. Her gloves cling and catch against the smooth surface of the flask as she swirls it like a glass of cognac. Warm water gushes from the faucet and into a Dutch oven. Twisting the knob on her stove to high, she places a ceramic bowl inside to act as a hot water bath.

The temperature rises in her kitchen, and sweat drips from her forehead into her eyes, burning them. She blinks to clear her vision before heaving open a kitchen window. When the steam starts to rise, the air becomes sultry like Miami in the summertime and it clings to her skin.

Elyse watches a YouTube video—someone named Jill making homemade caramel. Her MacBook rests on the kitchen counter as she follows along, her gaze bouncing between the screen and her ingredients, the screen and her stove. She turns a bottle of cream upside down over a deep pot, and it glugs rapidly until it's empty. One, two, three sticks of butter. *Sheesh.* If the oleandrin doesn't stop his heart, all this butter and cream will.

Elyse slowly stirs and stirs the smooth, bubbling concoction. She jerks her head over her shoulder to catch Jill pouring her finished mixture into a glass dish. Her mouth waters, and she chuckles to herself at the thought of absentmindedly licking the spoon and dying in the dumbest way possible. *Worst. Assassin. Ever.* Laughter is released through the respirator in breathy hisses, which makes her laugh harder.

The cream froths and boils. Vanilla extract pools in a brown puddle before she folds it in and pours the molten poison into the buttered dish. The thick confection oozes from the pot in skinny ribbons until it settles, the ripples on the surface sinking flat. She leaves it to cool in the fridge.

The mask forms dents in her face. A sun is rising on her forehead. Red lines crease across the bridge of her nose and down her cheeks, like some kind of Nordic war paint.

She takes a deep breath and inhales the scent of warm sugar. *This will be your best work yet.* A professional presentation would improve the odds these caramels are eaten. Maybe they should be individually wrapped.

Finding her phone, she taps the Postmates app. Candy wrappers. *Add to cart.* Round candy tin. *Add to cart.* Fancy flakey salt. *Why not? Add to cart. Two-hour delivery, please.*

She reviews the meeting invitation again. *Untitled Seth Weidman Project Meeting - Charles King / Elyse Santiago - August 8, 2017 at 3pm, The Beverly, Room 325.*

Imagining what it would be like to wake up next to Ben every morning—feeling the warmth of his body radiate against her bare skin, inhaling his scent, feeling the bass of his voice against her neck—is dizzying. *Ahhh.* Just daydreaming about him is a thrill that makes her tingle all over. She longs for lazy Sunday mornings in bed, wrapped up in each other's arms. Life could be so sweet.

When the order arrives, she lays out the sheets of gold cellophane, then cuts out a square from the corner of the dish.

The caramel skin wrinkles against the blade of the knife. She rolls the candy into bite sized pieces, imagining what it will be like once she is the woman who gets to take care of Ben. She'll be the one to create a sanctuary where they can both find peace and happiness.

As she sets the caramels in the tin, an eerie sense of calm washes over her. Nothing is random, nothing is by chance. They were meant to be together. She was meant to save him, he to save her. Elyse sees this challenge as a perfect equation waiting to be balanced, and she is the catalyst that will make it happen.

Chapter Nineteen

"Mr. Deluca, Joseph Sierra's in the building." Janine announces Sierra's arrival through the intercom. Ben reviews his notes but he's distracted. Elyse has gone dark since they parted ways at LAX.

He pushes the intercom. "Janine, could you come in here for a minute, please?"

She enters with a bite of sandwich still wedged in her cheek, then swallows hard. "Yes, Mr. Deluca."

"Isn't Elyse supposed to come in to see Chuck later today?"

"No, sir. Carrie said the meeting is off-site. Do you want me to find out where it is?"

Seth Weidman's office is only a few blocks east. He's directing the picture. That's probably where they'll be. He was hoping to be able to prepare Elyse for her meeting, but she wasn't answering any of his calls and he was starting to get nervous.

"Has she called the office?"

"No. Did you want me to try her again?"

"No, that's alright. Thank you."

There's no time now. Sierra's on his way up, so he tries to focus on his meeting. They're rolling out the red carpet for him. The bottle of bourbon Ben plans to gift him costs more than his first car. It's a twenty-year-old WL Weller Kentucky bourbon—Sierra's favorite. Ben's tried it before. It's sweet, with hints of vanilla and a spicy cinnamon finish. He hopes it will dull the pain when Ben tells him the studio is done making his series of action films, *Bloodoath*.

Sierra strolls in wearing a tan, wide-brim hat with a tribal patterned band. He always looks the part. Last year, Ben helped him buy a cattle ranch in Colorado. Five hundred acres between a river and monolithic red rocks. It's incredible. Ben even made arrangements for the cows, which to his surprise, Sierra had no idea what to do with.

"Why would you buy a cattle ranch if you don't know anything about cattle?"

"To be a cowboy," he'd replied without an ounce of irony.

When Sierra says hello, he rests a palm on Ben's cheek. "Bennie Boy," he says with a smirk. It's his way of being overly familiar. It's one of the things Ben learned to tolerate because the guy made $35 million last year, ten-percent of which helped justify Ben's existence at King.

He pats Sierra on the back. "I like the hat."

"Merino wool from free-range sheep in Patagonia," Sierra says. "I'll pick one up for you next time."

Ben never thought to ask if the wool in his suit was free range or where the sheep grew up, but it sounds fancy so he makes a mental note.

They meet in the visitor room and sit on a turquoise, crushed velvet sofa between potted palms. The room is lit with soft light from recessed bulbs in the ceiling. A teleconference system mounted on a faux brick wall was once used for karaoke after visitors drank way too much from the fully stocked private bar. It's where Ben presents the bottle of bourbon to Sierra on his arm.

"I heard you like twenty-year-olds, so I got you a little something."

Sierra cradles it in his hands. "Let's crack her open."

It's not even noon. Ben knows what's going to happen—he'll be shitfaced by dinner. But the man is responsible for two-thirds of his income, so he grabs a couple of glasses and they clink together. Setting them on a concrete cocktail tray that rests on a large tufted leather ottoman in front of Sierra, Ben pours them each two fingers worth of the amber liquor. They settle into the soft cushions and take in the liquor's woody aroma. There are definitely worse ways to spend an afternoon.

He only just takes a sip, when his phone vibrates and he quickly yanks it from his pocket. *Nope.* He must have been imagining it. Nothing from Elyse. Maybe she's having second thoughts. He tries to push the anxiety from his mind.

Their short trip to New York was exactly what he needed. Elyse is sexy and affectionate, and their time together reminded him what it felt like to be happy. Seeing her up close in those little nude patches in the desert, he'd thought he could imagine what it would be like to make love to her, but actually having her was the difference between looking through a telescope and walking on the fucking moon.

The bourbon's cinnamon finish hits as Chuck strolls in with open arms. "Sierra, how are you?"

Sierra smiles and raises his glass. "Chuck."

Once, after several bourbons and a duet of *"Islands in the Stream,"* Sierra told Ben he thinks Chuck is an insufferable,

elitist asshole. Ben gets some pleasure out of watching Chuck go in for a warm handshake.

"You boys having a drink?"

"That we are," Sierra says.

Chuck sits with them like old chums and talks shop. Ben can tell Sierra isn't interested, but he lets Chuck tire himself out. He goes on and on until Sierra looks like he's going to cry from boredom.

"Well, I'm off," Chuck finally says. "I have some off-site meetings this afternoon. Always so good to see you."

"Always a pleasure," Sierra says, a sigh of relief relaxing his shoulders. He's a talented actor—he sounds like he means it.

Ben speaks up before Charles can make it out the door. "Hey, you're meeting with Elyse later today?"

Charles pauses and nods. "Yes, very pretty girl."

The urge to warn him, to give him detailed care instructions, is overpowering. Treat her gently. Please be kind to her. Be patient. She gets nervous and shy sometimes, she just needs a little reassurance. Make her laugh, it will put her at ease. But he doesn't say any of these things because it won't do her any good. Instead, he nods. "You're gonna love her."

Chuck waves dismissively and sees himself out, leaving Sierra and Ben alone. Not a moment later, Sierra blows a raspberry.

"What. A. Pill."

Ben gives him a knowing look and smirks around his glass.

They drink almost $10,000 worth of bourbon that afternoon and into the early evening before Ben finally decides it's the perfect time to break the bad news.

"I talked to Geller at Picturesque."

Sierra's shoulders slump and he deflates like the subject bores him to death.

"They're not renewing your option on *Bloodoath*." He waits for Sierra's reaction.

Sierra takes a long, hungry sip from his glass, then slams it down on the table before slouching back on the sofa. "I'm done man. I'm hanging it up."

Six years ago, Sierra was on divorce number three, which ended in a very brutal and public blaze of glory. All the critics were questioning whether he was too dysfunctional, too old, no longer relevant, or all of the above. He'd been ready to quit back then, but Ben and *Bloodoath* changed his career, while making him obscenely rich. He was one of the success stories Ben was most proud to tell. This can't be how it ends.

"You're not hanging it up. You had one loss after a hundred wins and you're gonna quit?" Ben pours them each another drink.

"I'm a wealthy man. I don't need this shit anymore. For what? To get richer? Money doesn't buy happiness."

Bullshit. Ben knows how it feels to slip into an $8,000 suit and pick from several $100,000 timepieces in a sprawling walk-in closet. To play golf at private clubs and ski at the King family lodge in Vail, Colorado. He's travelled to six continents and stayed at the world's finest hotels, sailed on private yachts and dined at Michelin-star restaurants. Maybe it wasn't happiness but it was awfully close.

"It's not about the money. You're Joe fucking Sierra, and you're not going anywhere. We both know *Bloodoath* wasn't the best you could do as an actor. When was the last time you really lost yourself in a character?"

Sierra gets misty eyed. Ben puts a hand on his shoulder and shakes him gently. "Come on, man. Don't make this weird."

"I just owe you so much." He's choked up. Some people are happy drunks. Not Sierra. Get enough drinks in him, and he'll weep all night.

Ben shakes his head and laughs. "You've compensated me handsomely. What are you talking about?"

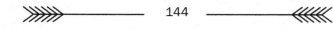

"It's more than that. You pulled me out of a dark place, got me *Bloodoath*. I wouldn't be here without you, Bennie Boy."

"Stop it. It was all you, man. You did the work."

Sierra sips from his glass and lets out a deep sigh. "Now what?"

"Eddie Sanz wrote a dark comedy based on *Prometheus and the Theft of Fire*, and you're Zeus. I'll send you the script. You've been doing this intense action thing for so long, it'll be a little unexpected. Your fans are going to love it. It's gonna open up a whole new genre for you."

Sierra holds Ben's cheek and winks at him. "I'll give it a read."

Putting that problem behind him is a weight lifted. The bourbon has made him warm all over and his worries drift into the ether. They're about to fire up the karaoke app when Ben's phone buzzes again. *Elyse!* Checking his phone, he sees it's Ana calling. He sighs with disgust.

Sierra smirks at him. "That's the sound I made when my ex-wife used to call me."

"Which one?" Ben jokes as he stumbles out of the room and into the hallway. Most of the office seems to have left for the day. "Hello?"

"Is Daddy with you?"

"No, I'm entertaining Sierra. Chuck left this afternoon for some meetings."

"He's not answering his phone for me or Mommy."

"Maybe he's busy."

"Come home. It's late." Her voice is soft and sweet. It's a trap.

"I'll try, but you know how Sierra is."

Ana sighs. "Come home."

Before he can argue, she hangs up on him.

Sierra is already standing when Ben returns. He tucks his hand around the waist of his pants and smooths out his shirt. "When the wife calls that means it's time to go."

"I'm sorry, man. She's a tough woman to argue with."

"Sounds like it. Boss's daughter. That's gotta be tricky."

"It's a nightmare." He points to the still-healing cut on his forehead. "This is what happened the last time I stayed out all night."

"Christ, kid. How'd she do that?"

"Threw a bottle at me. The woman has no self-control whatsoever." He's not sure why he's telling him this, but there's something about Sierra that puts Ben at ease.

Sierra pats him on the back. "You're a pacifist. I know it. I am too. But sometimes you gotta go to war, kid." It sounds like a line out of *Bloodoath*, but it puts a smile on Ben's face. Sierra's father was a television producer and he grew up in Hollywood, but he's really embraced the whole cowboy thing.

"You wanna see the girl I'm going to war for?"

Sierra's eyes get big and an intrigued smirk forms on his lips. He raises his eyebrows and Ben is already pulling up Elyse's Instagram account. Offering Sierra his phone, a smile stretches across his face. "Wow. This your girlfriend?"

Ben grins and nods. "Yeah. Isn't she perfect?" Thinking of her steals his breath, and he lets out a content sigh.

Sierra pats him on the back. "You're even dumber than you look playing with fire like that."

"I know, but I'm crazy about her." If only she'd return his calls.

In the parking garage, Ben escorts Sierra to his flamboyant lime-green Lamborghini, arrogantly sprawled over three spaces. Sierra cups Ben's cheek. "My Bennie Boy."

Ben grimaces. "Ah, come on. Don't be weird."

Suddenly, Sierra clasps Ben's face and plants a kiss squarely on his lips. Startled, Ben pushes him away. "Hey!"

"I know it was you, Fredo."

"I told you, no kissing. I was serious," Ben wipes his mouth with his arm.

Sierra laughs and pats Ben on the cheek just hard enough it borders on a slap. He crouches and crawls into his car. The doors lower and he revs the engine before pulling back and driving away.

Ben gets into his Range Rover and retrieves Elyse's contact card on his phone. It's after one a.m., and she's probably asleep by now, but he wants to know how things went with her meeting.

Hey, sorry to text so late. I was with a client all day. How did things go with Chuck?

Chapter Twenty

The curtains are drawn, and even though the sun outside is glaringly bright, it's dark inside where Charles sits across from Elyse in his white cotton robe.

When she'd arrived at room 325, Charles opened the door with a smug expression. He let her in, then sauntered across the room to rest in a cushioned hotel chair. The air smelled like soap.

"I just got out of the shower," he said, explaining the fresh steam in the air.

Unless she's a complete moron, his assistant, Carrie, might as well be an accomplice. Even though Kieran warned her, Elyse still finds herself distressed, poised between the window and king-sized bed, her palms slick with sweat. The only light comes from a razor thin crack in the curtains and two lamps on either side of the bed set to dim.

"You have a lovely body. Are you comfortable with nudity?" he asks.

It's literally the first question he asks. His skin is translucent. Dark blue veins branch through his chest and neck. His hairline seems to start at his crown and what's left of his white hair is slicked back.

"I...I don't know. I guess it depends."

He smiles at her. "Your breasts, are they natural?"

She laughs nervously and drops her head. Her cheeks warm up with a sudden blush of embarrassment.

"That's not an answer."

"Yes." Heat rises and her stomach aches with shame. It's not her who should be ashamed, but it doesn't stop her body from sending signals of its repulsion to her brain that twist up her insides with dread. The signals tell her somehow this is her fault, that she's foolish to meet him here. But she'd practiced all the things she'd say at home out loud, and in her head again on the ride there. He was the foolish one for underestimating her.

"The character has a couple of scenes that involve nudity. We're looking for someone who's willing to take risks."

As Elyse stands up from her seat, Charles's gaze follows her, surprised by her sudden movement.

"What kind of risks?" she asks in a voice that suggests her IQ is a negative number. She bends before him to retrieve the metal tin from her bag on the floor. When she stands back up, he's silently watching her, subtly rubbing himself through his robe.

"What's that?"

She's already begun to unwrap the candy when she sits on his lap. "Do you like sweets?"

His eyes light up, and her hand guides his mouth open to receive the poison confection on his slimy tongue like a communion wafer.

She smiles at him. "I've perfected the recipe."

The corners of his mouth perk up. "I bet you taste just as sweet." He cups her breast, and she suppresses her instinct to recoil in disgust. His grip tightens.

She drags her thumb along his bottom lip. "How was it?"

"Very yummy."

"I'm glad you like it. I made them special for you."

His eyes light up and a smile slowly creeps across his face. "You did?" His fingers glide under the hem of her top. "Take this off."

Her heart pounds. The oleander isn't an instant fix. It'll be a while before the effects start. She has to commit or this isn't going to work. She takes her time.

"Only if you have... one... more," she says with a coy smile.

He doesn't seem the slightest bit suspicious or distrusting. He's not even asking any questions. With her alone in his room, in his lap, the promise of a career-changing role hanging in the balance, he undoubtedly thinks he's the one in control.

He accepts another into his mouth, and she strokes his hair while the sugars dissolve and slide down his throat. Once it's gone, he presents his empty mouth to her, consideration for their trade. He looks her up and down. "Go ahead, honey."

She rubs his shoulders first and presses her bust against his face. *This should tide him over for a little while.* It only buys her a few minutes before he's groping her again with his wrinkled and spotted hands.

"Come on, don't make me wait."

"Can't we talk a little?"

He leers at her. "I've heard you talk. Now let me see you."

Shoot. Now what? She slowly twists and glides before him, his focus following her with anticipation. It's all part of the dance—inching up her blouse, lifting it over her head and flirting with him over her bare shoulder. She turns her back on him to carefully fold it and lay it neatly on the bed. By the time she turns around, his penis is out and he's massaging his testicles, squeezing them. It's like he's turning on a device.

The pink shaft sounds like it's vibrating, whirring and squeaking as his erection swells to a chubby stub. *Oh my God. It's bionic!* A gasp is trapped her throat. It repulses her, but her morbid curiosity refuses to allow her to look away. *Oh, I can't wait to tell Stella about this.*

"Take off your bra," he instructs.

"My bra?" She struggles not to laugh.

He nods. Her arms slowly bend back to grab the clasp. She makes a drawn-out tease of it before letting the lilac, satin fabric fall to the ground. This will be the last thrill he ever gets, and she makes it last. He strokes himself slowly, his gaze fixed on her breasts.

"On your knees," he says and taps his foot on the spot where he expects her to go. The thought of him coming on her or putting that ugly wrinkled thing in her mouth sends the contents of her stomach thrusting upward and she steels herself. "I'm not doing that."

"You don't have to do anything. I just want to look at you."

"You can look at me from over there."

He strokes furiously and his neck flashes bright red. Sweat dampens the white hair of his receding hairline and drips down his generous forehead. "Please. I'm so close. Just let me touch you a little."

Keep going, old man. Get that blood flowing and get those chemicals where they need to go.

"Please," he begs again, a vein protruding from his forehead. "You want the job, don't you?"

Letting him think she's mulling it over, she taps a finger against her chin. "I don't think you've actually told me what the job is."

He exhales with frustration. "It's a role in a Hollywood feature film. Any girl in your position would be begging for the opportunity to even be in this room. Now please, let me touch you."

"I don't care about the job."

Surprised, he pauses. "Of course you do. Why else would you come here?"

Without looking at him or saying a word, she squats to pick her bra up from the floor, as if she plans to storm out.

"No, please. I'm sorry. Just let me look at you a little longer. I'm almost done."

Buttoning up her blouse, she glances at her phone where it rests on the bed to check the time. He'll start to feel it soon.

Charles rises to his feet and tightens the strap on his robe before taking a step forward. He stumbles, extending out his arms for balance.

"Are you alright?" she asks.

The icy blue depth of his eyes flash with loathing as he meets her gaze. Gathering strength, he manages to move a few feet to the bed, then collapses at its edge. Beads of sweat glisten on his forehead, while the pallid skin of his neck is now flushed a deep shade of crimson. As his gaze transitions from resentment to alarm, he points a trembling finger toward the bathroom. "Please. There's medication in there. My heart," he says, struggling with each word.

"I'll go get it. Wait there."

Slipping her hand into her purse, she discreetly retrieves a pair of latex gloves. In the bathroom, she puts them on, her gaze darting around. An orange medicine bottle catches her attention on the counter. Digoxin. Just as she'd thought. The pills inside make a subtle rattling noise as she saunters back to him. "Congestive heart failure?"

"What?" he asks, panting.

She gets him a bottled water from the bar fridge and watches him take the pills. Grateful, he nods, his hands still trembling.

"Your father died from congestive heart failure. I thought you might too."

Once he notices her gloves, he squints at her, trying to make sense of what's happening. "I don't understand." He looks disoriented now. A confused expression weighs down his brow as he falls on his back.

"Are you okay?"

"Call 911."

"I'm sorry, I can't do that," she says. Pressing two fingers along his windpipe, she can feel the blood pulsing through his carotid artery. "Your heart is beating like a hummingbird, Charles."

He struggles to sit up, but he doesn't have the strength. "Please," he groans.

"You've seen my videos, haven't you?" She pauses for him to answer, but he just gives her a silent, fearful look. "Oleander. It produces something called oleandrin. It works like the digoxin you take for your heart condition. It's not overly sensitive to heat so it's easy to cook with. The problem is, it's very bitter, so having all that sugar in the caramel recipe really helps balance out the flavor."

He struggles again, thrashing his arms to get up like a turtle flipped on its shell. "Why?" he asks.

"Why?" She laughs. "Do you jerk off like this to all the girls who come here for a job? Do you rape them?"

"No, no, I don't," he says, his eyes fluttering.

"Lying isn't going to save you, Charles."

He spits at her, his eyes wild. "What do you want? Money?"

"I want Ben," she says.

He flinches, blinking in disbelief. "I don't know what he promised you," he says, struggling with every word.

"Ben doesn't know about this, if that gives you any peace." She strokes his cheek lovingly to calm him. "He told me you were his mentor, like the father he never had. He loved you. He just wanted you to accept him and teach him the things fathers teach their sons. But instead, you took advantage of that need and used it against him, used it to keep him married to your abusive daughter."

"No," he grunts.

"Don't pretend you didn't know."

A grimace etched in his face, he takes a short, shaky breath. "Ben," he whispers. He closes his eyes and his breaths start to shallow and quicken. A clenched fist falls to his chest and he winces in pain. Then, like his little bionic penis, his body deflates.

She presses her fingers along his windpipe. Nothing. She clicks her tongue and carefully gathers the caramel wrappers, tucking them into her purse along with her gloves. There's a mirror by the door, and she stands in front of it to straighten herself out before silently slipping out of the room.

Chapter Twenty-One

Ben shields his eyes from the assault of light flooding into his bedroom. *Jesus.* It beams brightly through windows unobstructed by curtains. Nice of Ana to open them so he couldn't sleep in. A dull ache in his head serves as a reminder he can't hang with Joe Sierra.

Dragging out a stool behind the kitchen island, he slumps on it, his face falling into his hands. Flora's breakfast making fills the air with the comforting aroma of coffee. He groans, his dehydrated mouth watering at the thought of a hot cup. As he takes the first sip, the warmth spreads through him, and his pulse pounds in his temple.

"Good morning, *mijo*," Flora greets him.

"Morning," he grunts in response. "Where's the boss?"

"She's gone to do exercise, but she'll probably be back soon," she says, scrambling an egg with a fork before pouring it into a copper pan. The blue flames beneath it heat up, causing the egg to sizzle.

Nodding, he sips his coffee, trying to ignore his throbbing migraine. Flora would support him if she knew the truth about his plans, but a part of him wonders how she would feel about his infidelity. The thought lingers in his mind as Flora turns to face him, holding a spatula upright like a torch.

"*Conocí a alguien*," he says, his voice hoarse. *I met someone.*

Flora pauses for a moment, studying his face before responding. "*¿Una mujer?*" she asks, her voice laced with worry. *A woman?*

"*Sí, y yo la quiero mucho*," Ben replies. *Yes, and I really care about her.*

Flora looks at him with concern, eyes silently warning. He suspects she's worried Ana might find out. The thunderous slam of the door to the garage interrupts their moment, causing both of them to jump. Flora hides behind the refrigerator door as Ana storms into the kitchen.

"Have you talked to Daddy?" Ana asks, her voice trembling.

Ben tenses. "No, why?"

"He didn't come home last night," she says, clutching her stomach.

Hmm. His hazy mind struggles through possible explanations. Chuck probably just needed to blow off some steam. Colette is as big of a pain in the ass as her daughter and maybe Chuck wanted a night off.

"Relax. Let me call Carrie. I'm sure she'll track him down."

Ben phones Chuck's assistant, Carrie. When she answers, it sounds like she's in a hurry and a child is fussing in the background. "I'm sorry to bother you. Do you know where Chuck

went yesterday after he left the office? Nobody's heard from him and we're a little concerned."

"Uh...he was off-site."

"I know, but where?"

"Oh... uh...I have to call you back."

"Wait," he says, but she's already hung up. *That's strange.*

He knows Chuck had a meeting with Elyse, but Ben really doesn't want to drag her into this. He checks his watch. It's not even noon. He'll turn up eventually.

"Carrie's going to look into it and call me back, okay?"

Ana's eyes fill with tears and she clings to him. "I have a bad feeling."

"Everything is going to be okay," he tries to reassure her, yet he fights the urge to recoil from her touch. It's the first time she's sought comfort from him in a long time, longer than he can even remember. She's never vulnerable like this.

"He's not answering. He always answers for me. He'd at least call me back, but he hasn't. I called so many times." Her heart is beating fast against him.

Even if he doesn't love her, being here for her is the decent thing to do. Though, it's a struggle to release any words of consolation against his tightening throat. "Shhh, just relax. Breathe."

Ana's tear-filled eyes meet his, and a swell of sympathy for her fights against his bitterness. Hesitating, he knows she doesn't deserve his pity, but he surrenders to it, and defeat sinks through him.

"Come on, do something to take your mind off of this." Resting his palm on her shoulder, he leads her to the couch.

"Sit with me."

Reluctantly, he takes a seat beside her. When she climbs into his lap, a twist of repulsion knots his stomach. How he wishes he could turn to stone when she cries instead of letting

her crawl into his lap for his comfort. His body can muster no desire to hold her, to touch her, but it's not worth the fight.

With a tug, Ana collects a blanket from the back of the couch, draping it over them, then lays her head against him. "Put something on." she whimpers.

A quiet sigh escapes him. *Sucker. Chump. Patsy.* Picking up the remote, he switches on the television.

***

The drone of *Keeping Up with the Kardashians* plays in the background. Ana is curled up in his lap, and from her stillness and soft breath against his neck, it seems she's fallen asleep. Ben's phone vibrates with a text from Elyse.

It went okay, I guess. Kind of weird meeting in a hotel room.

A hotel room? Carrie just said it was an off-site meeting.

I thought it was at Seth's office. I'm sorry. Thanks for letting me know. I'll check in soon.

Feeling Ana shift, he slides his phone into his pocket. Waking with a stretch and a yawn, she asks, "Did Carrie call back?"

"Not yet."

She exhales with a mix of annoyance and concern, disentangling herself to pace the room. He watches her, hoping there's a logical explanation for all of this. Before he can dwell further, his phone buzzes again. Carrie's name flashes on the screen.

"Mr. Deluca?" she says. It sounds like she's been crying. A tight knot of anxiety forms in his stomach as he braces for whatever comes next.

"Hey, what's going on?"

"I'm so sorry. I don't know how to tell you this."

The line goes silent and he holds his breath. *This can't be good.*

"Mr. King passed away," she says, her voice hushed.

His body goes cold. *Oh God.* How is he going to tell Ana?

"What happened?" he asks.

Ana freezes in place and stares at him with worry.

"He...he was at the Beverly. After you called, I asked them to do a wellness check and they found him. They need a member of the family. I wasn't sure who to tell them to call."

"I'll call them right now. Thank you, Carrie."

Hanging up, he turns to Ana. As much as she deserves to suffer for the things she's done to him, the shots she's taken and all the pain she's caused, this news is devastating, and he gets no pleasure from destroying her with it.

Making his voice soft, he starts, "Sweetheart, I'm so sorry."

Her eyes are wide and distant, as if she already knows the truth and is still holding out hope she's wrong.

"Chuck passed away. He was at a hotel in Beverly Hills."

Ana's face crumples, and she collapses onto the couch, embracing herself tightly. Ben, acting on instinct, holds her as she dissolves into tears. The news leaves them both paralyzed in shock.

By the next morning, Chuck's ugly mug is all over social media and national news.

Charles King, Hollywood Mogul, Dead at 65. The entertainment world was shocked and saddened to hear of his

sudden death after suffering a heart attack in a Beverly Hills hotel room Friday.

Ben went through the motions of comforting Ana and Colette, sorted out the logistics of how Chuck's body was to be carried from the hotel to the funeral home.

He goes into the office on Monday to phones that won't stop ringing. People look panicked as they filter in and out of his office with questions. Carrie is crying at her desk. Photographers with long lenses congregate outside the building.

Everyone is coming to Ben as if there's some natural line of succession, but nothing was ever discussed, at least not with Ben. Chuck probably planned to live forever. Even after retirement, he was going to stay on the board and pull strings. Now the board is meeting without him, but in the meantime, Ben can't get anything done.

Just after sunset, his phone vibrates.

When are you coming home? I need you.

He eyes Ana's text with skepticism. But she's grieving, after all. Despite the endless list of tasks before him, he rises to his feet and gathers his things. He nods to Janine on his way out of the office.

As he passes through the motor court, he can see the lights inside the house glowing softly. The grand door creaks open to the palatial, dimly lit interior. The aroma of a fresh-cooked meal wafts through the air.

Ana stands in the entryway, her silhouette illuminated by the gold light from the dining room. The sweatpants she'd worn for days have been swapped for a satin slip dress the same color as her fair skin. Her hair is down, falling in blonde ringlets against her shoulders. For a second, they just look at each other.

"You're home," she says, her voice weak and laced with need. He follows her to the dining room, where she's lit candles.

They flicker against the lustrous fabric of her dress. "I waited for you," she whispers, pulling out his chair. The usual edge to her voice, the one that had cut him countless times, is absent.

She pours wine into two glasses, handing one to him. Taking a sip of the deep red liquid, he watches her over the rim, the taste bittersweet.

They share a meal, mostly in silence but for the gentle clinks of silverware on porcelain. "I thought we could use a quiet dinner together," she says. She clears her throat as if she's been working up the courage to say something. "I know I've been difficult. But I wanted you to know that I'm so glad you're here with me," she says, her voice quivering. "Especially now, with Daddy gone. I don't know what I'd do without you taking care of everything."

His heart begins to race like a cornered animal. Images of Elyse's body, the day they spent in bed, cause his throat to tighten with shame. He's at war with himself, his mind pleading with his heart to put an end to this nonsense and learn his lesson, but looking into Ana's vulnerable eyes, his heart wants to believe her.

Elyse is special. They shared a connection unlike anything he's ever felt before, but Ana is his wife. They have years of history, they took vows.

Reaching across the table, she takes his hand and locks eyes with him. "We've both made our mistakes." The way she looks through him makes him wonder what she knows. "I want us to leave the past behind. Can we start fresh?"

They've been here before—the clean slate. The temptation to trust her again is powerful, even if every ounce of logic warns against it. An unexpected weight of guilt, previously unnoticed, presses on him. With her, his misdeeds, spoken and unspoken, might find absolution.

His fingers intertwine with hers and he lets out a heavy sigh. "Let's take it one day at a time," he says, drawing her hand to his lips.

"That's all I ask."

After, she stands and beckons him, leading him to their bedroom. There, she leans in, pressing her mouth to his with a desire he hasn't felt from her in a long time. Despite the unease he feels, caught between the memories of the pain, his deep feelings for Elyse and the present warmth, he responds, wrapping his arms around her, allowing himself to give in to the moment, the dangerous allure of hope.

***

It's after hours when Ben walks past the motion sensor in the darkened King office building. He'd waited for Ana to fall asleep. As to not disturb her, he stealthily slipped out of bed, pulled a blanket over her bare shoulder and pressed a kiss to her cheek before whispering. "I'll be back in a bit."

The lights flicker on in rapid succession. He strides past vacant offices and empty chairs toward a dim glow from the hallway. It lays a thin path to where Janine sits, an unexpected silhouette against the brightness of her computer screen.

"What are you doing here?" Ben's voice breaks the quiet.

She doesn't look up immediately, focused on finishing the sentence she's typing. "Final touches on the transition notices."

Ben nods, processing the information. He's distracted by the emotional turbulence of the last few weeks and the mountain of work it's made for him.

"Oh, Elyse called earlier," Janine remembers. "Just after you left."

He freezes, momentarily taken aback. *Elyse.* The very name sends his pulse skyrocketing. Memories of New York, of her skin against his and their whispered promises invade his mind.

"She say what it was about?"

"No." Her eyes scan his for a hint of reaction. "She asked if you were in. When I said you weren't, she said she'd try again later."

A brief pang of guilt stings him as his phone buzzes. Not Elyse, but another work email. He silences it, that unmade call seeming to grow heavier in his pocket. He'd promised himself to call her. Every time he thought of her. But not now, he decides, there's too much to do.

"Send me the notices when you're done." He slips into his office and shuts the door.

***

The next morning, he's working from Chuck's office, having been tasked with reassigning his clients and picking up whatever was left on his calendar.

"He had meetings scheduled all week. Did you want to take any of these over or should I call and cancel?"

Ben looks through Chuck's old-fashioned leather day planner. All of the appointments were in hotels. *Tiffany: 2 p.m. Alissa: 4 p.m.* The guy had stamina. These women didn't know how lucky they were he died before he could trick them into giving him a hand job in exchange for a shitty background role.

"Cancel these."

Carrie nods in acknowledgement and leaves Chuck's office. While looking for files, Ben opens a drawer and hears a clank. There's a steel lockbox tucked away behind rows of hanging folders. He looks around before setting it on the desk and examining it. It has sliding knobs that unlock with a three-digit combination.

Taking a stack of files, he rests the box discreetly in between before carrying the stack to his office. There, his curiosity piqued, he pulls it from the pile. It isn't Fort Knox. With a few wiggles of a paperclip on each side, the rinky-dink clasps pop open with ease.

Inside are stacks of envelopes and Polaroid photos bound together with a rubber band. Ben's eye is immediately drawn to a pair of large, natural-looking breasts. *Oh, what do we have here?* He scurries to close the blinds before hurrying back to his desk with excitement.

The old rubber band pops under the slightest pressure, and the photos fan out in his hand like a deck of cards. One falls on his desk, revealing a photo of a naked woman Ben recognizes as an actress Chuck used to brag about representing back in his UCLA teaching days, Marjorie something. As he shuffles through, there are several more of her. Marjorie on a desk in an office with her legs parted, posed on a nude beach, smiling at the camera while wrapped in a sheet. Ana and Colette would be crushed if they ever saw these.

He keeps digging. The other photos look recent. They're all taken in hotel rooms, often the same hotel room it seems. *Jesus.* Was he collecting these like trophies? Chuck gave Ben so much shit for his minor indiscretion with Elyse, all the while he was baiting and trapping dozens of young women like a big game hunter.

Elyse. Would Chuck have...? No, she would have said something if he'd been inappropriate with her. Wouldn't she?

His thought is interrupted by a knock at his office door. "Come in," he says.

Peter Boyle, senior managing partner, strides into the office as Ben quickly tosses the photos back in the box and shuts the lid. He rises to his feet.

"Peter," he says, surprised.

"Please, sit."

Ben's heart starts to race. Is this what the end of the road looks like? Cutting the dead weight Chuck lugged around all these years now that he's gone?

Peter rests in a chair and leans forward with his spray-tanned hands clasped between his knees. His silver hair is gelled into a Lego brick. "First, let me extend condolences on behalf of myself and the other partners to you and your wife during this difficult time."

"Thank you."

"I know this isn't ideal timing, and it probably seems fast, but Charles owned a significant share of the company and we're tasked with making arrangements to pay the value of his shares to his estate. We called a meeting this morning and felt this could be an opportunity to bring in some new blood. I know with Charles as a masthead there were some...*reservations* about bringing you to the table."

"Reservations?"

Peter smiles. "Charles is not a saint now just because he's dead. He didn't want you there. You had to know that."

It's a punch in the gut. All this time he was passed up, he thought he was just coming up short. Not a good enough earner. Not a reputable enough pedigree. Chuck was his mentor, the closest thing to a father he ever had. How could he have been the one holding him back all these years?

Ben fortifies himself and smiles politely. "I didn't know, actually."

"Well, that's in the past. We've put it to a vote and we want to invite you to the table. We trust the buy-in won't be a problem."

"What's the buy-in?"

"Five million."

Ben nods. Ana would write that check so fast it would give the partners whiplash. "No, it won't be a problem at all. Thank you for the opportunity."

"Good. We're meeting at the end of this week. Bring your checkbook." They stand, and when Peter smiles and shakes

Ben's hand, his teeth radiate white light. "Send my regards to your wife. I know they were very close."

"I will, thank you."

He walks out and Ben is alone with the weight of what he's just learned.

Wow. Chuck is a real prick.

No. He was—and now he's dead.

A surge of energy bursts through him. Chuck is dead and suddenly that's excellent news. Ben is going to be a partner after all and there's not a thing Chuck can do about it.

Watching the clock the rest of the day, he counts the minutes before he can in good conscience rush home to celebrate. There's still work to do. Contracts to review. Clients to call. He has to tell someone. Janine is just outside.

She's been working her ass off. He's about to have a ton of extra work and responsibility. All Ben ever wanted was a small chance to prove himself, and he never even made it in the room. Maybe he'll throw her a few low-revenue clients and see if she can turn things around. He hits his intercom button. "Hey, Janine. Come in here when you have a sec."

She dashes in. "Sir?"

"I just got some good news."

"Oh?"

"I made partner."

"Oh, congrats, sir."

"Thanks. Look, I know you've been wanting to get into this side of things for a while now. I was thinking maybe now that I'm a partner, you could take on a client or two. If you want."

"Are you serious?"

"Absolutely. If that's still what you want to do."

"Oh, it is. Thank you. Wow. Thank you so much." She beams and bounces onto her toes, but seems to catch herself mid-celebration. "Oh, I'm so sorry. You just lost your father-in-law, and I'm in here whooping it up."

He smiles at her. "You earned the right to celebrate. Just try not to look so excited out on the floor. Alright?"

"Yes, sir."

Despite his own advice, he later catches himself whistling a merry tune down the hall. He surveys the floor. Aside from Carrie, everyone is going about their day, business as usual. Sure, it was a little more chaotic. But once the news gets stale, and some other titillating headline grabs the town's attention, everything is going to be just fine.

At dinner, Flora uncorks a bottle of Chateau Margaux 2000 at Ben's request. He pours Ana a glass. She's wearing her hair down the way she used to and it gathers on her shoulders like swirls of honey.

She tells him about her day at the funeral home, how she and Colette got into an argument over whether Chuck should be cremated. Ana couldn't stand the thought of him being burned up. In the end, Colette won.

Ana needed good news to lift her spirits. "So, Peter came by my office today," Ben starts. Hardly able to contain himself, it's everything he can muster to keep a neutral expression.

She doesn't look up. Instead, she sulks over her meal, her silverware scraping against her plate.

"He offered me partner."

Her mouth falls open and her eyes light up at him. "Oh my goodness, babe. That's great news."

Savoring a long sip of wine, his lips form a smile against the glass. As he settles back, contentment evident in his posture, he says, "I'm glad I finally had some good news to give you."

"How much is the buy-in?"

"Five million."

She jerks back with surprise. "Five million?"

"Yeah. What's wrong?" That's nothing to them—a rounding error.

The Manchineel

Ana slices into the lamb, revealing a pink, juicy center. As she brings a bite to her lips, she lets out a soft moan of pleasure. The candlelight flickers in her eyes, turning them into flames. "You know they're only giving you partner now that they're having to pay out Daddy's share. They'll probably let anyone buy in now. Janine will probably be a partner next."

The comment strikes a nerve. Pushing his untouched plate aside, he rises from the table. The clatter of glass emphasizes his anger, and he's hit with the familiar sting of Ana's rejection. *Shame on you, you big fucking dummy. Fell for it again.*

"Where are you going?"

"I'm gonna go work out."

In the gym, he lifts his head and shoulders up and over where his hands squeeze around a steel bar and imagines himself hanging from it by his neck. How does she do it, he wonders—lure him in with emotional appeals, make him feel needed and wanted just long enough for him to expose a plump vein for her to sink her teeth into.

After years of belittling Ben and nagging Charles over the status of a partnership, he finally achieves it and practically levitates home he's so excited to finally tell her. He couldn't wait to see the look on her face—the one that tells him he's good enough. But she can't even give him this victory. In fact, it seems she takes pleasure in denying him of it.

The muscles in his hands and forearms flex as he stabilizes his body weight. Pushing himself harder, he hopes the physical pain will overpower the wound inside him. How is it possible it can still hurt so badly? By now his heart should have fully calloused over, and yet an ache resonates in his chest and he fights back the heat rising to his eyes. Watching himself in the mirrored wall, he sweats and struggles through the last few reps until the pain is unbearable and he's too spent to keep going.

Chapter Twenty-Two

With a flick of his wrist, Ben checks his watch as Ana presses her face against him, wetting his black dress shirt with her tears. At the head of the room, Chuck lies with a powdered nose in a glossy mahogany coffin, surrounded by massive sprays of red and white roses.

The church is stunning and vast with high ceilings and a kaleidoscope of stained glass. It features a grand façade with a soaring bell tower. They're ushered outside, and Colette weeps behind a black lace veil.

Ana wouldn't weep for Ben like this. She might even smile as they push the button on the incinerator and watch him roll on a conveyer belt into hellfire. She'd probably be the one to put him in that wooden box.

Photographers line up across the street. Each time she wipes a tear, the clicks are so fast and furious he can hear the clattering from the church steps. It's a performance. He plays the role of a loving husband, and she pretends to be comforted by him.

They'd been arguing all morning after Ben mentioned there would likely be photographers at the funeral.

"Is this just a photo op for you?"

"I just thought you should know what to expect." He slid a comb through his hair in front of a full-length closet mirror. Medium-hold pomade held it perfectly in place at $160 an ounce. He extended his arms to settle into his Tom Ford suit jacket. A black Audemars Piguet timepiece peeked out. It had an open-heart face that put its delicate inner workings on display.

"You're one of them now. This is just a job to you."

He scoffed. "I'm exactly who you wanted me to be, Ana. Let's not do this today."

"Of course, because you know I'm right."

He'd lost his temper. "No, I don't want to do this because you're a fucking hypocrite. You pushed me to do all the bullshit that these guys do—all the club memberships and the golf and bullshit parties you threw—and now you want to resent me for it? Fuck you. You begged your father to elevate me for years. I was finally asked to be partner now that he's not around to hold me back."

He knew it was cruel the moment he said it but he couldn't help himself. The days of biting his tongue were over.

She narrowed her eyes at him. "If he held you back, it's because you weren't good enough. You're not even a fraction of the man my father was. You can complain about him all you want but you never had a problem spending his money."

"You ever wonder, Ana, why the infallible Chuck died in a Beverly Hills hotel room when he had an office, a home and

every other luxury in this city? It wasn't for the room service. How many actresses do you think auditioned on their backs for your father in that room? That's his legacy."

Her palm cracked against his face and he was certain he deserved it. He took a deep breath and left the room. It was wrong to be so harsh to her on the day of her father's funeral, but she'd hit a nerve. She was right. He was one of them now.

Even now, at the celebration of life party at the King house in Calabasas, he surveys the crowd. There's hundreds of people there. Familiar faces and new ones—actors, musicians, athletes, producers, directors, and financiers, all in their black suits and dresses. His pupils dilate, his mouth waters and his dick gets hard imagining the money that could be made in this room. Ana clings to his arm and corrals him through the crowd.

"Ben," he hears a man call.

Looking toward the voice, he spots Seth Weidman tugging on the lapel of his boy-sized blazer. Annoyed, Ana huffs away leaving Ben behind. When he approaches, Seth is rubbing his scruffy beard and shaking his head, clearly agitated. To avoid causing a scene, Ben takes Seth aside. They find a private spot near a pair of French doors opening to a terrace.

"The Untitled Seth Weidman Project is suspended indefinitely."

"What? Why?"

"Chuck was the guy with all the clout with the private investors. The financing fell through."

Ben sighs. "I'm sorry, man. This is your baby. We'll make it happen." He gives him a brotherly pat on the back and squeezes his petite shoulder.

Seth leans in, close and intense, and Ben lurches down to meet him.

"Chuck always had to be in control. He never let me establish relationships with these guys so he could justify his

own existence. Now look. Left me with my dick in my hand, that piece of shit."

Ben whips his head around to see who's listening. "Relax. We're getting this thing figured out. How much do you need?"

"Ten million."

"I'll see what I can do," he says, smoothing out his tie.

Seth holds up prayer hands in appreciation. "That would be phenomenal man and so appreciated."

"Look, I need a job for a girl I brought on. Very beautiful. Chuck was scheduled to meet with her, but then..."

"I'll find a part for her. I'll make one up if I have to."

Just then, Ana snatches Ben's arm scoldingly. "Are you seriously orchestrating deals during my father's memorial service? You are un-fucking-believable."

"Excuse me, Seth. I'll catch up with you when I'm back in the office."

Seth bows to Ana apologetically before turning and disappearing into the crowd.

"Benny boy!" a familiar voice shouts.

Oh shit.

Ana seethes through a long, bitter exhale before turning to smile at Sierra.

Ben shakes his hand. "Sierra, thanks for coming. It means a lot to us."

"Ana, I'm so sorry for your loss. I was just talking to him that afternoon. It was so sudden. I can't imagine what you must be going through."

"Thank you, Joe."

"You mind if I borrow your boy Ben here for a minute?"

"Of course not, go right ahead."

Sierra and Ben stroll several feet away toward a group of guests. "Ben, let me introduce you to Russell Wilkes. He's the best damn blues musician you'll ever hear in your life. I was

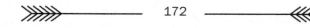

stunned to death he doesn't have a manager. I was telling him you're my hero."

Russell is a little shorter than Ben and heavyset. Ben extends a hand. "That's quite an endorsement. Ben Deluca, King Management. Nice to meet you."

Russell nods politely. "What do you do?" he asks.

Ben is already reaching into his jacket for a card. "I'm an attorney. I handle all aspects of my client's careers—contracts, negotiation, promoting talents, major life decisions. Maybe I could take you to lunch. We should talk."

Chapter Twenty-Three

The ground is damp from a light morning rain. It's still overcast as Elyse's fingers dig into the earth with a vicious pain eating at her heart. It's been a month since they returned from New York. Ben warned her he'd be tied up for a while, but as each day without touching him passes, she grows more troubled. Her loneliness becomes suffocating, and she spends every moment of daylight in her garden hoping to ease the pain of his absence. She even planted a pot of lilies in honor of his mother, Liliana.

Humiliation turns her stomach at the thought of telling Stella the plan backfired, that Ben has been so preoccupied with tending to Ana in the wake of Charles's death that he hasn't had time for her. But then Stella calls one afternoon and she can't avoid it anymore.

"How's Ben?" she asks.

"Fine, I guess." Hearing his name makes her ache and her words come out strained. "I feel like all I do lately is think about Ana. How she gets to lie next to him every night. He told me they don't have sex anymore, but I see all the pictures online of the stupid funeral and they're together. She's crying and he's holding her, and all I can think about is how I wish I was her. I just have this sick feeling. Like he got everything he wanted from me, now he's moving on to the next project."

"Oh, honey. Don't say that," Stella assures her. "King is probably turned upside down. He's a partner now. Trust me, I bet he's just overwhelmed with work."

"Yeah." She wants to believe her, but the acid brewing in her stomach tells a different story. "I think I'm in love with him, and I'm having a nervous breakdown."

Stella chuckles. "You need to relax. You know it's the stress that triggers you. Don't overthink it. Ben is a good guy. He's not ghosting you."

After their chat, she distracts herself with pulling and trimming, watering and feeding. *Did you really think he could love someone as broken as you?* George's voice slithers into her consciousness, venomous and mocking. Closing her eyes, she recalls the soothing calm of Ben's embrace, a panacea that once silenced George's cruel taunts. But since Ben's been gone, George's voice has amplified, chipping away at her sanity.

Monsters don't get fairy tale endings, Elyse.

Planting flowers for a man who's probably forgotten you. God, you're pathetic.

Gullible as always. First me, now him. Haven't you learned?

A furious cry escapes from deep within her belly as she thrusts her shovel into the earth. Stabbing over and over again, each plunge into the ground a release until her hands throb, she's gasping for air, and George's voice fades into the faint strain of music from a passing car.

The sun is setting, and she's driven inside by the night to her empty house. Soon she finds herself back in front of her computer, scrolling through photo after photo of Ben and Ana. It's so dumb to fall in love, to become so obsessed.

The shirt she kept barely retains a hint of his scent, even in the airtight plastic bag where she'd kept it as if it were a piece of crime scene evidence. She took it out only at night to press against her nose, her vibrator flipped on to the highest setting, droning like a prop plane engine.

She stands over her kitchen counter wearing a pair of nitrile gloves, separating the petals of a freshly picked lily. Her hands move with skillful grace as she carefully extricates the required parts of the plant, placing them into a copper mortar. Her phone buzzes.

Ben!

"Hello?" she answers, her voice laced with hope.

"Hi, Elyse. It's Janine at King."

"Oh." The disappointment is so palpable she could cry. "Hi, Janine."

"I was calling to let you know we're shuffling some things around, and I'll be your primary contact at King now." She sounds excited about it. As if this is good news.

"Oh." Her heart plummets like a lead weight. "Does that mean I'm not working with Ben anymore?"

"He'll still be involved behind the scenes, but it'll mostly just be you and me from now on. I'm excited to be working with you."

The sting is immediate and all-consuming. She wants to throw up. Ben didn't even warn her. He had his assistant break up with her. It's a cowardly act, a betrayal. She hangs up without saying another word.

One minute she's watching acid dissolve the plant material, and the next, she hears the *ding* of the elevator on the twentieth floor of the King Management building. She wanders through the floor, passing cubicles and glass-walled offices with only a vague recollection of how she got there. Eventually, she finds her way to Ben's door. The name etched in glass reads, *Ben Deluca, Partner*, and she brushes her fingertips against its gentle ridges.

"Elyse," Janine says, surprised. "I don't have you on the calendar today."

"Oh, I know. We spoke on the phone." She peeks through the glass and sees him inside with someone, hears the muffled bass of his voice even though she can't make out what he's saying.

"About yesterday, I'm so sorry about that. But Mr. Deluca is booked all day. What can I do for you?" she says and looks at her monitors.

Yesterday? A disorienting rush of nausea sweeps over her and her pulse quickens. It felt like only moments had passed since she hung up with Janine. Maybe she should just leave. Get a handle on herself before this gets worse. But she can't. He's just inside. She can see him, hear him. She's so close to her chance for relief.

"It's private. I'll just wait here."

Janine stiffens and tilts her head slightly. "Why don't I just schedule you for the next available appointment? How's that?"

"Okay."

Janine clicks her mouse and scans with her lips pressed tight together. "How's next Friday?"

"That's...almost two weeks from now."

"I know, I'm sorry." Janine grimaces apologetically. "But I'm available now if there's something you want to talk about."

"No," she snaps, then takes a breath and corrects her tone. "It's not that. I just... I need to talk to Ben."

Janine stares at her, unblinking. Her attention darts back to the screen. "I'm so sorry. He has meetings."

Elyse can't stop the tears that burn and threaten to spill. A pang of unease twists inside her. Did Ben tell Janine not to let her see him? Why would he do that? Why is he doing this?

Janine softens her voice. "Why don't you have a seat, and I'll check back a few minutes." She waves her over to long leather sofa in an open spot between offices. It's a minor relief, although she half expects for security to show up and carry her outside.

The canvas bag in her lap is filled with flowers from her garden and a box of guava pastries from a Cuban bakery. People walk by in their suits and dresses as she waits, all looking so important. A phone rings every few moments, and the tension constricting within her twists tighter with each incessant ring. She doesn't even know what she's doing here, how she got here.

Oh. Right. Antigua in a Chevy Volt. The facts of the morning blur together.

"Elyse?"

She looks up and there he is in a chambray suit looking handsome as ever. A lump gets trapped in her throat. She forces it down.

"Is everything okay?" he asks. His eyebrows pull together, and he checks his watch.

Elyse stands, and they obstruct the flow of bodies milling through the office. It looks like a hectic day. He's just busy, that's all.

"Uh...Janine called, and I...I was surprised. You didn't tell me."

Resting a hand on her shoulder, he gently guides her to his office, where he shuts the door and closes the blinds.

The silence makes her nervous. She reaches into her bag. "I brought you pastries. And flowers from my garden." Her vision blurs as he takes the gifts and sets them on his desk.

"Thank you. That's sweet of you," he says, moving closer to her. "Are you sure you're okay?"

"The flowers... I brought lilies because, well, your mother's name and the sky lupine. They just looked so pretty together. They're native to California, you know. The sky lupine, I mean." Hot tears roll down her cheeks. She can't look at him.

Rubbing his palms down her arms, he looks distressed. "You're kinda scaring me, sweetheart. What's going on?"

"You don't want to work together anymore?"

He drops his head and sighs, slumping on the edge of his desk. "I'm so sorry. I should have told Janine to hold off until I could talk to you. It's just the business side of things that's changing. I'm a partner now, which means more responsibility. Janine has been doing really great work, and I wanted to help her out. It has nothing to do with you and me. Our relationship doesn't have to change."

"It already has. I never see you anymore."

His expression fills with concern. "I know, baby. I feel terrible. But you saw the office out there. Since Chuck passed, we've been scrambling to reassure everyone that we're fine. I've been here day and night all week."

Of course that's what happened. It's a perfectly reasonable explanation. It makes her feel worse to show up unannounced like this, crying and bearing pathetic gifts.

"El, look at me."

It's painful to hold eye contact with him. The shame wants to draw her gaze to the floor once she sees the worry in his expression.

He places his hands on her shoulders. "Do you need money?"

"What?" She repels away, straightening her posture. "You think I came here for money?"

He holds up his palms defensively and shakes his head as he realizes his error. "I didn't mean it like that. You just seem like you're struggling with something, and last time I saw you this way, your power had just been shut off. I was just trying to help."

This was a mistake. Not just coming here, but all of it—calling him, meeting with him, signing a stupid contract, sleeping with him, falling in love, killing for him. "Do you still love her?"

His expression grows serious. "Elyse, listen to me." He brings his face to hers. "I meant what I said. I want us to be together. I promise I haven't forgotten about you, and I'm sorry it probably feels that way because I've been working so much. But I need you to trust me. Don't you trust me?"

"I want to."

"Have a little faith, okay?" He drags a comforting hand down the back of her head and looks her up and down with worry. "Have you been eating?"

She looks down at her body. Her clothes do feel a little loose, now that he mentions it. In fact, she struggles to remember the last time she ate. "I've been working outside a lot. Sometimes I get so focused on one thing I forget everything else."

"You've got to remember to take care of yourself." He strokes her cheek with his thumb. "My beautiful girl is fading away. You need to feed her," he says sweetly.

She nods. "I will."

He grins at her and turns to open the white bakery box. The plastic window bows and crinkles. Each golden brown turnover has a sugar glazed top and little sliced windows in its belly revealing its candied, rouge-colored filling. He grabs two and hands her one, then takes a bite. Flakey pastry dust falls onto his shirt and he brushes it aside. "Mmm, very good. Your turn."

She takes a bite. The sweet tang of the guava slides across her tongue, and her stomach responds with loud gurgles. How has she not noticed her hunger? Now that she's eating, she's

ravenous. Being here with him. His hands on her. Eating food. It all seems to have a calming effect, and the gravity of her behavior comes into focus. A knot forms in her belly.

"I'm sorry to show up like a psycho," she says, her voice small.

Lowering his mouth to hers, he kisses her tenderly, and the warmth of his mouth sends electricity through her. "Don't worry about it. I'm late for a meeting, and I don't want to cut this short, but I need to get going. Talk to Janine about some time for us to have lunch. Okay?"

Lunch? She wants to see him now, tomorrow, every day. Ana gets him every day. It's not fair.

He pulls out his wallet, counts out twenty hundred-dollar bills and hands them to her.

Holding them in her hand, she looks up at him, offended. "I don't want this."

"El, please," he says, taking her hands and closing them together to secure the bills inside. "I feel better knowing you have a little money to take care of yourself."

"This isn't why I came here."

"I know that."

"What about EcoFX? Did you ever hear about doing more work? The social media stuff? I can earn the money."

"No, sweetheart, but I'll call Mateus this afternoon and follow up. Okay?"

"When am I gonna see you again?"

"I don't know. Soon." His tone grows impatient.

The tears well up again. This is impossible. She can't live like this.

He gathers her into an embrace. "Just trust me, okay?" His nose brushes her neck and the heat from his breath caresses her skin. The sound of his hushed, deep voice in her ear sends tingles down to the soles of her feet. His kiss overtakes her. Any gumption she'd found to reclaim herself and her sanity is gone.

"Okay."

***

There isn't a gate. Elyse always pictured Ben's house would have a gate. She planned on going home after leaving his office, but his address ends up in the Uber app instead. It's as if her fingers were possessed as they typed 1994 Tower Grove Drive.

The driveway is long and curves up a hill. A mailbox encased in stone bears the number 1994 in brushed nickel. Opening it, she shuffles through the mail inside—car wash advertisement, takeout menu, credit card offer, an almond-toned envelope from The Beverly Oaks Country Club addressed to Ana King.

A pang of jealousy hits her, and she shakes her head. Elyse would gladly take Ben's last name if Ana doesn't want it. The envelope has a green crest, the text written in a fancy font. She rolls her eyes, picturing Ana with her little tennis racket and pleated skirt. Her and Ben hand in hand on the golf course. The image makes her blood boil, and a rush of heat surges through her. Every muscle tenses, her breathing becomes shallow and rapid. It's as if some force of nature within her takes over, filling her with a power that frightens and exhilarates her.

2837 Belladonna Road.

All the sounds of lawnmowers, birds singing and dogs barking fade to absolute silence. Color drains from the world and she's watching herself do the things she knows are wrong, until she's standing in a parking lot and Khaled in a gray Toyota Camry is driving away.

Men and women dressed in light, business-casual attire filter in and out. A skinny young man with blonde hair approaches her with a smile. "Can I help you, miss?"

He wears a canary-yellow polo with a green emblem on it. The same crest from the envelope. It drapes over his diminutive chest and bony shoulders. His khakis sag around his narrow

waist for lack of a belt, and his leather shoes look well-worn but clean.

"How does someone become a member here?" she says, but she barely recognizes the sound of her own voice.

"The club is invitation only."

"Oh. Of course it is."

"Are you alright?"

Why would he ask her that? She's fine. "A friend of mine is a member. Ana King. Have you met her?"

His face lights up when he hears the name. "Oh, Ms. King. Yes, of course."

Cool air from inside is billowing out. It smells like cedar wood and money. "She plans to extend an invitation, but before I make an investment like that, I thought I might take a look at the property."

Glancing around as if to see who's watching, he lowers his voice. "We don't really do tours." He pauses as his eyes briefly drift over her form then adds, "But I'm on lunch in ten minutes. Would you like to have lunch here?"

From his cherub-like face, the boy couldn't be older than seventeen.

"With you?"

A chuckle escapes him, tinted with a hint of unease, and pink colors his youthful cheeks. "I hope I wasn't too forward," he admits, using his forearm to dab away the sweat forming on his brow.

"That's okay," she says. "Lunch is fine, thank you."

Brightness returns to his eyes. "I'm Matthew by the way."

"Nice to meet you. I'm Sarah."

She lingers by the valet stand, watching as Matthew informs another attendant about his break. When he signals her, they stroll together down an open corridor. An ornate table holding a vase of white hydrangea and peonies catches her eye.

Ahead, dark wood floors lead them to a short flight of stairs, and beyond that, the patio.

The sky is gray and the rolling greens are muted, drained of their vivacity. They sit at a table with a view of the golf course and the buildings of Los Angeles jutting up in the background like jagged teeth. It's different from any place she's been to, a symbol of opulence and privilege. Ben would fit right in here.

"I hope you don't mind sitting out here, they get a little touchy about staff eating in the main dining room."

"This is perfect."

Drumming his fingers on the table, Matthew studies her intently. He makes small talk and Elyse tries to maintain the ruse. When the server arrives, Matthew orders a chicken cobb salad. "What would you like?" he asks.

She hasn't looked at the menu. She's been too busy scanning the faces of the people who walk in and out. What will she do if she sees Ana? Attack her? Follow her?

"I'll have the same," she says.

They eat together, and Matthew talks about the film classes he's taking at the community college. How he plans on being a member here himself one day. When the bill comes, he puffs up and unfolds his wallet. She sets down a twenty-dollar bill, and it takes the air out of him. Despite his apparent disappointment, he persists.

"Could I get your number?"

"You're very sweet. But I don't think so. I'm sorry."

A subtle slump in his posture doesn't deter his final offer: "Well, you know where to find me if you ever change your mind."

Walking out of the dining room into the lobby, she stops them near the main entrance with a gentle hand on his arm, causing him to blush.

"Where's the ladies'?"

"Oh, it's right down that hall," he says, pointing toward an archway.

"Thank you. It was nice meeting you, Matthew."

"Nice meeting you too, Sarah," he says, offering a dopey smile before sauntering back to his post.

Elyse walks down the hall to the ladies' room and finally gets a look at herself. Colors are more vibrant. The fuzziness in her brain has faded. She's worn her amber tank dress, but she doesn't remember putting it on. It used to cling to her, but now it hangs flaccid like loose skin. Her hair is pulled back into a messy ponytail. Her complexion is sallow, cheeks gaunt, eyes stained with fatigue. *Geez. Look what you've done to yourself obsessing over this man. Just let him go.*

She lets cold water gush through her fingers, then pats her cheeks. Just a little exploring, that's all. Then she'll go home.

Wandering through a corridor past the dining room to a lounge, Elyse spots a woman carrying a gym bag and follows her to a locker room. Silver plates with etched numbers affix to each dark wooden locker. Maybe they're assigned.

Pushing through the swinging door, she notices an unstaffed desk just outside. She peeks behind the counter. There's a laptop with a Beverly Oaks Country Club wallpaper background and its unlocked. An app is already pulled up. It's a gray window with five tabs. One of them reads *Member Lookup*. She clicks it and a page with a long row of search fields pops up. First name *Ana*. Last name *King*.

Ana's club member identification photo appears. Elyse snaps a photo of the information screen on her phone. An older woman in a yellow polo approaches just as she clicks out and leaves.

"May I help you?" the woman asks.

"Sorry, I'm just waiting for my friend."

She nods politely and walks up to the laptop. Elyse's heart pounds as she pushes through the locker room door again. It's quiet inside except for the sound of a shower running nearby and a woman humming.

Elyse consults her phone. Locker number 352. She scans the room. The rows of lockers go on and on, dividing the room into skinny slices. She moves swiftly, but not too fast as to draw attention. Here it is—352.

The country club community is so trusting the dummy doesn't even bother to keep a lock. *Stupid cow.* She opens the door to find an aluminum water bottle, a makeup kit, expensive perfume and a pair of clean size six and a half sneakers.

Elyse fishes through her bag and retrieves a glass vial of calcium oxalate crystals. *This one's for you, Liliana.* They won't kill Ana. Probably. But they'll make her mouth and tongue swell just enough to cause some concern. Maybe a bought of diarrhea. The thought brings a wicked smile to Elyse's face as she opens the bottle and spreads the invisible needle-like crystals around the rim and inside. She wipes the water bottle and locker door of her fingerprints and hums her way toward the exit.

Chapter Twenty-Four

It's Ben's first official partners' meeting, and he's late. It's poor form, but the unexpected visit from Elyse threw him. She seemed scattered when he saw her, and he couldn't leave her that way.

Hurrying into the conference room, he sidles up to the table, hoping not to look as out of place as he feels. Peter Boyle stands at the front, addressing the fifteen partners in their black, blue and gray suits and dresses. Their dull color palette matches the dim pallor outside.

They sit around a large, glossy mahogany boardroom table. A wall of windows behind them display a wide view of the Los Angeles skyline and surrounding hills.

Before them is a vote on whether to sell a minority interest of King to Angele, Forrest & Phelps, a global media conglomerate. Ben only had a chance to skim the agreement over coffee this morning. From the looks of it, it was a fine time to become a partner. The stock price would be bought at a generous premium. These rich men and women were poised to be become even richer.

The allure of the vote for Ben was intensified by Chuck's clear opposition. Before his death, Chuck had argued AFP wasn't a cultural fit. Ben suspected what Chuck really feared was having the company renamed given Chuck's well-known vanity and narcissism. Sharing the marquee with three other names might diminish the prestige of the 'King' name. His corpse was barely cold when the partners put the decision up to another vote, and Ben was all too eager to deliver a final *fuck you* to Chuck, wherever he was.

After the meeting, Ben returns to his office. Turning the corner, he finds Janine on the phone.

"Oh, hold on. He just walked up." She presses the handset to her breast. "I have Mateus at First Robin for you."

"Sweet. Put him through." He walks to his desk and answers the phone. "*Que bola.*"

"I've officially heard it all," Mateus answers without any of the enthusiasm Ben had hoped to hear.

"What do you mean?" He sits and braces himself for bad news.

Mateus sighs. "This is insane, but EcoFX doesn't want to use her again."

"What? Why not? The ad is perfect. She's tripled her followers since July." The image of the asshole photographer who gave Elyse a hard time flashes in his mind, and his grip tightens involuntarily on the phone.

"Apparently, they're getting harassed by some lady who keeps calling every day."

"What does that have to do with Elyse?"

"Bro, you won't believe it, but she's saying Elyse murdered her son."

Ben's laugh is a reflex. "So some random woman calls and says the model in your ad murdered my son?" Confusion furrows his brow as he tries to wrap his head around the ludicrousness of the statement.

"She knew Elyse by name. Look, I don't want to freak you out or anything, but that's just what their marketing guy told me."

He's not sure what to do. "What's the name of the person she supposedly killed?"

"I wrote it down, hold on a sec. Ramos was her name. The lady's name is Eileen Ramos. In Miami. I didn't get her son's name."

Miami? Maybe some old rival is trying to get back at Elyse for something. Ben scribbles the name on a Post-it.

Hanging up, he rubs his face. Elyse has the worst luck. Who is Eileen Ramos? He spends the rest of the afternoon trying to solve this bizarre puzzle. An internet search returns a *Miami Journal* article from a little over a year ago titled: *Mother of George Ramos Demands Further Investigation of 2008 Death.*

In 2008, 22-year-old George Ramos's body was found in his bed. His death was ruled as a fatal anaphylaxis. His mother believes he was murdered. Ramos family attorney Chris Taylor also believes there was foul play at work. "This family has been through so much over the last decade and they deserve answers."

George Ramos worked various construction jobs across Miami-Dade county and was beloved by many friends and family members, who want to know the truth about what happened to him. "I truly believe he was poisoned," said his mother, Eileen Ramos.

The last person believed to have seen George Ramos alive is identified only as Elyse, according to a police document. The document also points to rape allegations raised by a neighborhood minor shortly before George Ramos's death.

The family denies these accusations and believes the claims have made law enforcement unwilling to reopen their investigation. Police officials confirmed the case is closed, concluding George Ramos's death was not a homicide and there is no active investigation concerning the matter. The Attorney General's office had no further comment.

Shock courses through him. Although, she did move here a year ago, it has to be a coincidence. The Elyse he knows isn't capable of any of this. And yet, considering the dates, it suggests she was still a child back then, perhaps twelve or thirteen. Was she the minor referenced in those allegations?

Fingers tapping impatiently, he quickly types "Chris Taylor attorney Miami" into the search bar. Miami Lawyers' website pops up, showcasing a slew of attorneys. As he scrolls down, a professional headshot of a middle-aged man with salt-and-pepper hair labeled "Chris Taylor" appears. Ben narrows his eyes at the image, a surge of frustration making the back of his neck heat up.

A hot wave of anger courses through him as he scribbles the email address from beneath the image on a Post-It. This motherfucker is going to explain why his client cost Elyse a job with her defamatory bullshit. The police investigated and concluded it wasn't a homicide. The case is closed. He starts an email.

I am writing in my capacity as legal counsel for Ms. Elyse Santiago. It has recently come to our attention that damaging and factually unfounded statements implicating Ms. Santiago in the death of Mr. George Ramos have been circulating, largely

owing to comments and insinuations made by your client, Eileen Ramos.

He types furiously, writing a strongly worded cease and desist letter, stopping short of threatening to fly to Miami to personally kick his ass.

Let me be abundantly clear: Ms. Santiago had no involvement in the death of George Ramos. The case is officially closed according to the investigating authorities, and any attempt to suggest otherwise is not only false but malicious in intent.

"Janine," he shouts.

She dashes into his office. "Sir?"

"I need you to run my meetings tomorrow. I have something I need to take care of."

"Run them?"

"You know everything I know. You don't want to?"

"No, of course I do. Thank you."

"Good. Go home."

As Ben packs up his laptop bag, he glances at the lilies on his desk, still wrapped in paper. It's sweet Elyse remembered his mother's name, but she worries him. She appeared frail and vulnerable when he saw her earlier. Unwell. Now this. He'd been so consumed trying to prove himself at work and falling back into Ana's bullshit that he'd neglected her.

"Janine," he calls, hoping to catch her.

"Coming." She enters with her bag hanging off one shoulder.

"Do you know how to turn off location services? I need to turn it off without the person I'm sharing with to know I turned it off."

Ben catches a glint of amusement in Janine's eyes before she quickly composes herself. "I can do you one better," she says. He hands her his phone. "There's a spoofer app. You can set the location and it will show you on the map like you're there."

Raising his eyebrows, he imagines the possibilities. This would have been helpful to know sooner. "You're a lifesaver."

He waits for Janine to leave before calling Ana. "Hey, I've got a problem I'm working through at the office. Don't wait up."

***

Elyse opens the door in her pajamas and ushers him inside. It's stark. A flickering ceiling light casts a sinister pulse on the hardwood floor. Ben wonders how anyone can live like this. Even during his darkest days, he had a place to sit and eat.

He kisses her cheek. "We need to do something about your furniture situation."

"I'm working on it," she says and takes his arm. "Come up."

He follows her up the stairs to her sparsely furnished bedroom, where a mattress, made up with floral sheets and comforter, lies directly on the floor. A single lamp lights the room from a bright corner. "I'm so glad you're here," Elyse says, her face lighting up.

Ben marvels at how easy it is to please her. Nothing he does is ever good enough for Ana—no achievement prestigious enough, no romantic gesture impressive enough—and yet Elyse always seems so content just having him around.

After taking off his shoes and jacket, he crouches to lie on the mattress. It brings him back to his college days where this sort of a living arrangement was still acceptable. Nestling beside him, she rests her palm on his chest as if to feel his heartbeat. "You make me so happy."

A profound ache spreads through him; he's missed her.

Whispering against his neck, her voice is soft and fragile. "I'm not sure how to explain it. When we're together, I feel safe, like nothing bad could ever happen to me. My mind. It gets quiet." She exhales a weary sigh. "Ben, do you think...you know...now that Ana's father isn't your boss anymore, do you see a way out?"

He hates how his blood pressure rises, the instant panic that sets in at the sheer thought of untethering himself from Ana. It makes him pause, careful to keep the apprehension from his voice. "I want to believe there's a way out," he says. "But it's complicated."

"I know." He hears a sadness in her that makes his throat constrict with guilt. As magnetic as Elyse has been since the day they met, he's disgusted by the realization her pull is no match for Ana's grip on him. For better or worse, appeasing Ana has kept the fragile life he's found in stasis, and any change threatens to destroy it or throw it into chaos.

He brushes his fingers through her hair, pressing his lips to her temple. "You make me happy too," he mumbles against her. "I told my housekeeper about us."

She gasps. Eyes widening, she props herself up on one arm to face him. "Aren't you worried she'll say something?"

He shakes his head and chuckles. "Nah. I know it sounds strange, but she's kind of like a second mother to me. Knows how unhappy I've been."

Settling against him, her hand caresses his belly. "What's her name?"

"Flora."

"Flora," she says wistfully. "I love that name."

He drags a finger down her arm and up again. Their breathing syncs, and it's a welcome rest after a stressful day. But a question still lingers in his mind. One he needs to ask her, but he's not sure how.

"I talked to Mateus."

She sits up again excitedly. "Oh, how is he?"

"He's good." He hesitates. "It was about EcoFX."

She reads his expression and her shoulders sink a little. "They didn't like me, huh?"

"No, sweetheart, it's not that. It's just...it's the strangest thing." His body tenses. "Apparently, the company got some calls."

"Calls?"

"Yeah. Some woman saying crazy things about her son—George Ramos."

Her face changes. It hardens. She turns away.

Ben waits with bated breath for her to speak.

"I knew something like this would happen." Her voice is low and measured, weary. "That woman won't ever leave me alone."

"You know her?"

"Mm-hmm. She lived across the street from me in Miami. Her and George."

He remembers the young girl from the article. "This happened so long ago. You were just a kid. Right?"

Taking a deep breath, she slowly sits back on her heels. Her hands shake slightly, and she presses them together in her lap. "When we met, he was twenty-one and I was only twelve." As she speaks, she doesn't meet his eyes, instead gazing at a distant point on the floor, lost in the painful memory. "At the time, I was so neglected at home, I was just happy to be getting some attention. I didn't think he'd want to hurt me."

A knot forms in his stomach. "Did he...hurt you?"

"He'd knock on my window at night. At first, he'd just hold me and tell me how special I was. I actually looked forward to his visits. Then, one night..." She trails off, hesitating. "He kissed me. I pushed him away, and he told me I'd been teasing him. That he was a man, and he needed more. It could be nice if I didn't fight him. I did fight, for a little while. But I was also scared

to scream because...I don't know...I guess I feared what my father might do even more."

"But you let him in again?" he asks. "Even after?"

The question seems to wound her. Her head drops and she stares down at the bed. She coils her body in the way she did in Kieran's RV, like a pill bug—knees to her chest, arms wrapped around her. She looks at him with a haunted expression, her eyes wet with tears.

He sits with her and wraps her up in his arms. "I'm sorry. I didn't mean it like that. I just want to understand."

"He was all I had," she says against him. "I was already in a bad situation at home. He'd become this light in a very dark place, and I was afraid it would go away. There were days it was nice again. He'd just hold me. And I thought, maybe things could go back to how they used to be. I know now he was just trying to confuse me so I'd be emotionally attached and keep letting him in. But then it started to pile up and I couldn't find ways to live with it anymore."

"I told my mother. She told me not to tell my father because he'd get angry. She tried to make it seem like it could be a good thing. Maybe we could get married in a few years."

Laughing incredulously, tears pool in her eyes. "I was thirteen and she was talking about grandchildren. But she was practically a child when she had me. She was suffering in that house too. It took a while, but I've found a way to forgive her. But back then, I thought if my mom won't help maybe if George's mother knew she'd stop him." Her voice takes on a cold, pained edge. "But she just called me a liar."

As she recounts the gruesome details, a sharp sickening feeling wrenches his gut. Each word sends pulses of revulsion, disbelief. How could adults in her life know what was going on and do nothing? Even today, George Ramos's mother is still harassing her.

"When George died and the police got involved, I told them about what he'd done to me. Child services picked me up and I ended up in foster care. It wasn't as bad as that house, but it was still pretty terrible."

The memories flood his mind—the ill-fitting overworn clothes, waking up in beds that weren't his, that sick feeling of filling a backpack with the few things he owned before being thrust into the next strange place. The constant intruder, a burden. No one wanted to raise a grieving teenager. All his suffering was only a fraction of what she'd experienced.

"I am so sorry," he says and holds her close, feeling the pain as if it were his own. "We can sue this woman for harassing you, for defamation—"

"No." She draws away and faces him. "I don't want to do that."

"But she's lying about you."

"She's not lying."

"She's saying you killed him."

Looking away, she seems to struggle with it. Her breaths are shallow and quick. The silence ticks on into eternity, each unanswered moment tightening its grip on his heart.

"El?"

Closing her eyes as if to gather her courage, she clasps her trembling hands together to steady them.

"El, did you?"

She nods. Tears escape from beneath her closed eyes, tracing paths down her grief-stricken cheeks.

Shock courses through him. Elyse, the gentle, loving soul he knew, had taken a life? And got away with it? Although, there's no statute of limitations for murder.

"How?" he asks, wiping a tear from her cheek.

As she rocks gently, her fingers tug at each other. "Poison," she whispers. "A fruit from the mangroves behind our house. It made it seem like a fatal allergy."

Stunned and conflicted, he struggles to find the right words. Of course, murder is a terrible act. But as chilling as her confession is, he can't help but empathize with her. The burden of this secret she's carried all these years is unimaginable. What this man did was unthinkably evil. She was just a kid.

"He got what he deserved," he says, pulling her into a tight embrace.

Her body relaxes against him, and she opens her eyes with surprise. "You don't think I'm a monster?"

"No, of course not. But as long as this woman is out there, I think it's better not to draw more attention to yourself."

"Alright," she says quietly.

He holds her, the only sound between them the soft hum of their breathing.

"Have you talked to someone about this? A therapist?" he asks.

"Mm-hmm. I had a therapist in Miami for a really long time."

"Good. How are you doing with it? Now, I mean."

"I still struggle with internalizing the blame for letting him in. Sometimes when things get really stressful, I disassociate. It was a lot to go through. Not just what he did but everything that came after. I never really felt like I belonged anywhere until I met you."

The word *belonged* reaches inside and clenches his heart. In that second, every broken piece of his past, the loneliness he felt, the hunger for belonging—all of it clicks into place. That inexplicable connection he's felt since the beginning, the magnetic pull toward her, isn't just desire; it's a longing for the home they were meant to be for each other.

Pulling her tighter, he presses his lips to her temple. "You belong with me."

She offers a weak smile, her eyes glossy with tears.

Her doubt is palpable, and it stings. He's letting her down, letting himself down. Looking at her, her gold eyes gleaming back at him, he resolves to take action.

With her hands on his shoulders, she follows him down the stairs. Surveying the emptiness evokes a sudden pang of pity. Meanwhile, Ana has an enormous storage unit filled with barely used treasures she was too selfish to give away and has long since forgotten about. Janine does have his day covered tomorrow.

"You know, I know somewhere you can get a bunch of free furniture with same day delivery."

She lights up. "You do?"

"Well, it's used. Kind of. But it's nice. I can take you in the morning if you want."

She throws her arms around his neck. "I'd love that."

Chapter Twenty-Five

The clouds gather outside, a thick blanket of gray foreboding a coming storm. He has a task to complete, one he should have done weeks ago. That morning, he drives to Highland Park to fix Elyse's furniture problem. Rubbing the fatigue from his eyes, exhaustion weighs on him. The sofa Ben slept on in his office last night was not designed for a man his size to get a good night's sleep, but he refuses to lie beside Ana ever again.

When he arrives, the scent of flowers greets him. Nature's cacophony is unusually absent. There are no birds chirping or insects hissing. In the daylight, he can see that her yard, once a mound of mud and dirt, is now blanketed with green leaves and stems in dense bunches a foot high.

The Manchineel

She'd only just planted the seeds the day he picked her up for New York, yet now they sway in the wind, on the brink of sprouting buds. That trip, Ben and Elyse overflowed with promises, with visions of a future together. Standing at her doorstep now, the weight of his neglect presses down on him.

The doorbell buzzes. As he waits, the doormat catches his eye. *Trespassers will be composted*, it declares in bold capital letters. Even though it makes him smile, it takes on a darker meaning now that he knows what she's capable of.

The door swings open revealing her radiant expression, which quickly morphs into concern. With a gentle touch to his cheek, she asks, "Are you feeling okay?"

"I haven't been sleeping well. I'm just tired, that's all."

"Come with me."

Leading him through the stark bungalow, they reach her garden. He's never seen it before, not really. Only in small glimpses from her social media accounts. It's magnificent. Even under the cloud cover that seems to dull all of Los Angeles, brightly colored flowers and fruit-bearing trees are vibrant, each planted in their perfect place. He's amazed she was able to do all this herself. It's full of life and thriving from her love and care.

She tiptoes through the rows of plants to dig out patches of yellow flowers and snip green herbs. They're thrown into a colander she rests on her hip. A wind chime clinks and twangs, and he wonders if being with her like this, in a humble tract of paradise, could be enough for him.

When they return to the kitchen, he watches her rinse her bounty to rid it of all dirt. The ingredients are added to a blender—greens, dandelions, lemon juice. He watches it spin. She isn't going to make him drink this, is she? His question is answered when she pours it into a mug. A fleeting thought of George Ramos passes through his mind.

He stares at it with concern.

"Come on. It'll make you feel better."

His pained expression and whine is met by Elyse resting her fists on her hips. "*Bébalo*," she insists. *Drink it.*

"Oh, you've been practicing your Spanish." Chuckling, he's charmed by her accurate pronunciation and endearing effort. To humor her, he takes a cautious sip. *Ugh*. It's bitter, grassy, and utterly revolting, but her bright laughter makes it worth it.

By the time they arrive to Ana's storage unit, he's rejuvenated. He's not sure if it's her magical concoction or time spent close to her, but he's alert and filled with energy again.

"I thought we'd check here first just in case you saw anything you liked," he says. "If you'd prefer something new, that's okay too. But anything in here can get delivered today."

He punches a key code into the lock pad and it clicks open. The gate lifts and he guides them into Ana's "treasure room," a massive storage warehouse filled with all the furniture and home decor items Ana had accumulated over a lifetime of keeping up with the latest trends and never wanting to give anything away. They paid thousands of dollars a year to ignore a warehouse full of pretty things.

Elyse takes in the surroundings in awe. Her fingers graze the fabric of a blush velvet sofa that used to sit in Ana's office. He doesn't think anyone's ever sat on it. Standing back, she considers it with a finger at her chin. "I suppose I could burn some sage over it. Request the evil energies within it to vacate the premises."

He laughs, but maybe she's right. Maybe these things still hold Ana's energy somehow. If that were true, they'd need to burn enough sage to take the whole unit down. "Come on, we'll check out some stores and get you something new."

"No, I was only joking. You're right. I need something now, and anyway, it's temporary."

She picks out everything she needs, and some things she doesn't, from the unit—the blush couch, a gold and glass coffee

table, some flowery artwork, a flat-screen television with a stand, an area rug, a large mirror, dining table and chairs.

Ben points and the storage facility staff lift each item into the back of a box truck. By the early afternoon, the movers are gone and her house looks like someone actually lives in it. Elyse proves she was serious about "cleansing" the furniture. An iridescent abalone shell rests in her hand, a bundle of dried sage burning a smoke trail from the lit end. The air fills with a pleasant, sweet and earthy smelling smoke. Her lips pucker up and blow at it, exciting the orange embers.

He grins at her as she slowly wafts white clouds around the dining table. "I purify any negative energy from this table," she says adorably.

His urge to laugh is quickly suppressed by a memory of Ana berating him at that table. Once while sitting at it, he wiped his mouth with a napkin at a time she found offensive, so she picked up his dinner and poured it into the trash. When she was done, she sat back down and finished her meal. Whatever swamp witchcraft Elyse believes is fine with him as long as it works.

"I thought you were a scientist," he teases.

She quietly cleans up her kit with a hint of a smile on her lips. "Burning sage releases negative ions that produce biochemical reactions in your blood that increase serotonin. Puts you in a good mood. Doesn't your energy change the way you interact with the world? It is scientific."

Were these the kinds of things she was talking about on her channel? Had he ever really listened or was he just ogling her like everyone else?

She slowly waves the burning sage around his shoulders like a magic wand. He bites his lip to conceal a smile.

"I purify you, mind, body and spirit, releasing any worries from your heart."

As the smoke billows around him, a warmth spreads within him. All humor fades, replaced by a deep sense of earnestness.

Placing the sage into the shell, she allows it to smolder on the table. Rising, she finds him there, waiting to pull her into an embrace. "Thank you. That was very sweet," he says, showing his gratitude with a tender kiss.

As their lips meet, her hands trace a path down his body. The warmth radiating from her makes him melt under her touch. His tongue brushes hers, and his fingertips graze the velvety skin of her thighs where the hem of her dress rests, making their way up until they find the fabric of her panties. The way her body responds to him is a thrilling reminder of his forgotten power. Every delicate shiver running through her, the eruption of goosebumps across her skin, magnifies their connection.

He drags the soft fabric down her thighs and she steps out of them. Drawing back, she makes her way to the couch. His eyes follow her as she bends over, hikes up her dress and presents herself to him on all fours. Gazing over her shoulder, she invites him. "Hard, please."

Oh fuck. All the blood leaves his head. His senses, once dulled, are now honed to a predatory sharpness. His hands work faster than they ever have to unbutton his pants and shove them down just enough to thrust into her like it's an emergency. Elyse has awakened something in him. It may be wrong, but there's something so satisfying about fucking her on Ana's couch.

His hips pound with exponential force, every movement a declaration of reclaiming control—an act of defiance that carries the weight of his stolen dominance. For her, this sweet, loving woman who finds comfort in his scent, having been starved of him, it's a deep hunger finally satiated.

Their connection is primal. He finds purpose in soothing her ache, and she, in turn, revels in their reunion with fervor. Her cries, a mix of pleasure and release, sound possessed. The light

skin of her back flashes pink, and she stares back at him like she's drunk or drugged or both.

His eyes close to focus on the sensation—how her silken flesh yields to his grip, the pulsating rhythm of their bodies, the overwhelming urge to bury himself so deep inside her he bursts through the other side. The pressure builds until its unleashed with a wild cry and relief crashes over him like fresh blood after a long hunt.

When his soul returns to his body, he sees she's frozen like a contorted Picasso.

"Are you okay?"

"I can't move," she mumbles into a cushion.

First, he takes a lovely mental portrait of her fucked senseless. Helping her up, her bottom falls against the couch, electrified, her hair in disarray. Smoothing it and combing through it with his fingers, he says, "That's better," then kisses her softly.

Resting together on the couch, he holds her, his heart full. She's perfect, and he's so content, enjoying the softness of her skin and the gentle rise and fall of her breath.

His life has been a series of temporary situations. With Ana, he was always working to earn his spot in her world, a world he was once in awe of. It was a painful irony that the more he tried to prove himself to her, the more he felt he didn't belong.

In Elyse, he sees a need that mirrors his own, a connection that draws them closer. It was a mystery before, but now he knows Elyse has felt as unloved and unwanted as he has. With her, he feels seen, understood, and most importantly, he feels at home. But he had abandoned her, consumed by a desperate need to prove his worth in a world that always made him feel worthless. She's been so patient, so forgiving. Even today, it was if she invited all of his baggage into her home and purified it. He can't ever let her go again.

As he presses his lips to hers, her stomach growls for attention. Chuckling at the sound, he pulls her closer to him.

"Hungry?" he asks.

Elyse nods. "I'm starving, actually."

"Let's go to our place."

"Our place?"

"Little Havana."

She smiles at him with a love-drunk expression. "Okay, let's go to our place."

***

On the patio, couples dance to romantic boleros. Clouds obscure the sun, and white-filtered light brightens the gold and amber hues of Elyse's eyes. A haunting melody begins to play. It's familiar. He recognizes the melancholy progressions of the piano and places it. It's "Dos Gardenias," a song he decides while gazing at her across their small lunch table will be theirs.

He's been staring so long, her eyes widen and she smiles bashfully. "What?"

"Dance with me."

"Oh, I don't know. This is different than what you showed me before."

Ben doesn't care if she makes it up as she goes along, he simply wants her close. Standing, he holds out his hand. She takes it, and they move to the patio. The gray haze threatens to rain down on them at any moment. He positions her into a waltz-like stance. Their bodies pressed together, he says, "Do you see their feet? Just follow my lead."

He gently guides her with whispers in her ear. "Slow, quick-quick, slow, quick-quick, slow." She steps on his feet and sighs in frustration. "It's okay," he reassures her, guiding her to the rhythm again.

The singer croons with yearning. *Te quiero. Te adoro. Mi vida.*

Elyse struggles, but eventually, she starts to move in step with Ben. He smiles against her cheek. "There you go." The slow, sensual bolero continues, and Ben loses himself in the moment.

"What are they saying?" Elyse asks, sweeping her fingers over the hair above his ear.

"He's giving the woman he loves two gardenias, one for each of their hearts," Ben explains. "By giving them to her, he's telling her, I love you, I adore you, you are my life."

"That's so beautiful."

"It's our song now."

Elyse's chest rises sharply as she takes a deep inhale, marking the swell of emotion within her. Her eyes, shimmering pools of light, meet his with an intensity that speaks of deep adoration. The silent weight of her gaze, coupled with the soft curve of her lips, tells him everything he needs to know.

As they sway to their song, everything finally feels right. Like two once-broken pieces, they now fit seamlessly together. He sings to her in Spanish, slightly off key, in a low hush. Despite the rational part of his brain telling him to slow down, his heart races with the intensity of his feelings for her. He knows it's love; she's the sanctuary he never knew he sought. He would give anything, fight any battle, to protect what they have together.

Eventually the music fades, and they break apart. Raindrops begin to fall. Ben's phone vibrates—it's Ana. Before he can ignore the call, Elyse insists, "Please. Just take it."

He concedes, walking through the restaurant and out onto the sidewalk, away from the romantic music. "Yes?" he answers, annoyed. Specks of moisture from the misting rain collect on his shirt, and the pleasant aroma of roast pork and spices gives way to the stink of car exhaust.

"Mr. Deluca?"

It's Ana's number, but it's not her voice. He glances at his phone again just to be sure.

"Uh, this is Ben Deluca, who's this?"

"Hi, Mr. Deluca. This is Angie from Cedar Sinai Emergency Department. Your wife came in with an allergic reaction. She's stable, but we need someone to pick her up."

Shit. "Okay." He wants to hang up. Let Ana find her own way home and deal with her bullshit by herself. But that would be cruel. There's a proper way to end things and abandoning her in the hospital is not it. Exhaling with defeat, he responds, "I'll be there as soon as I can. Tell her I'm on my way."

When he returns to Elyse, deflated, she must notice the shift in his demeanor.

"Is everything okay?"

"I'm so sorry, sweetheart, I have to go. Ana's in the emergency room."

"Oh no." She takes his hand. "It's okay. I'll be at home. Call when you can."

If the tables were turned, Ana would insist Elyse call somebody else. He's grateful for her understanding. That this doesn't have to be a fight, that she trusts him.

"I love you," he says. "I'll call you tonight."

Chapter Twenty-Six

Beads of rain pelt the windshield, and the wipers on Ben's Range Rover turn on automatically, sweeping back and forth across his view. The hazard lights of the car ahead of him blink on and he shakes his head in frustration. Nobody in LA knows how to drive in the rain.

It's forty-five agonizing minutes of bumper-to-bumper traffic before he arrives to Cedar Sinai. The ride should have taken less than fifteen minutes, according to his location services, which showed Ben in Beverly Hills.

When he finally sees her, Ana's appearance is shocking—her lips have ballooned and the skin around them is stretched like a plump grape. She communicates her frustration with her wild eyes, but when her mouth opens nothing but a hoarse gasp escapes. Despite the seriousness of the situation, he can't help but savor a thrill of satisfaction, giddiness even. It's wrong, but there's something poetic about this form of justice.

"What happened?" He feigns concern and tries to dim the glee in his eyes.

Tapping furiously on her phone, she writes out a message then hands it to him to read.

I don't know what happened. I was playing tennis and my mouth and tongue swelled. They told me I need to follow up with an immunologist.

Ben was with Elyse all day. Even if he wasn't, she doesn't have access to the club. She couldn't have done this. Could she? It troubles him that he instantly suspects her. The nurse returns and hands Ben a printout.

You have been diagnosed with anaphylaxis, a serious allergic reaction. Common causes include medication reactions, bee stings, contrast dyes, nuts, and latex products. Make a follow-up appointment with your healthcare provider. Call 911 right away if symptoms return.

"Well, they seem to think you're allergic to something," he says and folds the paper in half. He waves her on with it. "Come on, let's get you home."

At home, Ben follows Ana upstairs. As they pass Flora, she catches a glimpse of Ana's swollen face and her eyes get big. Her lips press into a thin line, and she averts her gaze, but he notices the corners of her mouth twitching, and her face lights up with humor.

Their bedroom is shaded gray from the storm outside. Helping her into bed, he covers Ana with a thick blanket. Her eyes plead for comfort, her swollen face heavy with drowsiness

from the antihistamines. Despite all the bitterness he feels, seeing her this way surprises him with a small swell of pity for her. As he runs his palm across her arm affectionately, his show of warmth is met with a deep pang of guilt.

Elyse.

It's only a kindness. His instinct to comfort means more about who he is than how he feels about Ana, but deep down, he knows he cannot continue to nurture them both.

"I'll let you rest." Leaving her alone, he closes the door quietly behind him. He walks into his office to catch up on everything he's missed today tending to the women in his life. There's a reply in his inbox from Ramos's attorney.

I've attached the evidence we gathered in support of reopening the investigation into Mr. George Ramos's death. I think you'll find any statements allegedly made by Ms. Ramos would not have been unfounded, even if they were made.

Asshole. He clicks the file. It's a large PDF binder with documents and photos. Blood and vomit coat George's face and stain his shirt. His mouth and eyes are nearly swollen shut. His cause of death by all official accounts was acute anaphylaxis. The hairs on the back of Ben's neck prickle up. The woman he loves deliberately did this to another human being. Even the law recognizes a distinction between crimes of passion and premeditation. There's something cold and calculated about a planned kill that makes it worse than self-defense or a moment driven temporarily insane by rage, love or betrayal.

He's not sure how, but he knows now Elyse was the cause of Ana's reaction.

Descending the stairs in a haunted daze, he enters the game room where Flora is vacuuming a Persian rug. Facing him, a mischievous grin perks up her cheeks. He leans against the pool table, and the vacuum powers down. Flora creeps up, then

playfully puffs out her cheeks and pushes out her lips like a duck. Though Ben drops his head with a laugh, his stomach quivers with unease.

This isn't funny. Maybe there's a little schadenfreude to be had. But if it's true, if Elyse really did do this, then it's also fucking terrifying and Ana is in danger.

Reaching for a bottle of Buffalo Trace behind the bar, he serves himself a pour. It warms his throat and coats his tongue with tingling flavors of oak and caramel. Outside, the rain batters the windows.

Even now, with all the gruesome facts dancing in his mind, he can't explain it, but he warms thinking of her. It's like she's under his skin, deep in his bones. Beyond reproach. When they're together, her every action carries an air of grace, a touch of something ethereal. And yet, within her lies the chilling capacity to kill. Did she think this would be some kind of romantic gesture? Justice? Her way of protecting him?

As he takes another sip of whiskey, he makes a decision. He's going to confront Elyse, to ask her directly. Did she do this?

Chapter Twenty-Seven

The dark clouds finally make good on their promise and let down some heavy rain. Elyse lies on the floor after returning home from Little Havana. Thinking about Ana makes her sick to her stomach. It's strange to have that woman's things here, for Elyse to claim them as her own.

It's late afternoon and it's already dark as she stares yearningly at her garden from her window. The thick clouds shroud any hope of sunlight breaking through. Rain is good for the plants at least, but all she wants to do is work in her garden. She needs a distraction.

Every object in her house offends her. She can't bring herself to sit on the couch, or eat at the table. Instead, she climbs the stairs to her bedroom, but even there, Ben's scent lingers on her sheets. There's not a safe place for her in this house anymore. The ache hurts too badly. Tears spill down her temples and into her ears as she lies on her back. Pressing the buttons on an app, she places an order and waits for her vodka delivery.

Feelings are awful. She's always tried to avoid having them and then Stella had to meddle, introducing her to the most wonderful man in the world so they could fall in love. She just made things worse.

Downstairs, the doorbell rings and she opens the door for the delivery man. Flashing her ID, she takes the bottle from him. He nods at her sympathetically, her red eyes and puffy face a dead giveaway for the ailment his delivery is intended to cure.

Standing in her kitchen, she pours herself a mug. It's warm. The sharp flavor hits her lips. It heats and tingles against her tongue and burns all the way down.

She'd promised Ben she would control her drinking, but he'd promised her they would be together. He would do anything it takes, he said. It was a promise he'd made over and over again all the way from New York to Los Angeles. What's his excuse now?

On her laptop, she finds their song and listens to it on repeat. Finding the lyrics online, she reads them again and again in Spanish, then finds a translation online in English to fill in the gaps of what she doesn't understand. *But if some darkening day, the gardenias of my love die . . .these blooms will speak to you as if I were still by your side.*

A shiver runs through her.

How romantic, George teases. *It could have been our song, my love.*

"I never loved you."

If that were true, I wouldn't be here. Indifference never drove anyone to kill.

He's right. It's love that's driving her mad. Elyse's thoughts blur with intoxication, drifting from the specter of George to the very real fear gripping her heart.

"I can't lose him."

You already have. Ben only loves whatever glittering thing is directly in front of him. Out of sight, out of mind. He's holding her right now, you know. It'll be another month before his assistant reminds him you exist. It's over. He's already bored, and Ana's dusty secondhand furniture is your consolation prize.

"She doesn't deserve him."

Deserve? Nobody ever gets what they deserve. I didn't deserve to die, and you should be in prison. The universe doesn't give handouts. If you want something, you take it. Simple as that.

It's late, she's drunk and contemplating murder.

Before she snuck her way into the club, Elyse thought Ana's circle was impenetrable. But now that she's gotten to her, wounded her, she's filled with confidence. If she can get to Ana at her private club, what else could she do? Once she has her where she wants her, then what?

It gets late. He promised he'd call. She sits on the floor in front of Ana's couch and waits by her phone. Her leg bounces, her gaze fixed on the television screen. No amount of vodka or television is a helpful distraction from George's voice. She bites at her cuticle until it bleeds.

He's with Ana, tending to her. Holding her. The image is an insult she cannot ignore a moment longer. She gathers things into her bag and calls an Uber to take her to Beverly Hills.

***

They really should have a gate. With their kind of money, a gate seems like a basic security feature. Some barrier to keep out the common riffraff. Yet, Elyse is grateful for their trust in the

safety of their affluent neighborhood as she stumbles into the driveway and sneaks through a thin patch of woods up a steep hill.

Crickets chirp and air-conditioning units hum amid the darkness. She crouches and sits on the wet earth. A light illuminates the entrance to his house beyond the trees. Everything she's ever wanted is just beyond that door.

She imagines the two of them inside, entwined in bed, losing themselves in shared laughter and whispered promises. As the fantasy deepens, the world around her starts to blur, merging dream with reality.

A blink, and the sun rises over the mansion, blinding her. She puts on sunglasses to shield herself from its intensity. Her head aches. She must have had too much to drink. Has she been here all night?

As Ben's Range Rover backs out of the garage, Elyse ducks behind a thicket of trees. She waits for him to drive off and begins to plan her exit. But then she notices an older woman with short dark hair sweeping the doorstep. This must be Flora, Ben's beloved housekeeper.

Despite the itch of crawling insects and the ache in her back from sitting upright on the ground for hours, there's something oddly comforting about being here. This is Ben's house. It's full of secrets and new discoveries about the man she loves. What might the inside of his closet be like? Maybe she'd grab the sleeve of a hanging dress shirt and drag the soft fabric across her lips.

Her fantasy is interrupted when Ana drives out of the garage in a white BMW and her brakes screech to an abrupt stop in the motor court. Ana runs inside. When she returns, there's a yoga mat slung over one shoulder. Elyse checks the time and makes a mental note—*10:32 a.m. Yoga.*

Once Ana drives away, Elyse summons some courage. If she knocks on the door, Flora will answer and she can introduce

herself. Flora is an ally after all. They have a security camera that will capture her, but if there isn't anything eventful to record, they probably won't even notice.

Blood rushes to her legs as she stands, making her feel pins and needles. The hat from her canvas bag will have to do for a disguise. Its stiff bill is pulled down low when she treads warily toward the door. Holding her breath, she presses the bell.

The click of the lock sets her heart racing. The door swings open.

"Can I help you?" Flora stands at the entrance peering through the narrow opening, just wide enough to be polite, yet cautious.

"Hi, are you Flora?"

Her eyebrows furrow with suspicion. "Yes. Do I know you?"

"We haven't met before. I'm Elyse. I think Ben might have told you about me. I'm so excited to finally meet you."

Flora's face lights up with warmth and surprise, her eyes widening in recognition as she opens the door further. She surveys the motor court and lawn to see who might be watching, then relaxes once she confirms they're alone. "He didn't tell me to expect you." Her voice is light and friendly. The cool air from inside wafts against her carrying the smell of warm vanilla.

"He doesn't know I'm here. I'm so sorry to show up unannounced like this. I've just been so worried." She motions to the camera. "I don't think I should say more standing right here."

"*Claro*," Flora says, then gently grabs Elyse's forearm. "*Ven conmigo.*" *Of course. Come with me.* She invites her inside.

A surge of exhilaration pulses through her. *I'm in.*

The foyer is grand, with towering ceilings. A round, wooden table at its center is adorned with a giant potted orchid. A water feature is recessed into a wall, casting soft light on the marble surface. Ben has an honest-to-goodness waterfall in his house. Elyse shakes her head in disbelief, taking in all the details.

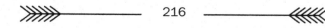

The house smells fresh and clean, with light-colored wood floors cut in a herringbone pattern. It's so elegant, she wants to laugh out loud. No wonder Ben hasn't left the Princess of Monaco. She gets it now, and she's only made it a few feet inside their palace.

Flora leads her to a kitchen with a giant stainless-steel stove, sparkling white marble countertops, and cabinets that stretch up to the ceiling. It's spotless, and sunlight floods the room. This is where Flora undoubtedly prepares Ana's meals. But the worst possible scenario Elyse can imagine is inadvertently hurting Ben. This needs to be airtight.

Through glass double doors, Elyse can see the terrace and glimmers of light reflecting off the crystal-clear water of a swimming pool. The views of Los Angeles from the hill are spectacular. A sharp pain comes with the realization she can't compete with this. She never stood a chance against it all.

Stop this. Focus.

Her eyes follow along the countertops. A sleek stainless steel coffee maker. *Hmm. No.* Ben loves his coffee in the morning. A collection of ornate ceramic canisters. A large butcher block, adorned with an array of gleaming knives. *Too messy.*

On the outer corner of the island is a wooden pedestal holding colorful fruit. Nearby, Elyse notices a steel box with a series of buttons and dials. It's the base of a blender. A heavy handled jar rests in the sink, caked with the remnants of a brown sludge.

Elyse traces her finger over the skin of a green mango blushed with hues of orange and red. It makes her mouth water when she presses against its tender flesh, imagining the juicy sweetness inside. She picks it up and holds it in the palm her hand.

"You caught me while I was cleaning up," Flora says, walking to the sink. She runs the water and rinses out the glass

vessel, her delicate fingers forcing a sponge around the sharp silver blades inside.

"Were you making smoothies?" Elyse asks sweetly, returning the mango to its place at the top of a mound of exotic fruit.

She shakes her head, smiling. Her eyes focused on the sponge working its way in and out of the container. "No. Ms. King. She put a bunch of stuff in there. Fruit. Vitamins, I think."

"Mm."

Once its rinsed, she sets it to dry in a rack, then dries her hands on a towel. "Can I get you something to drink? *¿Quieres un café?*" Would you like coffee?

"Yeah. Uh...*si. Gracias.*"

She wanders toward the kitchen table and slides out a chair. "I can't believe how beautiful this place is."

The coffee maker whirs and squeals. The sharp nutty aroma fills the space. "It's a lot of cleaning," Flora jokes.

"I bet."

Ambling toward the table, Flora sets the mug in front of Elyse, then sits with her. Giving her a warm smile, she rests her manicured fingers over Elyse's hand. "*¿Qué te trae por aquí, querida?*" What brings you here, my dear?

"Um." She's been practicing, but her Spanish needs work. "Ben, *dice que*...you know." Her face warms up. "He told me he trusts you, Flora. And I don't know who else to talk to about this."

Elyse gives her an incomplete history. How they met, the things she's observed about his relationship with Ana, how she's never loved anyone this much and how terrified she is to lose him. "He's never going to leave her. Why would he? Look at all this," she says.

Flora nods with a haunted expression. "I love Ben like a son. I see the way she treats him. I tell him, all of this can be replaced, but he only has one life."

"That's why I'm here," Elyse says softly. "You know Ana better than I do. Do you think she could really hurt him? I mean...like *really* bad?"

Flora sighs and cradles her coffee cup with both hands. "Sometimes she screams at him so loud I can hear it from across the house. She throws things, breaks things." Her eyes become glossy and she clicks her tongue with regret. "The police have been here, you know."

"The police?"

Flora nods emphatically. "They look at him, this big man and then they look at her, a small pretty woman, and they make him leave even though he doesn't do anything to her."

A knot tightened in her throat. "No wonder he feels helpless." Elyse leans close. "Who else does he have but us? Who's gonna stick up for him?"

Her appeal makes Flora's face warm with humor. She pats Elyse's hand affectionately as if she can appreciate the place her concern is coming from, but shakes her head in disagreement. "He can stand up to her himself. He can go. He's just stubborn."

Elyse leans closer. "Imagine growing up, being passed from place to place and feeling like no one loves you enough to keep you, that everyone else gets to have things of their own and you only get to share. Can't you imagine what that must feel like?" Elyse had tried to tamp down her emotions, tried to suppress them, but now they bubble up to the surface and burn her eyes.

"He thought he'd finally earned something good and secure for himself. Ana knows the fear of losing it all is too terrible to imagine. I know that he's a man, and a big man at that. But, Flora, inside he's just as vulnerable as anyone."

"I'm sure he's ashamed every time it happens. But then she apologizes, doesn't she? Maybe they have a few good days or weeks, and he holds out hope that it could be good again. It's a cycle. And from the outside, it seems like he keeps making the same stupid decision, but I promise you he feels like he has no other choice."

Flora watches her intently, the air thick with silence. For a moment, she seems to consider the gravity of the situation before letting out a defeated sigh. "I don't know what else to do for him."

"I do. But I can do it alone."

Chapter Twenty-Eight

The manchineel is rare. In the US, it only grows in South Florida. It was the manchineel fruit that led George Ramos to his death, and by its grace, Elyse is still a free woman. Now that the need for Ana to die weighs heavy, Elyse can't shake the images from her memory—her childhood backyard retrieving the fruit; searching for Ana to eat the fruit. In her dreams, in her waking nightmares, a grim solution emerged. It was the manchineel all along.

The danger of Eileen Ramos lurking just across the street from her former home flashes in her mind. There will be trouble if she notices Elyse back in the old neighborhood, but the fear of losing Ben is infinitely greater than the risk of facing that horrible woman again.

Saturday evening, Monica in a maroon Buick takes her to the Greyhound bus terminal. The wind is beating against the US and California flags high up on a pole outside the short building painted in colorful community murals. She slips on her hat and sunglasses and tucks her hands into the front pocket of her thick hoodie.

Inside, she follows along metal handrails toward her bus zone. She'd checked in online as Sarah Flores with her prepaid ticket. Her senses are bombarded with sounds and smells. Families and children gather around piles of luggage, sitting on benches and on the tile ground. The sounds blend together— coughs, laughs, babies crying. The sounds of people talking with tense voices. The hiss of an air brake. They swirl around her.

She clutches her canvas bag against her body. It's all she has for this journey home. Her pulse races as she finds a seat on a bench near her boarding zone. She practices a grounding exercise—zeroing in the things she sees, smells, hears. She gets to *motor oil* and *gasoline* when she's interrupted by a woman.

"Can I sit here?" she asks.

Surveying the area, every other seat is full. People are sitting on the ground. "Sure," she says, but it makes her tense. What if she wants to rob her? Trick her? *Breathe. Just breathe.*

A man in a blue button-down shirt and chartreuse vest shouts at the people gathered at the terminal. Did they announce boarding? There are too many sounds happening all at once.

Casting her eyes around, she notices people are starting to get up. They're lining up near the doors. She hops up and hurries over to the man, the ticket on her burner phone extended. "Is this the bus that goes to Miami?"

His gaze shifts from the screen and back at her, then nods. "That's the last stop," he says and waves her on.

Elyse walks through the metal gates outside, where the bus doors are open. As she makes her way down the aisle, a few faces pop up to glance at her before shifting their apathetic gaze out the window or to their device. Somewhere in the middle, she finds a window seat.

Her seat belt sticks. She tugs and tugs but it won't budge. Seats are filling all around her. She yanks harder, again and again until sweat begins to form on her forehead.

"Excuse me, miss," a woman in a yellow vest says. "That seat belt doesn't work."

"Oh," she says.

"Would you like to move?"

Raising her eyes to the woman, she tries to ignore all the bodies moving in her periphery, but she can't seem to speak. "Uh..." she says. There's too much going on, too many variables to consider all at once.

"Come on," the woman says kindly and guides her across the aisle to another seat.

When she sits by the opposite window, the seat belt glides with ease and clicks into place. Just as she sighs with relief, her stomach grumbles. *Shoot.* She'd forgotten to eat. It'll be fine. It's a three-day trip; they have to stop for food at some point.

"Can I sit here?" a voice asks.

Elyse is plugging in a burner phone, paid for with the cash Ben gave her. She raises her head. It's the woman from inside. Is she following her? Suspicion lingers as she notices other available seats. Why does this woman want to sit here? It would be rude to say no. She seems harmless enough. "Okay," she says.

The woman smiles and sets her purse down. She doesn't have any luggage. Maybe she checked it. She's short and petite with eyes that are a little too close together. When she finally sits, she turns to Elyse. "I'm Mira."

"Sarah."

"Nice to meet you."

"Mm-hmm."

Elyse's attention drifts down to her phone. It's charging now. Maybe she'll listen to some music so this woman will stop talking to her. When she finds her headphones in her bag, they're a tangled mess.

"Where ya' headed?" Mira asks.

Elyse presses her thumbnail against a white knot. "Baton Rouge."

"Oh, that's a long way. I'm heading to Houston myself."

Elyse's only response is a non-committal hum. Untangling the last of the knot, she seals herself in a musical cocoon and finds solace staring out the window. She's been trying not to think about Eileen Ramos—in her open garage, crammed into a plastic patio chair and chain-smoking cigarettes to the nub. She was always out there surveying the street, her face locked in a dumb perpetual squint. Although, she tended to stay inside more often during hurricane season when heavy rain, lighting and want for air-conditioning forced most everyone inside. It's late August, and this is when the stormy South Florida weather hits its peak.

She closes her eyes and thinks of her Ben. Tall and broad shouldered, sweet, handsome Ben. Even now that he knows her deepest secret he loves her. He's worth every bit of danger. There's nothing she wouldn't do for him.

They stop in Arizona, New Mexico and make six separate stops in Texas. The thick humidity she's longed for is felt against her skin somewhere in Louisiana. Each stop offers a chance to stretch her legs and binge fast food.

There are seven stops in Florida. The very last arrives sixty-two hours later at the Greyhound station at Miami International Airport, where she washes up at a sink in the bus station bathroom.

Jessica Carrasquillo

Walking outside around noon, she has the urge to spin around like Maria von Trapp in *The Sound of Music*. The humidity. The moisture clings to her skin like slipping into a warm bath and it restores her. Dark clouds are moving rapidly overhead. She doesn't have long to celebrate. Her bus home leaves tonight at seven, and she has work to do.

Chapter Twenty-Nine

Through the window, Ben can see Elyse's living room and parts of her kitchen. His face nearly pressed against the glass and a hand shielding his view from the light, he scans the room, spotting an array of flasks, beakers, and chemistry equipment cluttering the countertop.

What the fuck is she doing in there?

The lights are off. In the dimness, he spots a vodka bottle on the coffee table, and possibly, the silhouette of her phone on the sofa. *Strange.* She wouldn't leave her phone behind. Not on purpose. He presses his ear to the door and listens to the bell ring. The power is on at least.

The door shakes as he pounds his fist against it. "El," he shouts.

Nothing.

It's late morning. Ben paces her porch under a cloudless sky, heart racing. He dials her number, only to hear her voicemail message again. The anger he hopes to leave out of his voice gets pushed through flared nostrils and exerted through a tight clench of his jaw. He takes a deep breath. "El, I've lost count of how many voicemails I've left you. Can you please call me? I'm worried about you. If you don't want to see me anymore, fine, but it's not cool to just disappear like this."

Huffing around the wooden fence, he finds the side gate and pushes it. It's locked. He gives it a shake, then stands on his toes to peer over the top, searching for any sign of her in the garden. Only a gentle breeze rustles through the leaves.

Is she hiding from him? Does she feel guilty? He doesn't want her to hide. If the worst case is true—if Elyse did poison Ana—his heart tells him he'd forgive her if she was remorseful. He can't imagine his life now without her laughter and her smile, without the way she looked at him like he was the only person in the world who mattered.

When he returns home, he tries to tread lightly past the kitchen, where he hears Ana making herself a smoothie. Her eye catches him. "Oh, it's you. I thought you were still at the office."

An unexpected jolt reminds him of the spoofer app. Leaving Elyse's house, he'd forgotten to update it. With a feigned glance at his email, he swiftly updates his location to correct his oversight. "Finished up early."

"Good. Maybe we could spend some time together today."

He forces a tight-lipped smile, concealing his dread. "Sure. What do you want to do?"

"I was thinking about taking out the boat."

"Just you and me?" His smile vanishes at the thought of being lured on a boat to his death, his body dropped into the ocean.

"Yeah, I could pack a picnic," she says dreamily.

Ben opens up cabinets and closes them at random. He's not even really looking for anything. "I don't know. I'm not feeling all that great."

Her annoyance is accentuated by the loud, gravely whir of the blender grinding up her açai berry and kale into a slurry. It blends to an off-putting color.

"Fine. Can we at least have lunch at the club together?"

He checks his phone. Still nothing. Panic swells within him. *Goddammit, Elyse, where are you?*

"Uh...yeah, sure. Alright."

It's a five-minute drive from their house to the club, and they walk together from the parking lot. As they walk past the valet stand, a young man calls out to them.

"Ms. King."

Ana scowls at the blonde boy. "Yes?"

The valet runs up to her excitedly like a golden retriever. "Good afternoon, Ms. King. I was wondering if your friend has decided on becoming a member?"

"My friend?"

"Sarah. She said she was considering becoming a member."

"I don't know who you're talking about." She clings to Ben's arm, pulling him inside. He gives the valet an apologetic half smile for Ana's brusque tone.

They only make it a few steps before Ben has a realization. "You don't know anyone named Sarah?"

She shrugs. "I'm sure I do, but no one I invited to the club."

"Hmm," he says. "Why don't you grab a table. I need to use the restroom."

He turns toward the men's room and watches Ana disappear inside the dining room before turning around and heading back to the valet stand.

"Hey," he says to the valet. Retrieving his phone, he finds a clear photo of Elyse's face from her Instagram. "Is this the woman you were asking about?"

"Yeah, that's her."

"She was here?"

"Uh," the valet says and shifts nervously. "Yeah, just for a bit. We had lunch."

He's not sure whether to be frightened or impressed, but he's a little of both. Smiling, Ben asks, "Had lunch with her here?" He gestures at the building for emphasis.

The valet's face pales, concern evident. "Yeah. I was on break. I'm allowed a guest for meals."

Holding up a reassuring hand, Ben says, "No need to worry. Just curious. Ana and Sarah had a little...blowup. It's a touchy subject."

Understanding dawns on the valet's face. "Oh, sorry. I shouldn't have mentioned her. I just wondered if she'd come around again."

Clearly, Elyse left quite an impression. The young man looks like he's going to cry. Ben, sympathizing, assures him, "Don't stress. You couldn't have known." He offers a comforting pat and a kind smile, which seems to help the valet relax.

As Ben makes his way to the dining room, curiosity gnaws at him. How did Elyse know about their membership at this club? He'd never brought it up. The events leading up to Ana's reaction, especially when he spent the whole day with Elyse, still mystify him.

Seated by a window, Ana waits. As Ben settles beside her, he tries to hide his distress. She catches his mood immediately, her pout deepening and eyes widening. "So, how's work?"

Rubbing his eyebrow, Ben responds, "It's, uh, good. Busy." He avoids mentioning AFP, leaning into the table and resting a cheek on his fist.

Unexpectedly, food arrives. The waitress places their meals on the table.

"Did you ever figure out what caused that allergic reaction?" Ben asks.

Ana shakes her head and casts her napkin over her lap. "No. They stuck me full of needles but they have no answers. It's ridiculous. They tested me for allergies to nuts, penicillin, aspirin, you name it. Everything was inconclusive." She takes a long sip from her water glass.

"Did you eat or drink anything before the reaction?"

"Just water."

It doesn't make any sense. Elyse is smart, much smarter than he probably ever gave her credit for. Ben taps his fist against his lips. He's been fidgeting in his seat, eyes darting around the room. "What's wrong?" Ana asks.

"I'm worried, that's all."

Ana extends her hand. "I'm okay, babe. Don't worry about me."

After lunch, the rest of the day passes in a blur. He finds himself unable to focus on anything but his concern for Elyse. The image of her at the club haunts him. How could she have pulled off such a dangerous stunt with Ana, and why has she vanished without a word?

As evening falls, Ben finds himself pacing restlessly through the house. He knows he won't be able to sleep, not with so many unanswered questions swirling in his mind. Ana retreats to their bedroom early, leaving Ben to his own devices. With a heavy sigh, he decides to seek solace in the one place where he can still find Elyse: her YouTube channel.

Retreating to his office, he shuts the door quietly behind him. There, in the dim glow of his phone screen, he opens up Elyse's channel and begins to watch her videos, one by one. The sound of her voice, the passion she displays for her work,

provide some small comfort to him, even as the mystery of her disappearance continues to consume him.

Boughs of colorful pink, orange and gold flowers bend over her head, and she pulls a vine down with a gloved hand. "The thorns of this bougainvillea are meant to defend it against getting eaten by predators," she says. The video cuts to the bunches of colorful blossoms. "The pretty, bright blooms attract pollinators so it can reproduce." Her face comes into frame, and her big doe eyes glitter with excitement. "Isn't that neat? No matter what obstacle, nature will find a way to remove it so life can go on."

There are dozens of videos like that one. Plants and science, what they teach about life, death, and hope. It's actually beautiful.

Even if she did mess with Ana, if Elyse really wanted Ana dead, she'd be as dead as George Ramos. Instead, Ana just had a bad day. Elyse was punching up, probably in his defense. But that doesn't explain why she's not returning his calls.

He tries her again.

"Sweetheart, it's me. Again. If you're getting these messages, please call me back. I miss you. I'm worried about you. I'm not mad, if that's what you're worried about. And if you're mad at me, well, give me a chance to fix it, whatever it is." He sighs. "I love you, El. Please call me back."

Chapter Thirty

It's just after noon and raining by the time Yaritza in a Blue Chevy Malibu picks Elyse up outside the bus station. She'd installed the ride share app on her burner phone and funded it with a prepaid debit card. Her lungs pull in the sweet sultry air. She's missed this, the ozone and earthy oils mixing and rising off the hot ground. It smells like dirt and sparks of electricity. She's home. It's dangerous here, but she's glad to come back, even if it's for the last time.

"Sarah?" Yaritza confirms.

"Yeah, I need to make a few stops, is that okay?"

With bold false lashes and vibrant magenta tendrils peeking from her nape, Yaritza glances at Elyse in her rearview mirror. An *azabache* and a silver cross hang from the mirror as signs of protection. Yaritza replies in Spanish. *"¿Claro, a donde?" Of course, where to?*

"Can you take me to Walmart? I only need twenty minutes."

"Claro."

Traffic is congested. Yaritza stops in a loading zone outside Walmart just after one o'clock, and Elyse slips on her hat. She heads inside through the automatic double doors and yanks a cart from the corral. Her wet sneakers squeak against the shiny white linoleum floors. *Gloves.*

The double dipped latex gloves she needs are between the hardware and garden sections. In the home section, she finds a six-cup sized plastic canister with an air-tight securable lid. A section near the registers is set up for tourists, and she grabs a clear plastic poncho. She goes to self-checkout, scans the items and pays in cash, then heads back to Yaritza.

The rain hammers down now in heavy warm drops. The shopping bag crinkles as she shoves the items into her large shoulder bag. Sharing the address of her childhood home with Yaritza, she checks the time. The car clock flashes 1:35 p.m.—shopping took longer than expected.

Colorful cinderblock buildings are painted like flags—Colombian yellows and Cuban blues stand out among the sleek and freshly gentrified modern construction. They pass stores that end in vowels and start with La or El, a church in a strip mall. The streets are lined in tall, skinny palms that provide no shade. The windshield wipers are at full speed, and the rhythmic high-pitched screeches loop endlessly until they pull up to her street just before 2:30 p.m.

"Viente minutos," Elyse promises. *Twenty minutes.* Yaritza nods and Elyse puts on the clear poncho and gloves. As she emerges from the car, she turns her focus to the Ramos house. The garage door is closed and the gravel driveway empty. This might be easier than she anticipated.

The Manchineel

The rain is now coming down so hard and fast, it's like looking through a wall of beaded curtains. She sneaks through the wrought iron gate, stained with white streaks of calcium. A posted notice from Miami-Dade County calls attention to the condemnable condition of the house, which becomes more apparent as she trudges deeper onto the property through the side yard. Pink stucco crumbles off a wall, revealing shattered wooden bones that splinter and tangle into gnarly patches of grass.

Her bedroom window is still the only one not covered in iron bars. She peeks through the glass to see the blinds broken and dangling like a mangled mobile in a child's nursery, offering only fragmented glimpses of the damage inside. The ceiling peels down with moisture. A blue tarp is crumpled uselessly against a section of roof, held down by a cinderblock. It must have been damaged in a storm.

The backyard is the same, only more vibrant. Palms, bushes and vines interlock into a wall of green against a tall chain-link fence. Invasive kudzu vines have claimed the trunks and branches of oak trees behind the property and drape over their irregular shapes like a thick, verdant blanket.

The fruit trees have grown so much since she last saw them. Her poncho hood pulled into place, she creeps toward the mangroves and approaches the manchineel tree. Strong winds force the palms to arc eastward, blowing dense mists of toxic water in that direction. It keeps her from getting too close. *Shoot.* Coming home with blisters all over her skin will be a dead giveaway that she's been up to something.

There's a shed in the yard, and she forces it open. A family of rabbits are nesting inside and hiding from the rain. "Hey, little guys. I won't bother you," she says and reaches in for a rusty pole saw. She closes the metal door, stands back from the manchineel as far as the metal rod will let her and starts to cut. Her arms grow sorer with each violent jerk. It's harder work than

she expects, and she's out of breath when a limb eventually falls to the ground. *Finally.*

She drags it toward her with the pole's hook and carefully collects the precious fruit with a gloved hand before dropping each one into the canister. When she's gotten what she needs, she removes her gloves and abandons her tools in the yard. Her sneakers sink into the wet earth as she leaves. The hood of her poncho flies back with the wind, and by the time she can fix it, the rain has soaked through her hair. Her shoes are heavy, saturated with mud and water.

Elyse waits to approach the front of the house and peeks around the corner, zeroing in on the Ramos garage. Still closed. She exhales with relief and starts toward the front gate. She only takes a few steps into view when she realizes Yaritza is gone and Eileen Ramos is standing inside the gate with her cane, staring through her. Elyse freezes as Eileen takes a step toward her, never breaking her gaze from under a blue umbrella.

Backing away, Elyse fumbles with her phone, but the device is unresponsive to her wet hands and there's nothing but a wall of rain in either direction on the road. Eileen inches closer, her breath coming out in short, labored huffs. "I know who you are," she says, leaning forward to get a closer look at her. Years of smoking have made the crepe-like skin around her mouth a matrix of crisscrossing lines. The intense hatred behind her pitch-black eyes sends Elyse's back pressing against a cold stucco wall.

"You have some nerve coming back here."

"Why won't you leave me alone?"

"If I can't have peace without my George, then neither can you."

The rain pelts Elyse's plastic poncho. "What do you want from me?" she shouts. "I moved away. I left you alone. What do I have to do?"

Eileen hobbles closer until they're face-to-face, inches apart, and stares into her eyes. "Tell me the *truth*. Tell me what really happened to my George." Her voice is garbled and deep, as if she's speaking through a pool of rocks.

Elyse takes in their surroundings. They're all alone on the street. No cars are passing by.

"Fine. But can we get out of the rain?"

A bright jagged bolt of lightning breaks through the clouds, followed by a deafening boom and rumbling thunder that echoes on and on into the distance. It causes them to jump. A neighbor's dog barks and yips. Static ripples and cracks across the sky. It's dangerous to stay out here, and Elyse would rather not get struck by lightning.

Eileen silently glares at her, letting the shock of the noise dissipate until she simply turns and walks unsteadily toward her house, her discolored legs swollen with fluid. Elyse follows her, shoving her hands into the plastic poncho as they approach the garage.

The door rises, revealing the familiar room filled with bins and cardboard boxes, old furniture, and storage shelves lined with dusty knickknacks. She catches a whiff of cat urine. Eileen pushes a button resembling a doorbell near the interior entrance, and the garage door motor starts loudly whirring and creaking the steel door shut. Elyse's pulse begins to race. She's trapped.

Following Eileen inside the house, it takes a moment for Elyse's vision to adjust to the dark. The only light is from a small desk lamp beside a blue corduroy recliner in the living room. Being in here is so surreal she bites the inside of her lip to confirm it's really happening. The quick, painful pinch from her incisor lets her know that it is. An old digital clock sitting on a plastic tower of drawers reads 3:35 p.m. No wonder Yaritza left. Elyse lost all track of time.

The recliner swiftly rocks back and forth as Eileen collapses into it. Elyse doesn't want to sit, doesn't want to touch anything. Her eyes dart to Eileen's surroundings, ensuring there's no immediate threat. It seems like they're alone. No weapons. A cell phone is plugged into the wall above the kitchen counter five feet away.

"What do you want to know?"

"Why did you do it?"

She grips her stomach. "Ms. Ramos, like I've told you before, your son was hurting me."

Eileen clutches her cane and slams it down, causing Elyse to flinch despite the rubber stoppers dampening the sound it makes against the tile floor. She points a thick, bulbous finger at Elyse. "My son wouldn't hurt anyone. He was a good boy." Eileen studies Elyse's face and sneers. "I'm alone here because of you. I should have George. I should have grandchildren. This is all I have now."

"I never wanted to hurt anyone."

"But you did, didn't you. You killed my son."

Her mouth dries but the nape of Elyse's scalp is damp with rain and sweat. The air-conditioning blows against her and a shiver prickles up her skin, her thin plastic poncho offering no warmth or comfort. "Yes," she admits. "I killed him. That's the truth."

Cupping her face, Eileen hunches over and weeps into her hands. "I knew it. I always knew you did this." The muffled words barely escape through her choked sobs.

It makes Elyse sick. George isn't worth blubbering over, even if she is his mother.

Once the wailing subsides, Eileen stares at her darkly. "You need to pay for what you did."

Wrapping her arms around herself, Elyse trembles. She's so cold, her legs shake and her teeth chatter. If she leaves, Eileen will call the police. They'll know she was there, there will be a

record of it. This won't work. She's not even supposed to be here. It's all over.

"I'm so tired of running away from this," she says, her voice strained. Eileen jerks back with surprise, her eyes narrowed at her. Elyse drops her head and presses her hands to her belly as her body shudders. "I keep trying to move on, but I keep getting pulled back here somehow. I hear him, you know. In my head. Every day he reminds me of the monster I am."

George has been with her so long, she struggles to think of a time when she was truly free of him. But he was insidious. Since his first day in her life, he began to dig in deep, each day rooting further into the recesses of her mind.

He's isolated her, driven her to a life bereft of connection. Perverted any moment of joy. Before Ben, she was adrift and alone, belonging to no one. But now that Elyse has failed here, what ephemeral love affair she's shared with Ben will likely fizzle out. When they're together, he makes the most beautiful promises to her, but as soon as he goes back to Ana, it all slips away. Her hold on him is too strong.

"I think...maybe finally telling the truth might be the only thing that'll make it stop."

Eileen sits up straighter, the tension in her expression easing. "We'll call the police. You can talk to them here. Together."

"Okay."

"You will?"

"Yes." She reaches for her phone and clutches it in her trembling hands. "Can I please just make a quick phone call first? My boyfriend. He's going to be worried if he doesn't hear from me soon. I just want to let him know I'm okay."

Eileen stares at her silently, then lets out a heavy sigh. "Alright. Make it quick."

"Thank you," she says, before turning down the hall.

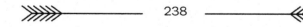

Seeking a moment of privacy, she walks toward a bathroom. Standing in the hall in front of the open door, she stares down at her phone. Her finger quivers over Ben's name and her gut tenses and aches. What will she say?

A light flickers in the corner of her eye and she quickly glances at it, noticing the laundry room door is ajar. A fluorescent light inside buzzes and strobes. Below it, a wire shelf full of cleaning supplies is mounted to the wall, holding big bottles of industrial cleaners. She takes a step closer to scan the labels. Yellow liquid sanitizer. *Sodium hypochlorite.* Pink scale remover. *Acid.*

A spark of realization ignites within her. In a hurry, she dons a fresh pair of gloves from her bag then picks up a bottle of scale remover. The pink, thickish fluid bobs around inside as she rests the bottle gently in the bathtub. Turning, she paces softly back to the laundry room for the liquid cleaner.

"I'm calling because I don't want you to worry," she says loudly to no one. Her voice echoes down the hall. She yanks a metal chain to plug up the bathtub. "I'm going to be okay. I've got to go. I love you so much," she says.

Her shirt over her nose, she holds her breath and quickly unscrews each bottle, dumping the contents inside the tub. Suppressed air pulses in her lungs as the chemicals mix and bubble. A yellow haze of vapor flows from the rising mixture, lifting like a soufflé as the room fills with gas. She throws a towel on the floor and steps onto it, wiping her wet shoe prints from the tile. Her lungs quiver. She needs to breathe. Now.

Backing out quickly, she closes the door with a gloved hand. Her heart is beating loudly in her ears. Once outside, she exhales and desperately sucks fresh air. She kicks the towel at her feet into the laundry room and waits. Gas is expanding inside the small bathroom, poisoning every cubic inch of space. After counting sixty Mississippis, she slowly walks to the living room.

"Ms. Ramos?" she calls sweetly.

Eileen turns from her recliner and squints at Elyse. Her phone is still plugged in and sitting where it was before. *Good.*

"Um, your toilet...it's overflowing."

Eileen rocks and flounders over her stomach until her feet touch the ground, and she uses the momentum of her recliner to stand up. She shuffles past Elyse down the hall in a hurry. Elyse follows behind her and gets a running start when Eileen pushes the door open.

"What is that?" Eileen asks, staring into the tub.

Elyse holds her breath, tackling her around her waist and pushing her into the bathroom. Losing her balance, Eileen collapses forward toward the toilet. In an attempt to stop herself, she grips onto the counter. Her cane falls to the floor, and she grasps at air reaching for it. Tendrils of toxic gas float in the air. One good inhale could be fatal all on its own. Eileen is coughing when Elyse seals the room shut, holding onto the doorknob tightly.

Exhaling again with relief, she then draws unpolluted air back into her lungs. The coughs from inside become groans and raw hacking.

"You should have just left me alone!" Elyse shouts to her through the door. "I moved across the frickin' country to get away from you, and it wasn't good enough. Now look what you made me do."

Eileen gasps and struggles for air. Elyse can hear her hand slapping against the tile floor, the shower curtain hooks scraping against the metal bar as Eileen tugs it in a futile attempt to get on her feet. The smell of chlorine grows stronger as it seeps through the gaps in the door frame. Elyse can't stay much longer, or she might get hurt.

Letting go of the handle, she slowly backs away from the door. She wipes her sneaker prints from the tile in the living room and down the hall. The pungent odor is apparent now,

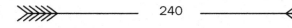

even from several feet away. The coughing has stopped. Her body relaxes, and she slips out of the house. Entering the garage, she locks up behind herself, then raises the metal door.

When she was a kid, her mother showed her how to leave this way. Every exit was a challenge of speed and agility. She pushes the garage opener and the door begins to lower. Keeping her bag close, she runs toward it. The trick is in bending low enough that the door doesn't hit you, while also kicking your feet out far enough that your stride doesn't flag the sensor to stop.

She makes it to the other side and waits for the metal to make contact with the concrete. All the doors are locked. There aren't any cameras. Eileen's phone is inside charging and untouched. It's like Elyse was never here, and Ms. Ramos just made some unfortunate household cleaning decisions.

It was the most fundamental of all chemical reactions—simple neutralization by combining an acid with a base to form a salt. It just so happens this reaction also makes toxic chlorine gas.

It's stopped raining, and Elyse decides to walk. It takes a little over two hours to make it five miles west. Her gloves and poncho are discarded in a McDonald's parking lot trash can along the way, where she also washes up in their bathroom. She orders a ten-piece nugget and fries and takes a rest, watching the sun start to evaporate the water on the ground from the dining room window.

It's 6:22 p.m. when she approaches the bus station with sore feet and a blister forming on the back of her right heel. She puts on her sunglasses and hat from her bag, tucks her arms into her oversized sweatshirt, and keeps her head down all through the terminal before taking a seat at her gate.

***

It's late when she gets home. Exhausted, she sets the container of manchineel fruit on her kitchen counter and stares at it for a while before heading to bed. In the morning, she slides on her full-face respirator and a pair of latex gloves, tugging them at her wrists.

She quarters the green death apples, then dices them into tiny bits. The bits half fill a large Erlenmeyer flask. A gallon bottle of ethyl alcohol sits under the sink. She pours it over the fruit and covers it with tin foil.

This should be a special blend. She shops around her garden. Ana is young and her heart is strong. An autopsy is likely, although Elyse hopes the combination of toxins will appear consistent enough with her prior allergic reaction that, with a bit of luck, a forensic exam won't be required. But if the coroner is analyzing, Elyse wants them confused. These toxins should be difficult to identify. She picks and prunes with gloved hands and sets her bounty into a bucket. This will be her masterpiece.

After cutting, grinding with a mortar and pestle, and soaking in ethanol, the chemicals need time to be drawn out. It's going to be a while, so she pulls off her protective equipment and shoves her gloves in a trash bag.

Turning on her phone, it vibrates with an alert—twenty-one voicemail messages. *Oh no.*

"Hey, baby. I just got home. I've been thinking about you. I miss you. I'll see you Sunday. Love you. Bye."

"Hey, it's me. I'm just confirming I'm coming by tomorrow. Call me back."

"El, it's me. I'm on my way this morning. Please be awake."

She listens to voicemail after voicemail and they're almost all from Ben.

"El, it's me. Please. It's been a week. I've called, I've come by and you're not answering. I'm worried about you. Is this about the furniture? I'm sorry, okay. I'm an idiot. I never should have offered you her furniture. I get that now. I'll make it up to you, I swear. Just, please, please call me."

Oh frick. She calls Ben back. It rings and rings before it goes to voicemail. *Great. Now he's mad at me.* She hadn't accounted for this. It hadn't occurred to her that he'd even notice she was gone.

"Hi. I'm so sorry. I did the hyperfocus thing again and forgot about everything else. Please don't be mad. I'm home. Call me back."

Elyse can't shake the sound of desperation in his voice. He was so sincerely worried. Pacing her bedroom, she bites at her nails, the taste of regret bitter on her tongue. Has she pushed him away? The thought of Ben out there in the world thinking that she's abandoned him crushes her.

She leaves her science experiment to work its magic and goes to him.

Chapter Thirty-One

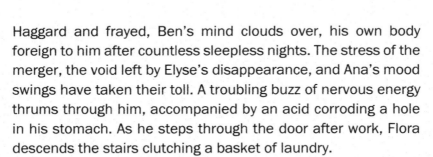

Haggard and frayed, Ben's mind clouds over, his own body foreign to him after countless sleepless nights. The stress of the merger, the void left by Elyse's disappearance, and Ana's mood swings have taken their toll. A troubling buzz of nervous energy thrums through him, accompanied by an acid corroding a hole in his stomach. As he steps through the door after work, Flora descends the stairs clutching a basket of laundry.

"Are you okay?" Flora asks.

"It's Elyse," he says, rubbing his bloodshot eyes. "I think something's wrong."

"What do you mean?"

"She's not answering my calls. Something's going on, but I don't know what it is."

Flora furrows her brow and places a soothing hand on his shoulder. "Why don't you sit down and rest, *mijo*. You look tired."

He shakes his head, a tide of unease crashing over him. How can he rest when Elyse is nowhere to be found? The longer he misses her, the more certain he is Ana must be at the root of it somehow. "No, no, I can't sit. Has Ana mentioned her at all?"

"No." She sets the laundry down on the floor of the foyer. "Can I get you a drink to help relax you?"

He nods. He could really use a drink right now. They walk to the bar in his game room, and she pours him a glass of bourbon. Just as he tastes the smooth, cinnamon finish, he notices Flora staring at him, wringing her hands. *"¿Qué te pasa?" What's wrong?*

She sighs. *"Ella vino aquí la semana pasada." She came here last week.*

"¿Quién? Elyse?" Who? Elyse?

"Sí."

He can't believe what he's hearing. There is a tingling in his chest that spreads like wildfire, leaving his heart racing. *"¿Elyse vino aquí?" Elyse came here?*

Flora nods with a guilty expression and twists a bar rag in her hands. His stomach is a hard knot, clenched tightly and sending waves of nausea through his body. It draws all the air from his lungs. *Oh my God.* Elyse has lost her fucking mind. Is she trying to have him killed? Why would she show up to his house, where his wife lives? How could Flora betray him by keeping this from him?

"She came here and you didn't tell me?" His tone is harsh and Flora shrinks back.

"I'm so sorry, *mijo*. I didn't want you to be upset. She was just worried about you."

Flora cries and confesses every detail. Elyse showed up unannounced and they had coffee. They talked about him,

about Ana. She wanted to know all about her. Her schedule. What she eats. Where she exercises.

"Creo que quería confrontarla, pelear con ella, no lo sé. Le dije que no querrías eso y se fue." I think she wanted to confront her, fight with her. I don't know. I told her that you wouldn't want that and she left.

He becomes unhinged. With each breath, his lungs feel restricted, as if he's being suffocated by the weight of his own anxiety. What was Elyse thinking?

"I'm so sorry, *mijo*."

Now what? His eyes squeeze shut and holds his hand to his head. A migraine is starting to brew at the base of his skull. Ben leans in toward Flora, his tone serious. "If she shows up again, I want you to call me right away. Do you understand?"

She nods solemnly. He expects her to leave, but when she doesn't, he can tell she's holding something back. "What is it?"

"Por favor, no te enfades con ella. Te quiere y una joven enamorada puede hacer locuras." Please, don't be angry with her. She loves you, and a young girl in love can do crazy things. She shrugs. *"Me caía bien." I liked her.*

Ben's blank stare must convey his frustration, because Flora leaves him to drink alone.

For hours, he refills his glass wondering what Ana might already know, what she might have done. It occurs to him that the security camera footage is backed up on their server. Maybe that will offer some clue of what's happened.

It takes a little digging, but once he finds the video via an app on his phone, he sees Elyse creep to the door wearing a white University of Miami ball cap and aviator sunglasses. She fidgets outside the door until Flora answers. His throat constricts with emotion as he listens to her sweet voice. If she was upset with him, why would she show up and tell Flora how worried she was about him? No. None of this makes sense.

Elyse must have tried to confront Ana. Ana's been so lighthearted lately, wanting to spend quality time together. But why? Is she overcompensating for something? Is she happy now that she knows Elyse is out of his life? Maybe she's just trying to distract him, create a diversion. His finger traces the lip of his glass and his mind races with frightening scenarios.

"Ben?" He hears Ana call out to him. His body tenses as soon as he hears her voice. On instinct, his thumb taps the delete button on the video and it's gone.

Ana eventually stomps into the room to find him. "I've been yelling for you."

"Didn't hear you," he says, his tongue heavy.

She rubs his shoulders affectionately and his suspicion grows.

"What's wrong?" she coos.

He draws away from her in disgust. "Bad day."

She sits beside him on a barstool and beams. "Well, I had a great day."

Despite her chipper mood, he can't even manage to force a smile. "You set an orphanage on fire?" he slurs. "Tied a baby to some train tracks?"

Ana laughs and shoves him playfully. "No, asshole. I met with Seth on his project like you asked me to. I wanted to thank you for setting it up because it means a lot to me to carry out Daddy's work."

She's doing that thing again where she's easygoing and kind and it confuses him. He should know better by now not to fall for it. Ana's up to something. She knows about Elyse. She hurt her. He stares inside his glass and takes another burning sip of his drink.

Ana leans back into her barstool with a push, glaring at him, the edge of the bar pressing into her palms. "What's been going on with you?"

He focuses on the glass of bourbon, loses focus, refocuses again. "Told you. Bad day."

A mocking smirk flickers on her lips. "Did your girlfriend break up with you?"

The way she says it is taunting. A sudden chill courses through his body and something snaps inside him. His attention leaves the bourbon glass and turns to lock eyes with her. "What did you just say?"

"You've been moping around here all week like you had your heart broken."

He bends toward her until they're face-to-face. "What'd you do to her?"

"What?"

"Where is she?"

"Who? I don't know what you're talking about."

"Elyse!" he shouts and staggers to his feet. She jerks back, startled at the sudden boom of his voice. "You hated her from the start because she's good and pure and you're rotted from the inside out."

She slaps the glass from his hand. It shatters on the floor.

"I knew it," she says, her eyes sharpening. "How could you do this to us?"

"*How could I do this to us?*" he mocks her. "Are you fucking kidding me? You've made my life hell. You're constantly controlling me, hitting me, emasculating me. I've never been good enough for you. Elyse loves me, and I love her. And I swear on my mother's grave if you disturbed a hair on her head, you will regret the day you were born."

Her stunned expression twists into a contained rage. "Oh, she loves you. That's so sweet. You're the dumbest wetback piece of shit I've ever met in my life. How much money did you give her?"

"Fuck you," he says, brushing past her. He steps over the broken glass and exits the game room. She rushes to jump in his path.

"Get out of my way," he says, his voice calm. He sidesteps her and she trails behind him.

"You're a worthless piece of shit. Daddy knew it. You think she loves you? She doesn't even know you. Not like I do. I've seen who you really are, and you're not fooling me with that suit."

He tries to phase her out, to keep her words from seeping in, but she's relentless.

"Well enjoy it while you can, because when I'm done with you, you'll be right back in the ghetto where you belong and that gold digging bitch will have to move on to her next meal ticket. Everyone in this town is going to see exactly who you are. A nobody. You can't hide behind my family's name and our money and pretend you're one of us anymore. You were never one of us and you never will be."

He laughs and smiles, shaking his head. She keeps pace with him as he hurries down the hall toward the stairs. He's at the landing when she rushes ahead to stop him.

"You think this is funny?" She swings. Her fist makes contact with his jaw.

The pain is so sudden and intense that before he can stop himself, he grabs her by her throat and slams her against the wall, a shocked gasp escaping her on impact before she bounces and falls to the floor.

He pauses long enough to loom over her, an accusatory finger aimed in her direction. "I'm warning you," he says, his voice dark. "Stay away from me."

It gives him a head start, but in no time she's off the floor. She follows him up the stairs. Cursing. Screaming. She picks up a large candle holder from a hall table and throws it at his back.

It thumps against him, then explodes on the ground into purple granules of glass.

He locks himself in the office and tries to steady himself. The room shifts around him. All effort to silence his mind is made impossible from Ana's incessant banging on the door. He's so tired of this, of her. Tired of being manipulated. Mistreated. Tired of running away. He stumbles toward the door and opens it, then steels himself. She's standing there, waiting.

"Five fucking years," she says, her face streaked with tears.

He turns away, emotionless, as she weeps, groaning and sniveling with angry heaves. Fleeting moments of shame and guilt pass over him but are quickly overshadowed by the memories of violence.

This is usually the part of the fight where he apologizes, gathers her into a forgiving embrace and excuses her vitriol in exchange for peace. Not today. Never again. He's hardened, holding firm to his resolve like a deeply rooted oak.

Once she realizes he's unmoved by her emotional appeals, her breathing steadies, and she gathers herself. "I hate you," she says, glowering at him with eyes cold enough to freeze a flame.

"Good."

She pushes him. Shoves and punches at him. But he's too close, too sturdy. Her swings aren't landing with any force and his calm only fuels her rage. She raises her knee with a quick jerk. It hits him in the groin. The pain is sharp and immediate. A guttural gasp escapes from his clenched teeth as he's brought to his knees. When he falls to the ground, she kicks him in the ribs so hard he sees white, and the searing impact knocks the air out of him. Her kicks land again and again, harder and harder—ribs, chest, stomach.

He grabs her leg, yanking her feet from under her, and she tumbles to the floor with a hard thud. Flora must have heard the

glass shattering because she's standing in the hallway with her hands over her mouth. *"Mijo,"* she cries.

"Flora," he wheezes, "get help." His body is still reeling but the adrenaline takes over. It hurts to breathe; each inhale like a jagged shard of glass burrowing into his chest.

Ana is back on her feet. "Flora, don't you dare."

He grips the arm of the leather couch to climb up to his knees. There's not enough air. He can't breathe. His limbs are heavy. There's a sharp pain in his chest. He gasps and croaks a weak, "Flora." But she's gone. He coughs, and the taste of blood fills his mouth.

For a moment, Ana backs off, her posture relaxing. It's a short-lived illusion of mercy that evaporates when she pivots, her fingers closing around the grip of the Yankees baseball bat from his collection. *Oh fuck. Tonight is the night.*

The moment she lifts it off the shelf, a jolt of panic surges through him. He attempts to rise, but he can't get to his feet. She raises the bat over her head and lands a blow against his back. His hand instinctively reaches behind him, clutching on to the bat, and they engage in a fierce tug-of-war. She leans back, leveraging her body to try and jerk the bat from his hands. He lets go, and her momentum sends her reeling backward, her body falling to the ground.

He's numb when he climbs over her. "Is this what you want?" He pins her down with his body and his hands find her throat. She grabs his forearms but he's too strong. Every ounce of might tightens his grip. His blood drips on her face. She gasps for air but none comes, not even a sound can escape. Her disbelieving eyes beg for his mercy as a vein protrudes from her forehead, mouth open in a silent scream.

"Is this what you want?" It's a tormented cry from the depths of his soul, spitting with rage. His arms shake with tension as he squeezes harder. Eyes bulging, unblinking. A primal, cathartic growl rumbles from his belly as he wrings

tighter. Tighter. His vision starts to fade. He hears a strange sound. Bells. A sickening crack and gurgle emerge from the back of Ana's throat as he lets go, feeling a sense of release, a warm caress of the sun after a prolonged winter.

Her body is still. Lifeless eyes rimmed with blood. He recoils in horror and scrambles backward into the corner of the room.

Oh my God. Oh no. Oh no. What have I done?

His vision blurs. Everything is shrouded in a black halo that shrinks smaller by the second. The walls pull toward him. He can't breathe. He collapses onto his back, staring up at the coffered squares on the ceiling and watches them spin before everything turns black.

Chapter Thirty-Two

Devon in a gray Nissan Rogue takes Elyse to a block from Ben's house. When she makes her way on foot up the street and through the woods outside, she can hear faint screaming. With every step she takes, the booming voice sharpens with chilling clarity. It's Ben. His screams cut through the stillness outside.

Elyse's chest tightens in panic. She breaks into a run, her feet pounding against the ground in rhythm with the escalating cries. Reaching the front door, she finds it locked. Her mind is a whirlwind, and without pausing to think, her finger jabs repeatedly at the doorbell, each press a plea for entry. The bell chimes urgently until finally Flora opens.

"Is this what you want?" Ben screams from somewhere deep in the house.

Elyse runs past Flora and up the stairs toward the sounds of Ben's cries. A pair of doors to an office are open. Ben and Ana are on their backs, his mouth bloodied. She stares at Ana's torso to see if it rises even a centimeter with breath, but once her eye catches Ana's throat, death is a foregone conclusion. It's bent and crushed in like a paper cup.

I'm too late.

Sensing a presence next to her, she turns to find Flora standing there with her hands over her mouth. "He needs help," she cries.

Oh frick. What am I gonna do? If they call this in, they'll find Ana and he'll go to prison.

"Ben!" She runs to him. "Ben," she says again and shakes him. His eyes open and close. He's coughing and choking on blood.

Oh God. Oh God. Pull yourself together or he's going to die. Breathe.

Her mind goes fuzzy and she's not Elyse anymore. She's not anyone. The colors fade and she's watching herself grab his wrist and pull off his watch. Flora looks on, distraught.

"Flora, I'm going to need you to help me carry him down the stairs. Can you do that?"

"*Ay dios*, I'll try," she says and whimpers.

Elyse rolls him slightly and takes his wallet and cell phone from his pocket. She shoves them in her bag, along with his watch.

They lift him only a few inches off the ground. He groans and blood gurgles from his mouth. He must be so heavy, but her senses are dulled. The pain is happening to someone else. They manage to get him to the hallway before setting him down again.

Elyse catches her breath. Flora is unsteady on her feet.

"Come on, Flora. Just a little further. Okay? *One, two, three.*" They groan, lifting him up again. She grips him under his arms. "I'll head down first."

Flora has his legs and they struggle down the stairs. When they reach the bottom, Elyse watches from outside herself as they carefully rest him at the foot of the stairs.

Flora looks at her. "Now what?"

"Now, we get him in his car."

They lift him again, carrying him several feet before setting him down. They repeat the process, lifting and setting, through the massive house. When they finally get to the garage, Elyse lifts the keys off the hook, and they struggle to lift him inside.

Before she gets into the driver's seat, she shouts to Flora. "Hold things down here. I need you to get all the hydrogen peroxide you can find. Just whatever you have here, do not buy anything at the store. Got it?"

"*Santa Maria Madre de Dios.*" It sounds like she's reciting the rosary.

"Flora, please," she interrupts. "Do you want Ben to go to prison?"

She's weeping. "No, oh God no."

"Then do exactly what I tell you. And don't let anyone else in. I'll be back soon."

***

Elyse hunches over the steering wheel of Ben's Range Rover, squinting through the dark at a blur of fast-moving lights. Ben moans and wheezes from the passenger seat, his chest undulates with rapid shallow breaths. "It's okay, we're getting you help. But we've got to keep you out of trouble. Can you hear me?"

Incoherent mumbles escape his lips and he seems to dose off every few moments, his eyes closed, chin falling to his sternum. He's awake now, but she's not sure she's getting through to him. The light turns red and she slams on the breaks,

 255

bringing the Range Rover to a sharp halt. Ben lurches forward and he cries out in pain.

"Oh shoot. I'm so sorry."

It's been almost a year since she's been behind the wheel. Traffic whips by and they sway from the force and speed of passing cars. Her heart races and the air-conditioning chills the sweat on her back. Ben coughs and blood spills down his lips. The static begins to ripple against her brain. *Stay in control. Ben needs you.*

They pull into a dark alley between a Spanish-service Nazarene church and a tire shop around the block from the Community Hospital Emergency Room. This is as close as she can get to the entrance while staying outside the view of nearby cameras. She climbs out of the driver's seat, rushes to the passenger side and opens the door.

"Ben, baby, can you hear me?" she asks, quickly releasing his seat belt.

"Mm."

She drags her fingers affectionately over the hair above his ear, usually so neatly kempt, now mussed and drenched in sweat. "Can you walk?"

Beads of perspiration speckle his brow and he's wincing in pain. Streaks of blood drip from his mouth down his stubbled chin. She grips his thigh, applying gentle pressure to rotate his lower body out of the car. "Let's get you on your feet."

He struggles, grimacing and groaning as his torso twists toward the outside. Extending his legs, he stumbles onto his feet. He holds steady.

"Good, that's good." She wedges her compact body under his arm like a crutch, the top of her head barely reaching his shoulder. They hobble together, inch by strenuous inch, toward a white cinderblock wall. The wall stretches to the emergency room entrance roughly fifty yards away, with only a short gap

between the wall's end and a low boxwood hedge. Ben rests against the bricks, fading in and out of consciousness.

"Ben," she says, rousing him. "You just need to walk along the wall, okay? Keep going until you reach those doors."

The automatic double doors are just feet beyond the shrubs. He can make it. At least, she hopes he can. Taking his head into her hands, she forces him to face her. "Ben," she says sternly. His confused eyes struggle to find hers. "I need you to keep going on your own, do you understand?"

"Mm," he says. For a moment, his eyes find hers and seem to find a second of clarity. She takes his hands, squeezing them. "Go," she whispers.

Slumped against the wall, he creeps forward and drags the weight of his body. He takes a few steps, then stops to rest against the wall once more to catch his breath. Faint streaks of blood stain the painted bricks as he goes. She backs away and he pushes on, her fear for him swelling in her throat. *Please let him be okay.*

The Range Rover's engine runs as she waits, watching from the driver's seat. Ben navigates the small gap between the wall and the hedge just feet from the entrance. He takes only a few steps without support before his knees buckle and he crumples onto the sidewalk.

"Ben," she wails in a muted whisper. Every muscle, every instinct wants to run to him but that will only make things worse. Her fingers clench around the steering wheel. Will someone find him? He's so close, surely someone will. She glances around, helpless. Should she jump out of the car and help him inside? Lay on the horn until someone comes out?

Just then, from the corner of her eye she notices a police cruiser slowly turning the corner. She ducks down as the headlights briefly shine through the windshield. When the darkness returns to the cabin, she peers up, exhaling her held breath. The cruiser stops just across the street but the officer inside doesn't seem to take notice of Ben's fallen figure beside the hedge.

He's probably just on patrol, not searching for anything in particular, but what if he notices her? Takes note of the car? Sitting around out here too long would be suspicious. She can't be found here, not when it could cost Ben his freedom.

Elyse takes her foot off the brake and the Range Rover rolls forward at idle speed. Just as she passes the double doors, a young woman is emerging. She'll see him, won't she? Taking one last glance at Ben lying there on the ground, she tries to reassure herself. *Everything is going to be okay. Ben will be okay.*

She drives away. Once alone on the road heading toward Beverly Hills, all her thoughts collide. Six days on a bus. Cutting down poisoned fruit in the rain. Making chemical reactions in a bathtub and all the other effort she put in to make this clean and easy. All so Ben's temper could blow it in an instant.

The strength required to make a person's neck look like a crushed soda can is incredible. The sheer rage that must have fueled it—every injury Ana's ever inflicted, every insult and humiliation—tightened his viselike grip. This was exactly what she was afraid would happen. He'd put too much faith in the strength of his civility. There are limits to restraint and self-control. He'd let himself forget that, like all of us, he's an animal.

Nobody blames a lion for devouring a person with the audacity to throw themselves into its den, especially not someone who challenges it to a fight. Poor Ben had been so patient with her. He suffered so much. And now, he'll probably never forgive himself.

Yet if it was up to the law, he'd be in police custody. A jury of his peers too dumb to get out of jury duty would get to decide if he was justified. Any person who could see her head practically decapitated from the inside would lock him up for the rest of his life. It isn't fair. He's not going down for this.

Getting rid of a body is a whole new prospect. She's never had to do this part before. *Think*. She's running on pure dread and adrenaline. Her vision goes blurry.

Then it hits her, and in an instant, she sees a solution.

In her backyard, Elyse stands before a row of blue polyethylene barrels. She seizes one, unfastening its lid and releasing the plastic clips. Fifty-five gallons of rainwater meant for her plants slosh inside. With a strong yank, she tips it forward, emptying it. Once empty, she carries it and the lid back to Ben's Range Rover and loads it inside.

"*¿Eso es para ella?*" Flora asks with a dreadful look. *Is that for her?*

Elyse is in the garage unloading the car. "*Si...um...tengo que...*get rid of her...*de alguna manera.*" *Yes, I need to get rid of her somehow.*

"*No sé si puedo.*" *I don't know if I can.*

"It's okay. I'll handle it. Just stay down here."

Elyse carries the empty drum up the stairs and sets it down next to Ana's body. *She's dead alright. Oh lord.* Poison makes all this so much tidier. She pulls off the lid and lays the barrel on its side. How is she going to get her in here? The drum is just under three feet tall and less than two feet wide. Ana is close to Elyse's height.

She cautiously eases herself into the constricting confines of the barrel, the air inside feeling stifling and muggy. The dimness adds an overwhelming sense of claustrophobia. She bows her head between her knees, every breath and slight movement results in muffled, echoed sounds that resonate in her own ears. She climbs out, catching her breath and settles the barrel on the ground. Her eyes dart to Ana, then to the barrel. *Okay. This is going to suck.*

Ana's giant diamond wedding ring slides off her stiff finger with ease, her clothes sliced off her body with a pair of sharp scissors. Better not to have anything identifying survive this. Suppressing a gag, Elyse lifts Ana's legs and bends her. *You can do this.*

"It didn't have to be this way, Ana." She forces her legs back and presses her body weight against her until Ana's knees meet her shoulders.

"You could have been a decent person. Let Ben leave with what he's entitled to and that would have been it. You're so rich it wouldn't have made a difference to you. But, *no*, you had to be vindictive about it," she says, snatching Ana's arm with a huff.

She wrenches each one back and bends them around her knees, but she's not compressed tightly enough. When Elyse did it, she could make herself as small as possible with muscle pressure. Ana bends into place but there isn't any force holding her shut. When Elyse lets go, Ana's limbs fall back and out like a limp starfish.

She shouts downstairs. "Flora, I need that duct tape!"

"Coming."

Elyse climbs to her feet and meets Flora at the top of the stairs.

"*¡Ay, Dios mío!*" Flora cries, her curiosity causing her to peer over at the gruesome scene. "*Oh, my God!*"

Why did she look?

"Flora, relax. I know it's terrible, but this is the reality we're dealing with right now and getting rid of her is the only way to protect Ben."

Flora trembles with clenched fists pressed against her mouth. Eyes glistening with tears betray her terror and disbelief. The situation hinges on her ability to keep composed, and she's spiraling. Elyse tries to calm her down by softening her voice.

"No one will believe this was self-defense. A jury will look at him and look at her just like the police did, and he'll go to prison for the rest of his life. You know this wasn't his fault, Flora."

She's crying now but nodding emphatically. "I know."

"Okay, then. The only way we protect him is to do this correctly. We can't panic."

Elyse takes the duct tape from her hands and returns to Ana's body. She tries to sit her up and hold her while wrapping her tight with tape, but struggles. Flora appears and holds Ana steady while facing away.

"You don't have to do this, Flora."

"I want to help. Just tell me what to do."

Together they bend and press Ana's body until it's compact, and Elyse wraps her tight like a mummy in silver tape. The drum is on its side, and they slide her into it, curled up like a fetus in a womb. They set the barrel on its bottom, and Elyse puts on the lid for transportation. "Let's get her downstairs."

She's much lighter than Ben, thankfully, and they set her on the first-floor landing. "Go upstairs and clean like you've never cleaned before. If you see any blood, soak it with hydrogen peroxide and then scrub it up. No bleach. When you're done there, we need to get every fleck of blood out of Ben's car. He bled all over the passenger side. Whatever you use to clean, set it aside so we can get rid of it. Okay?"

Flora nods and hurries up the stairs.

The lights in the pool are on and there's a slight blue tinge to the glow emitting from the water. A small shed on the property is concealed with bushes. Elyse goes inside and scans the bottles of chemicals behind rows of tubes, poles and skimmers. She finds six gallons of muriatic acid and takes two trips to carry them to the first-floor landing next to Ana's drum.

She finds Flora upstairs scrubbing the floor with a brush and peroxide. "Do you know Ana's schedule? Will anyone be expecting her anywhere soon?"

Flora stops scrubbing and looks up at her. "She has a yoga trip this weekend. I think she said she was leaving tomorrow."

"Where is it?"

"I think she said Lake Isabella."

Elyse has no idea where that is, but if people are expecting her, she doesn't have much time. She goes through Ana's closet and puts on some Lululemon workout clothes, a hat and sunglasses and drags out a suitcase. If Ana was really going on a trip and police start poking around, her suitcases should be gone. Clothes should be missing. Makeup. Toiletries. Yoga mats.

She's packing a suitcase when it hits her. *Shoot*. Ana's car.

The tasks ahead of her seem to only get more arduous. Rushing downstairs to the garage, she assesses the sporty white BMW, wondering how in the heck she's fitting a fifty-five gallon drum, six gallons of acid, a suitcase, rope and a shovel in there. Ana's key is hooked on the wall and Elyse uses it to unlock the car and pop the trunk.

Dang it. She squeezes her fists and kicks the air. It's only slightly more spacious than she thought but not big enough to hold it all. As she scans the car's interior, her fingertips brush against a small latch. Pulling it releases the back row of seats, which proceed to gently fall flat.

The newfound space appears almost doubled, with the carpeted back of the seats now lying flush with the trunk floor. The windows are tinted at least, sparing her the anxiety of driving a luxury sports car with an obnoxiously bright, industrial-grade chemical barrel visible in the back seat. She can make this work.

After Flora and Elyse carefully lift the drum to the garage, Elyse takes Ana's phone from her pocket and removes the SIM card, bending it back and forth until it snaps. She finds a DeWalt in the garage and drills several holes through the mobile device, which she throws into the drum with Ana before resealing it with plastic clips.

 262

Together, they lift and roll the barrel into the backseat and load up the car with the gallon jugs. "I just need to finish packing a few things," Elyse says wearily. Upstairs, Flora gathers toiletries in the bathroom while Elyse rummages through Ana's closet. A shrill ring abruptly interrupts their concentrated silence. Elyse tiptoes out of the walk-in closet and looks at Flora.

"The phone," Flora whispers.

"Answer it like you normally would. Ben and Ana aren't home right now, okay?"

Flora dashes to the bedroom end table where a small handset rests, still trilling loudly on its base. "King residence," she answers with an imposed formality in her tone. The greeting causes Elyse to briefly stop stuffing clothes into Ana's suitcase and roll her eyes. Ana probably insisted she answer the phone that way.

"¡Gracias a Dios!" Flora's cry echoes off the walls. *Thank God!* Elyse rushes over to her, where she's nodding with an excited expression. "*Si, ella esta aqui.*" *Yes, she's here.*

Flora hands the phone to Elyse. She presses it to her ear. "Hello?"

"El?" Ben groans.

She sighs with relief at the sound of his voice. "Ben."

"I need you to get me the fuck out of here."

Chapter Thirty-Three

The first thing he notices is the green curtain, then the beeping. A cuff inflates around his arm and his torso has a constant dull ache. A tube carrying oxygen is hooked under his nose. His mouth is dry and the tip of his tongue is rough. He must have been sleeping with his mouth open.

Brushing a hand against his face, his cheeks and chin feel rough and stubbled. How long has he been here? What happened? He licks his lips, but his tongue is dry so it doesn't help. It hurts to move, but he turns his head around as best he can to see where he is. A woman in blue scrubs walks in, and he wants to call out to her but his throat is too tight. Instead, he coughs and it gets her attention.

"You're awake," she says and approaches him. She's short and petite with light brown hair and a narrow waist.

"Where am I?" His voice is weak and raw. He can barely recognize it.

She rests a gentle hand on his forehead. "You're at East LA Community Hospital. How are you feeling?"

"Like shit. Like I got hit by a truck." His hands survey his face and body to orient himself. Everything aches and his mind is blurry.

"You're on a morphine drip," she explains and gives him a plunger.

As soon as it's in his grip, he taps it three times and waits for the pain relief.

"How long have I been out?"

"A few hours. You came in without identification. Can you tell me your name?" She lifts a pair of reading glasses from around her neck and sets them on the bridge of her nose.

My name. The events from that evening replay in his mind. Ana's bloodshot eyes. The sounds of the last gasps of breath seeping from her throat. That awful cracking noise. Elyse's voice. Lying on the cold pavement. His pulse quickens. He's got to get out of here.

"Where are my things?"

She points to a nearby table where his clothing is folded in a clear plastic bag.

"I'm a little foggy. I'm sorry."

A man walks in. His dark bronze skin contrasts against the white of his coat. He squints at Ben's chart and pushes his silver glasses down the bridge of his nose. "I'm Dr. Rose, the attending physician." His voice is monotone and laced with exhaustion. "You have a couple of broken ribs. One of the breaks left a small puncture in your right lung. There was a small pocket of air that leaked into the space between your lung and chest wall, which is what caused your lung to collapse. The needle aspiration seems to have allowed the lung to re-expand, which should improve your breathing, but your blood oxygen is still lower than I'd like to see even with the oxygen therapy, so we're keeping you tonight."

Dr. Rose taps Ben's back to lean him forward. A shooting pain in his ribs causes him to wince and suck his teeth. The doctor presses a cold stethoscope against his back. "Breathe in gently for me."

Ben draws in air and the doctor moves the cold metal across his bare skin. "Fortunately the puncture is very small, so we've been able to avoid surgical intervention. But I'm still hearing some wheezing. We're going to keep you on the oxygen for now."

The thin hospital gown fabric is tucked over to cover his exposed skin. He settles back into the bed as the doctor hooks the stethoscope around his neck.

"How long am I gonna be in here?"

"At least a couple of days. The entire healing process takes time. Even after you leave here, you'll need to follow up with your primary for at least two to three months," he says before leaving and sliding the green curtain shut.

Goddamnit.

He'd been drinking, instigating. It was like he wanted her to blow up, and she delivered fantastically. He stares down at his hands.

An image of Ana flashes in his mind. He'd taken her home after the movies. They saw *Birdman* and she was under a blanket on his futon in his tiny studio apartment. She looked up at him, her eyes as blue as curaçao.

"I'm falling for you," he said, and she rolled her eyes, a small smile on her lips. He was always trying, going along with all the things he thought she wanted from him, trying to be who she wanted him to be. He'd held out hope all these years that one

day she'd finally tell him he was enough. But she never did, and now she never will.

Nausea overtakes him. Ana's dead. He killed her. And yet, underneath the sick, the dread and the horror is a deep sense of relief. *I'm such a piece of shit.* He cheated on her, strangled her to death and he's relieved. Emotion wells up inside, threatening to overflow.

"Can I make a phone call?"

The nurse drags a small end table that holds a corded phone closer. "Just dial nine to get out."

***

It's just after one a.m. when Elyse arrives to the hospital in Ana's white BMW. Ben is out front under a neon-red emergency sign. His body aches, he can hardly breathe, and he's holding on to his forearm to control the bleeding from pulling out his own IV line. With uneven steps, he approaches the car, the pain evident in his limp. As he crawls inside, searing agony pulses in his abdomen and up through his chest. "Fuck," he moans.

Watching Elyse navigate the back streets in the dark, something strikes Ben as odd. It takes him a second to put his finger on it. "Are you wearing Ana's clothes?"

She looks down at herself and back at him. "Yeah, in case someone sees me. That okay?"

"It's weird."

As they drive, he tries to lean the seat back but it won't move. Something is sloshing behind him. He turns with a grunt toward the back seat. There's a blue drum. Gallon bottles of acid. *Oh, Jesus Christ. Ana is inside that drum.*

"What the fuck is that?" he shouts.

Elyse swerves and narrowly misses a parked Mini Cooper. "Don't yell like that when I'm driving. *Geez.* We can't afford to get pulled over right now."

His gaze locks onto the blue drum and the sour taste of bile rises in the back of his throat, the grisly truth turning his stomach inside out. "Elyse, what is that?" It can't be. None of this can be real. She glances over at him and back at the road but doesn't answer. Why else would she be driving around with a giant barrel in the back? He's going to be sick. "Oh fuck," he says and covers his mouth. "Pull over."

Opening the passenger door, he starts to retch, vomiting in the street. Every heave sends stinging jolts through his injured body, forcing a grip on his side. "Fuck." With a weak wave of his hand, he signals for her to drive on, wiping the remnants of sickness from his mouth with a grimy sleeve. Sweat slicks his forehead, breaths come rapid and shallow. The nauseating slosh of liquid in the back shifts with each turn of the wheel.

"Maybe I should drop you off at home first."

"Drop me off? Where are you going?"

"I need to find a place to hide this barrel, then dump Ana's car somewhere."

An ache radiates in his chest. This is the most pain he's ever felt. Not just the physical agony, but the weight of having done the unthinkable. It shatters him. "Oh, God, what did I do?" The strained words muffle into his hands. "I killed her. I fucking killed her."

Elyse drives until she can safely pull off to the side of the road. She wraps her arms around him, his head pressed against her breast. "Shhh," she whispers. "Everything is going to be okay." She kisses the top of his head. "You were defending yourself, Ben. You could have died."

"I picked the fight," he sobs. "I was drinking. I could have left so many times. Why didn't I just leave?"

"Because she wouldn't let you. She's not innocent in this."

He cries against her for a few torturous minutes until the waves of distress subside. Her soothing strokes on his back

anchor him. Pulling away slightly, he casts another glance at the barrel and shudders. "Jesus. She's really in there, huh?"

"Yeah."

"And all the acid?"

She dabs the sweat from his forehead. "I'm doing what needs to be done to protect you. And we don't have much time before people start asking questions, so we need to do this now before the police start watching your every move. Do you understand?"

If he thought life was rough before, life on the inside of a cage is an unfathomable nightmare. How did it come to this? He's lost all control.

"Ben?"

"I don't know what to do," he says, hopeless and overwhelmed. The tears well up and he breaks again, sobbing against her breast.

"I know you're in pain," Elyse says, her voice carrying a maternal quality. "I know this is scary. But this isn't just going to go away. We have to take action. What we do now will determine how this all ends. Okay?"

He closes his eyes and tries to calm himself. His body is vibrating. His world collapsing. With a conscious effort, he draws in a ragged shallow breath and slowly releases it. The instant pain is a reminder he'd nearly lost his life. Were it not for Elyse, he might have. Her being there at his exact moment of need wasn't a coincidence.

His head turns, drawn toward her. Even in the dark, the warmness in her gilded eyes seems to radiate a strange sort of calm, grounding him. An angelic aura forms against her silhouette from the hazy glow of streetlights, and the turmoil inside him steadies. Something serendipitous is at work. Maybe it's a sign everything could still be okay.

"I'm expected in the office today," he says. "I can't show up to work looking like this. I...I have meetings, appointments—"

"I took care of it," she says, apprehension flashing in her eyes. "I used your phone and texted Janine."

His head rolls back and he closes his eyes, pushing out a suppressed scream with a sharp exhale from his nostrils. "Elyse. Why would you do that?"

"Relax," she says. "She thought I was you. I told her you had an accident and you just needed a couple of days to recover. She didn't suspect anything. Did you want me to give the police driving directions to Ana's body? I left your phone at the house."

"What kind of accident?"

She shrugs. "You fell down the stairs."

"Fell down the stairs," he mutters, shaking his head. "Jesus." He runs his hands through his hair, astounded by the utter dumpster fire his life has become.

"I had to make decisions," she says, gesturing toward the barrel in the back. She takes his hands in hers. "If we're going to do this right, you have to trust me."

She's right. Elyse is trying to save his ass, and he knows he can't do this alone. He tries to soften his expression. "I trust you."

Her lips turn up into a small smile and she kisses his cheek. She settles back into the driver's seat, starts the ignition, then slowly pulls away from the curb. A realization flashes across his mind. "Wait. How'd you get into my phone?"

Her grin widens, teasing him with a sparkle in her eye before returning her focus to the road. "'Yankee?'" Her tone makes it clear it hadn't been a difficult guess.

A chuckle escapes him, surprisingly genuine amid the horrific circumstances of the night. In this moment, despite everything, he finds himself grateful she's with him.

"Do you have cash?" he asks.

"The bag," she says, glancing down at the passenger floor.

Hoisting up a canvas bag from his feet, he peeks inside—his watch, wallet and a manilla envelope with several hundred-

dollar bills. "I've got an idea. It's a long way, but I think I know who can help."

Chapter Thirty-Four

He dozes off and wakes to a light so blindingly bright it looks like they're driving into the sun. Glancing at the clock on the dashboard, he checks the time—7:30 a.m.

Sunlight illuminates Elyse's eyes, and Ben's heart floods with affection for her. This is love—driving all night to save him. But he can't be saved. He's the husband. The moment someone notices Ana's missing, all scrutiny will be on him. Life as he knows it has ended.

Outside, they're surrounded by sand dunes. A green highway sign emerges. Henderson, Lake Mead. They're in Nevada. The desert is a stark and unforgiving place, an expanse of rugged terrain with distant mountains rising up on the horizon in shades of beige, tan, and brown. The desolate barrenness mirrors the void within him.

Elyse notices him awake and glances at him quickly before returning her gaze to the road. "Good morning."

"Morning." There's nothing good about it. His wife is decomposing in a barrel in the back seat and he's in agony. He misses that morphine drip. "You have any pain medication?" Leaning forward, he starts to dig through her purse.

"There's a bottle of ibuprofen in there." Her gaze flickers from him to the road. "Don't eat those caramels."

Digging through the bag, he's amazed by how much shit she has in there. She's like a deranged Mary Poppins. Finding a metal tin, he holds it up, shaking it slightly.

"These?" he asks, twisting off the lid.

"I'm serious. They're poisonous."

He quickly shuts the tin and drops it back inside, then wipes his fingers on his pant leg, lest he'd made contact with any deadly residue. "Poisoned caramels? Who are you?"

"They're for self-defense."

"Some women keep pepper spray in their bag," he says sarcastically. "You think a carjacker is going to want a little snack when they're robbing you?"

She laughs. "Hush. I need to focus on the road."

He digs until he finds a bottle of pills. *200mg Ibuprofen.* Rattling the bottle at her, he teases, "You sure this is just a regular painkiller and not cyanide capsules?"

"I'm sure."

Pills cascade into his hand, and he forces two down without water. Dark memories cloud his thoughts—Ana's final gasps, her body limp on his office floor. And now, stuffed into a barrel. It makes him ill. "You didn't...cut her up...did you?"

"No."

Although he sighs with relief, it's only a small consolation. "Thank you." He rubs her thigh. "For everything. If shit goes down, which it probably will, I will take responsibility for all of it. Okay? I don't want you getting into trouble because —"

"Stop it. The police are going to question you. You know all you have to do is shut up."

"What about Flora? She saw everything."

"Flora helped me. She won't say anything. She's part of this now too. If you go down, we all do. So just stop with the crazy talk. We'll get through this together."

He sinks into his seat. Poor Flora. She doesn't deserve this. Somehow, she always ended up in the middle of something between them. Hundreds of stupid fights and now this.

As they get closer to their destination, Ben tries to work out what he's going to say. Entrusting Sierra with this is risky, but it seems like the safest option. Sierra's ranch is over five hundred acres of private property. He has an excavator and other equipment that will make easy work of things. But with each passing mile, his doubt intensifies. He's just making a bigger mess. Bringing more people down with him.

"Sierra is one of my best friends, but I don't know if we're *help me hide a body* close."

The sun accentuates the tension in her jaw and the way her fingers clench the steering wheel. She turns to him, a crease in her brow. "Then let's pull over somewhere. There's miles of desert. I have a shovel."

"I won't be able to help you dig. I have a hole in my lung. If my lung collapses out here, I'm dead."

"I can dig."

"We'll be there all day. We're out in broad daylight. Someone might see us. It's too dangerous."

"But what if he turns you in to the police?"

The car falls silent. He deserves to be turned in. If Sierra is the one to do it, so be it. "Then I'll ask him to leave you out of it. Leave Flora out of it. I'll take responsibility for everything."

Elyse exhales sharply, her lips pursing. Of course she's scared. She's never met Sierra and has no reason to trust him. Drawing a steadying breath, she turns to him. "I'll do whatever you think is best."

"Thank you," he says. "They're all bad options, but I think Sierra is the safest bet right now."

***

Just outside Grand Junction, Colorado, Sierra's property sprawls in the middle of red-rock canyons, snow-topped mountains and a river lined with pines. A tall gate and call box conceal the entrance behind green meadows speckled with wildflowers and low shrubs. Sierra spends most of his time out here alone, and Ben prays they've caught him at home.

Ben gets out of the car, gravel crunching under his feet, and stands in front of the call box. There's a camera pointing at him. Pushing the button, he hears it ring as a cool breeze passes over him and rustles through the fragrant pines.

"Benny Boy, is that you?" Sierra's voice answers, sounding tinny through the metal box. The gate opens before Ben can say a word.

"I'm sorry to show up like this. I'm in some trouble."

"Come on up."

Ben gets back into the passenger seat and guides Elyse through the gate. He's been here before for hunting and fishing. They'd smoke cigars and drink bourbon and pretend to be cowboys.

The main house is behind a curved motor court. It's three stories tall and modeled after a fortified medieval castle, with gray and beige stone. Elyse leans forward and stares up at the house through the windshield, slack-jawed.

"Geez, this place is bananas."

Emerging through a sequence of gothic arches, Sierra greets them with a broad smile and open arms. But as they step out of the car, that warm welcome vanishes at the sight of Ben. Arms dropping, the smile wanes and deep creases mar his brow. "What the fuck happened to you?"

Rubbing his battered neck, Ben grimaces. The state of his suit tells a tale—wrinkled, stained with sweat and streaks of blood. A bruised and scabbed face and a limping gait. "Ana."

Sierra looks at Elyse and back at Ben. "This your girlfriend?"

Ben nods and turns to find Elyse standing bashfully in front of Ana's white BMW, sending an awkward wave Sierra's way.

"Why don't you two get inside and we can talk."

Elyse catches up with them, and Ben keeps his hand at her back. Inside, the foyer floor is made of intricate patterns of marble in various shades forming a sun and moon design. A staircase curves up and an elk-horn chandelier hangs above them.

Sierra leads them to a living room with flannel carpeting and large exposed wood beams across the ceiling. A worn leather sectional sits across from a giant stone fireplace. The walls are lined with windows, filling the room with light and exposing views of the expansive property surrounding them.

Ben sits with a groan and grips his ribs. "I'm sorry to show up like this, man. Is anyone else..."

Sierra sits across from him on an ottoman. "We're alone."

Where to start?

"Sierra, I'm in a world of shit. I'm so sorry to bring this to your doorstep, but I'm desperate. If you tell me to go fuck myself, I'll get out of here and there would be no hard feelings. I mean that."

Sierra leans in and they lock eyes. "Tell me what's going on."

Ben clasps his hands together and takes a deep breath. "Ana and I got into a fight." His voice wavers and his head falls

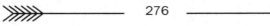

into his hands. *What the fuck am I doing? I cannot unring this bell.* "I shouldn't have come here."

Sliding a cigarette box from his pocket, Sierra offers one to Ben, which he accepts with trembling hands. He lights Ben's and then one for himself.

"You have a hole in your lung," Elyse warns gently.

Oh. "Yeah, you're right." He puts the cigarette out in an ashtray on the coffee table.

Sierra snuffs his cigarette out as well. "You have a hole in your lung? Why aren't you in a hospital?"

"I should be in the hospital. I was, but I left."

Unable to find the words to explain, Ben stands and his fingers work the row of buttons down his sullied oxford shirt. He slides it off, calmly draping it on the arm of the leather couch. Elyse's hand flies to cover her mouth and his posture stiffens. Varied shades of plum and merlot stain Ben's torso like spilled wine. A square of gauze and medical tape sit below his right clavicle from where a needle expelled the air trapped in his collapsed lung. His forearm is marred after pulling out his IV.

Sierra's jerks back slightly. A shadow crosses his face as his gaze roams over Ben's injuries, before settling, heavy and intent, on Ben's face. "Ana did this to you?"

"Yeah," he says, reaching for his shirt.

"Where is she now?"

In a barrel in the back seat of the car parked in front of your house. Those aren't the right words. There are no right words. Nothing he can say can make this any less terrible. "She's dead."

Sierra drops his head into his hands. "Holy fuck." He takes a beat, then looks up with realization, his eyes wide and wild. "She's not in the fucking car is she?"

Ben puts his shirt back on and buttons it up silently.

"Holy shit. Holy shit. Holy *fucking* shit," Sierra says, slowly rising to his feet. He paces the living room.

"I'm sorry, Joe. I didn't know where else to go. You have equipment. I can take it off the property. Find a spot to —"

"What? No. Are you crazy?"

He's not sure anymore. He might be. They drove over eleven hours to get here, and he's still not sure why he thought this was a good idea. "I'm sorry. You never saw me. I'll get out of here. I'll never tell a soul I was here, I swear."

"You drove here from Los Angeles with a body in your car? Are you fucking insane?"

Ben nods. *Yes. He is.* Elyse is fidgeting in her seat. Ben waves her over. "Come on, let's go." She stands and Sierra holds up a hand.

"Hold on. I'm not throwing you out. I'm...trying to think." He continues to pace.

Ben sits and Elyse joins him on the couch. She strokes his hair and he relaxes against her. Who knows how much longer he'll feel her touch.

"Everything is going to be okay," she whispers, and he wants to believe it.

Sierra returns to the ottoman and sits. "The land surrounding this ranch isn't my land. God forbid one of the other owners sells and puts a fucking subdivision out here and they dig up bones."

"They won't dig up bones," Elyse says. They turn to toward her. Her voice is soft and meek. "She won't be.... solid...by the time anyone finds her. If they find her."

Ben gags and winces. Sierra looks at Elyse with alarm.

She goes on. "With the heat out here, it's only a matter of days before the soft tissue dissolves. Although, it is a weak acid. The bones will likely take a lot longer."

Ben is on the verge of retching.

Human soup. Every cell in his body writhes with disgust. How can she be so even-keeled about this? It's frightening how calmly she can talk about the most gruesome subjects.

Sierra sighs. "I want to help you. I trust you. But I got to know that Morticia Addams over here isn't going to change her mind and get all mixed up about this whenever you decide to move on."

Elyse looks at him with a flat, unwavering expression. "I won't say anything."

"See?" Ben reassures him. "Sierra, please."

Sierra lets out a long exhale and takes Ben's cheek in his hand. His calloused thumb brushes his cheekbone. For the first time, Ben is comforted by it.

"Yeah, of course I'll help you."

Chapter Thirty-Five

It's Sierra's idea to load the acid and Ana's drum into the back of his pickup truck and drive it behind the stables. Elyse watches from the back seat as Ben squints against the sun. He turns to check on her and winks like everything is going to be okay. The sky is clear and bright. A giant rock formation towers in the distance, speckled with pines and aspens at its base.

They approach a stained-wood and stone stable surrounded by a low fence, where a white freckled horse swings its tail. Elyse jumps from the jacked truck two feet to the ground and catches a whiff of the air. It's ripe with manure, turned soil, and the sweet, earthy smell of hay.

She goes back and helps Sierra unload. They rest the barrel and plastic jugs in the grass, then he points off in the distance. "Excavator's out there. Wait here. I've got to drive over to it."

Ben's waiting in the passenger seat. He gives Elyse another reassuring wink and they drive away.

Sierra wasn't who she expected him to be. He's not at all like he is in his movies. He always plays the good guy. Jumping out of airplanes onto moving trains, running into a burning building to save the world or a beautiful woman from the bad guys. She never thought one day he'd be helping her hide a body. The whole thing makes her question her sanity. Still, it's such a bright and sunny day, she's grateful to be alive to enjoy it.

Her elbow rests on the barrel's lid. She pats it with her hand. "This is a lovely burial site, Ana. If it were up to me, you'd be somewhere in the Nevada desert." That's not right. If it were up to her, Ana would be sipping on a manchineel smoothie. "You're lucky Ben strangled you to death, because my way would have been a lot more painful."

And it wouldn't have required crossing state lines to dispose of a body. These are the consequences of split-second, rage-induced decisions. It's dirty work, and she takes this opportunity of solitude to save Ben and Sierra from the unpleasant job of filling the drum with acid.

Elyse holds her breath, unclips the barrel, then pries up the lid to reveal Ana's corpse. Even under the golden sunlight, her skin takes on a ghostly pallor, her mouth blotted with ink, slender neck broken and bruised. Elyse watches intently as acid pours down in glugs, wetting Ana's hair and eyelashes, her skin still wrapped in silver tape like a burial shroud. She bathes her in chemicals until the last gallon jug empties into the drum, completing the unholy sacrament.

When she's done, she clips the barrel sealed and sits on the ground beside it. There's an odd serenity amidst the

macabre scene. As she rests, she realizes something. The nagging, critical voice that had once constantly berated her, George's voice, has fallen silent. She takes a moment to reflect on it.

It's not the chaos or thrill of victory over her enemies. No, it's this—stepping up for Ben, shouldering burdens, taking charge of a situation she'd never imagined herself in. For once, she felt capable, no longer the victim of her past or George's manipulation. There was something empowering in the horrifying acts she was committing. In rising to protect Ben, she realized she isn't the fragile creature she once thought she was. There's a fortitude inside her, nurtured not by revenge but from love.

Lying there at peace, the earth is so welcoming and soft she nearly dozes off until the sounds of a giant yellow excavator approaching steals her attention. She stands to greet them. The tank-like track wheels grind and squeal across the gritty terrain.

Joe is in the glass cab of the excavator, and Ben drives the pickup behind him. Elyse rushes to help him out. It's a steep drop and he's weak.

"Are you alright?"

"I need a shower and sleep."

The arm of the excavator starts to move and Sierra shouts from the cab. "Stand back."

They back up against the stable and watch the arm and bucket move and crash into the ground, uprooting patches of grass and scattering gravel. The earth is picked up and carried aside, where it's dropped, and the process repeats until he's dug a hole nearly ten feet deep.

After, Sierra disappears into the stable and returns with a long rope. "Now we just gotta figure out how to tie up this barrel so we can lower it down without blowin' it up."

Ben grips his stomach. Poor thing. He looks green. She reaches for the rope. "Let me."

Joe looks at her for a moment with skepticism. "Alright, girl. Let's see what you can do."

Taking the rope, she lays it on the ground the way she'd once learned during summer survival camp. Guillermo thought it would help her self-esteem. If only he could see her now.

Shifting the barrel on top of the rope, she brings up either end and crosses it over the top. "It's called a barrel hitch." She spreads the crossed ropes out so it's hugging the rim of the barrel, then ties the ends together and lifts.

"Well, I'll be damned," Sierra says.

Without saying anything, Ben turns and stumbles away, and she hurries after him. "Hey." He's moving slow and it's not difficult to catch up. "Talk to me."

When he looks at her, he has tears in his eyes and his breath is ragged. He's clearly in pain, and she wants to fix it. But how?

"It doesn't make sense. I should hate her. I should be glad she's dead. But I'm not, Elyse. I loved her." He backs away, bows over and staggers to the ground, sobbing between his knees. "She needed help. I should have tried harder. She begged me. She begged me to help her, and I pushed her away."

It hurts to hear him talk about Ana this way, but she doesn't try to talk him out of it, or give him reasons why he should hate her. Instead, she strokes his back. He's drenched in sweat and his shirt clings to him. "I'm sorry. What can I do?"

"I want to die. I want to die too."

"You don't mean that."

"I do. I was supposed to be her protector, and all I did was hurt her. I killed her. I deserve to die."

"No, you don't. You are so loved. Me, Flora, Sierra. We all love you. We need you." She hears a rustling in the grass and notices Sierra has joined them.

He sits next to Ben and throws a comforting arm around him. Ben shakes his head. "My life is over. Everyone is going to

know I did this. It's always the husband. With all the money involved, there won't be any doubt."

Sierra nudges Ben with his shoulder. "Sure, you're gonna have a hard time, and you'll be under a microscope for a while. But this girl and me, we're doing everything we can to keep you out of trouble."

Ben turns his face toward the sky and takes a deep breath. "It's not too late. You can turn me in. You should turn me in. I don't want to bring you down with me." His voice is panicked. He's spiraling.

Elyse kneels and lifts his chin to face her. "You think turning yourself over to the police is going to magically absolve your guilt? You think giving those bastards power over you is going to atone for this? Fine, you did this. But surrendering to the system isn't going to bring Ana back. All it'll do is take you away from people who love you and are fighting to keep you safe. Right now you're free, and I intend to keep it that way."

She wraps her arms around him, and he collapses to her breast, weeping until the tears run out. Once he settles down, he slowly sits up and wipes his nose. Sierra stands and extends a hand to help him to his feet. They walk back to the gravesite, where they each grab on to the rope and slowly lower the drum into the ground, then let the rope fall into the pit.

Ben grabs a clod of dirt and scatters it. They each take one of Ben's hands until he nods to let them know it's okay to move on. The excavator engine fires on with a jarring growl and pushes the mounds of soil back into the hole. Each pass conceals the barrel more and more, until the dirt is nearly level with the ground. Sierra drags a bag of gravel from the stable and empties it over the spot. Then, it's like nothing ever happened.

Ben walks back to the main house in a daze with Elyse holding his hand. It's almost three p.m. and neither of them has eaten, slept or showered through the whole ordeal. There is still the small matter of Ana's car to be dealt with.

Elyse addresses Sierra. "What about her car?"

"Why don't you two get cleaned up. I'll get some supper ready and we can eat, get some rest and then we'll get it figured out in the morning."

They gratefully accept, and Joe shows them to their room. A king-sized bed with eight fluffy pillows is in the center of the room. The headboard is upholstered with velvet. A full desk and sitting area with matching red sofa and chairs sit opposite the bed. The room has a private bathroom with a soaking tub. A flatscreen mounted across from it makes it opulent.

"Here," Sierra offers Ben a stack of clothes—a pair of folded sweats and a T-shirt. "The ex's brother used to freeload out here. These might be a little big." Ben holds up the shirt which looks like it's the size of a beach towel. With a shrug, Sierra departs, leaving them alone.

Ben's barely standing as he unbuttons his shirt. She runs them a hot shower. Inside, Ben sulks under the shower head. Bits of dirt and grass rinse off their bodies and onto the shower floor. Reaching for a bottle of shampoo, he groans in pain.

"Let me," she says, pulling him toward a stone shower bench. He sits and she stands before him. Pumping the fragrant shampoo into her palm, she massages her fingertips into his scalp.

The corners of his mouth turn up, and he closes his eyes. He rests the weight of his head in her hands, and she scrubs in gentle circles along his nape, behind his ears, along his temples. It rinses out in streams of sudsy water. She combs her fingers through his hair and his head rolls back to rest against the cool slate tile.

"Where were you all last week?" he asks softly. His eyes reflect a mix of love tinged with hurt.

His question is unexpected, and she holds her breath as her mind races for the right answer. If he knew the whole truth, he'd be upset. She doesn't want to lie, but she has to. He's too fragile right now. But before she can come up with a plausible excuse, his loving gaze transforms into a penetrating stare.

"The truth," he says, his voice dark.

His tone makes her briefly lose her breath and her heart races. She holds still, hoping to keep the anxiety off her face. He knows something. Ana's emergency room visit? Elyse's impromptu coffee with Flora? Charles King? No. That's impossible.

"I went home."

"To Miami?"

"Mm-hmm." She nods.

"Without your phone?" he asks skeptically.

"I left it behind. I'm sorry. When I got back—all your messages. I felt awful. Honestly, I didn't think anyone would even notice I was gone."

As her words sink in, his shoulders slump slightly. He shakes his head and sighs. "I know when things got busy I kind of disappeared. I was just spread so thin between work and..."

His mind must go to Ana because he trails off and winces as if in pain.

"It's okay," she says.

Leaning forward, he rests his stubbled cheek against her hip. The hiss of the shower reverberates around them, a rhythm of droplets cascading against stone and skin. The steam carries the spicy, woody aroma of scented soap. He looks up at her with need, like a lost little boy who doesn't want to be alone, his eyes gleaming with unshed tears.

"Stay with me."

"Hmm?"

"When we get back. I want you to stay with me."

He must not be thinking straight, because he is a smart man and what he's suggesting is a terrible idea. At best it's suspicious, at worst its more motive to disappear his wife. And yet, she doesn't want to say no. "The police will be watching."

"I know. But if they're going to come for me anyway, I want to spend as much time with you as possible while I still can."

She bends so they're at eye level, her voice a low hush. "Flora's at home cleaning her little heart out. I'm going to make sure there isn't a molecule of physical evidence in that house. Your cell phone is at home. Have you researched how to murder your wife recently?"

"No."

"Okay then. No body. No physical evidence. The police will be watching, so you can't do anything suspicious. No big purchases. No attempts to collect on life insurance policies. No girlfriend moving into your house. Got it?"

Ben takes in a deep breath. "Yeah." He takes a beat. "But, El. Look at me. I'm a fucking mess. I can barely stand up straight. They're going to know something's wrong."

"You'll tell them the truth. Ana did this. You knew if you reported it, she'd be in serious trouble, and you wanted to protect her. She left you at the hospital. When you were ready to go, you called home, and she picked you up. Her car was in full view of the security camera outside the hospital. I wore her clothes. We're the same size. Did you ever tell anyone about us?"

"Just Flora and Sierra."

She smiles at him. "See? Everything is going to be okay."

"What about Janine?"

"Ana must have texted her. She knew you'd need time to recover and didn't want to risk people asking questions at work. She used your phone. Then once you were back home, recovering, she went on her yoga retreat as planned. She just never came back."

He nods slowly, and she can see the gears turning in his mind. "Okay."

They dry off and dress for dinner.

Sierra is on the terrace, where he's started a fire in a raised stone fire pit with red rocks surrounded by plush patio furniture. "Homemade brick oven pizza," he announces with a bit of flair and sets down an irregular shaped pizza in front of them.

"Mmm, looks good," she says.

"I'm not hungry," Ben says, ignoring it.

"You gotta eat, my friend. You can't heal without fuel, isn't that right, princess?"

She takes a bite. It's not bad. "That's right, buckaroo." She tried it on to see how he likes it, and it makes him chuckle.

"Joe graduated from Beverly Hills High School," Ben says flatly, then grins to himself. He's coming around.

Sierra raises a glass of brown liquor. "I'm a man of the ranch now."

Ben shakes his head and takes a bite. He chews slowly, staring off into the fire, his mind elsewhere.

Elyse looks at Sierra. "What are you going to tell the police if they show up here?"

He holds up an invisible shotgun and cocks it, making the clicking sounds with his mouth. But when he sees Elyse's serious expression, the humor disappears from his face and he quickly straightens himself up.

"If they want to search the place, they better have a warrant."

"Yeah, but if they know enough to show up here, we're already screwed. Don't go running to the phone to call Ben, or text him about what's going on. It'll seem suspicious. We need some kind of a code you could post somewhere. Like on Twitter or something." She mulls it over.

"It's a beautiful day at the ranch," he says.

"That's perfect. If we see that tweet, we'll know we're in trouble and we go to Plan B."

"What's Plan B?" Ben asks.

"We run," she says, raising a beer to her lips.

"Don't worry. I'm not selling you out, Benny Boy. If they show up here, I don't know nothing 'bout nothing."

It's a sweet promise, but Elyse knows better. Once Sierra watches Ana's barrel being lifted out of the ground, his life will flash before his eyes and all bets are off.

It's not long before every trace of amusement leaves Ben's eyes and he's drifted back to a preoccupied stare. The glow of flames flicker across his face and dance in his eyes. "What if I can never move on from this?"

Elyse grips his thigh and squeezes it. "It'll scare you how well you will move on from this." When they look at each other, it's clear he understands she knows what she's talking about because she's been here. More times than anyone will ever know.

After dinner, they say goodnight to Sierra and head upstairs to bed. She props Ben up on pillows and puts an ear to his chest. It sounds better than earlier. A little rest will do him good. She nuzzles up to him and presses her nose to his neck.

"Do you think we're going to hell when we die?" he whispers against her hair.

"I don't think there's any cosmic math happening. And I don't believe in hell."

"What do you believe?"

She props herself up on her side and they look at each other through the dark. "You know how when a bomb explodes the chemical energy converts to other forms of energy—light, movement, sound, heat."

"Yeah."

"Energy can't be created and it can't die. Every cell in every thing has little tiny bits of energy stored in it. Well, I think when a soul leaves a body it's like a bomb going off, and the energy converts to other forms of energy. It disperses somehow. Becomes something else."

She caresses his cheek with her fingers. "Sitting outside today, it was so beautiful. It was strange because everything else about today was awful, but there was a nice breeze. The sun was shining. On another day, there could have been a flood or a wildfire. It doesn't make one good or the other evil. It just is. It's nature. It doesn't know right and wrong. It doesn't care. It just goes on. That's what I believe."

Murder isn't *good*. She doesn't *want* to kill. But when faced with the option of shrinking, fading away, being devoured by predators, she'll choose to survive at any cost. That was the choice Ben had made for himself. He just couldn't see it yet.

Chapter Thirty-Six

In the morning, they strip Ana's BMW of anything important, pry off the VIN and remove the license plate, open all of the windows and doors, and push it into a deep part of a river on Sierra's property. They stand on the riverbank and watch it bob in the water for several minutes until the water gradually overtakes it and it disappears, sinking below the surface.

Ben and Elyse get into Sierra's Bentley Continental. It's the color of an eggplant and the diamond-stitched seats are covered in buttery soft, ivory Napa leather. Sierra buckles his seat belt. "I've been wanting to take this baby on a road trip."

This is hardly a road trip. It's a shameful journey toward a dark uncertainty that makes Ben want to throw up. But this car is much too nice to violate that way. He tries not to dwell in his dark thoughts. How his wife is now ten feet underground in a vat of acid covered with dirt and gravel. He'd woken up with that gruesome image in his mind and an ache in his gut. Not just from his injuries, but from the weight of his sin. His soul is stained.

Although if what Elyse says is true, he'll move on from this. The mind has a way of forgetting pain. It can't happen soon enough. He's barely passed the threshold into the hell he will be wading through. All of their talks about staying quiet are well intentioned, but he doesn't know how they'll fare under pressure. All he can do now is pray, and he's not sure anyone is listening anymore.

Elyse leans over the chrome and black-gloss center console from the front passenger seat. "Do you have a less flashy car we could take? We're trying to keep a low profile."

"This is his least flashy car."

Sierra rolls his eyes. "Oh relax. I brought my disguise. See?" He slides on a black baseball cap and gold aviators.

Elyse takes a deep breath and looks away with a long sigh. She's been surprisingly put together through all of this. An acting class will send her into a panic, but a real-life catastrophe is where she shines.

They drive all day and into the early evening. Somewhere in Utah, Elyse starts to quiz him. "What happened to Ana?"

"She went to her yoga retreat. We expected her back Thursday night. She didn't come home so I started to worry. When I called her, it went to voicemail. I called Becca, her girlfriend who was at the retreat, and she told me Ana never showed up. That's when I called the police."

It rolls off the tongue with a confidence that sends a chill through him. This is what he does, after all. He lies for a living. *Sure, she's an excellent actress. Have you heard her sing? She*

has the voice of an angel. Can she dance? Are you kidding? It's like I'm lookin' at Ginger Rogers. She's a triple threat.

It's one thing to blow smoke up a casting director's ass. But it's another to look a detective in the eye and lie about murder, all while he can still hear the sounds of Ana's last breaths, see the terrified expression in her impossibly blue eyes. The same shade of blue as the barrel they buried her in.

Ben's shirt is soaked with sweat by the time they pass Las Vegas. No one gets away with murder. At least no one like him. "Hey, crank the AC. I'm dying back here."

Elyse leans forward and her hand hovers over the dials. "This thing is like a frickin' spaceship." A *whoosh* of air blasts through the vent, and it smells like filtered gusts of purified air off the alps.

"It's a $300,000 car," Ben says.

Sierra smiles at Elyse like he's just heard some great news, fanning himself like a southern belle. "You embarrass me, Benny Boy."

Elyse looks at him like she could not be less impressed. "Why would you spend that much money on a car?"

Sierra snorts. "Why not, princess?"

As unbelievable as Elyse has been through all this, Ben can't stop thinking about how she could put a person in a barrel. How she knew just what to do. His mind wanders to George Ramos. To Ana's lips about to burst. It makes the hairs on the back of his neck stand up. But he loves her. More than he's ever loved anything or anyone. Maybe they're both monsters now.

"What happened to Ana, Sierra?" She turns to him, and Ben can't help but notice the shade of her eyes is as gold as the Nevada sunset.

"Ana?"

"Ana King."

"Oh, that Ana. Is she alright? I haven't heard anything."

It was convincing. *Jesus.* The company Ben keeps. Liars and killers. Now he's both.

Sierra leans toward Elyse. "What happened to Ana?"

She takes a deep breath. "I have no idea."

"Isn't she your boyfriend's wife?" Sierra says, peering at her over his sunglasses.

Ben's posture stiffens, betraying his unease. He exhales slowly, wrestling with the undeniable truth. The trail of evidence. He's been calling her like a madman all week. They traveled together. She's gorgeous. Security camera footage would show them kissing all over the hotel, the airport. *Shit.* Janine was probably onto him by now too.

"I don't know anything about her."

Sierra pats her arm. "Good."

"No, not good. El, just don't say anything. Not a word. They can talk to your lawyer. Period."

Sierra's brows raise at Ben in the rearview mirror. "Don't you think that's a little suspicious so early in the game?"

"If they know about us to the point they are talking to her about Ana, she's already a suspect. She could incriminate herself. No. Not a word."

It's nearly midnight when Sierra pulls up to Elyse's house in Highland Park. He walks them to her door. "I'm sticking around for a few days at my place in Malibu. Call me if you need a friend, alright?"

Ben pats his arm. "You have no idea how much I appreciate you, brother."

He puts a hand on his cheek. "I've got your back."

It's so sincere Ben could cry. He's not sure what he's ever done to deserve these people, or why they'd be so willing to help him, but he's grateful.

Sierra hugs Elyse with a sincere warmth Ben loves to see. As scary as she can be, as rough around the edges and a little crazy, she is good inside.

When they walk in, he's smacked with the potent odor of alcohol.

"Don't touch anything," she warns.

What the hell has she been doing in here? He's sure if he lit a match the whole house would explode into flames. They walk into her kitchen, where she has flasks and buckets of stems and exotic looking fruits, now a pile of soggy waste attracting fruit flies.

"What is all this?"

Tugging on a pair of purple latex gloves, a hint of pink appears on her cheeks. "Uh...you know. Science." She lifts tinfoil off a flask with a substance that has separated into thick clumps and cloudy water. Their eyes meet for a second before she pours out the liquid into her kitchen sink then pushes the faucet open with a bump of her wrist.

Even though he doesn't want to know, he can't shake his curiosity. "What fruit is that?"

"Manchineel."

"It's poisonous?"

"Very."

"You can't go around poisoning people, sweetheart." He grabs a pair of gloves from the box. They're tight on his hands.

As she sets a clean beaker in a drying rack, she holds back a smile, her pretty gold eyes glittering with humor. "I know."

He wants to tell her that he knows about her little date with the valet, but it seems pointless. If the police find out about Ana's reaction, they'll look into the club, interview employees. There's got to be security camera footage of his deranged goddess snooping around. Her social media accounts are rife with this sketchy *Poisoner's Handbook* shit.

"I mean it, baby." He presses his forehead to hers. "You promise?"

"Promise."

"Good. Do you have any other poisons in the house? A hemlock blackberry pie? Strychnine Sauvignon Blanc?"

They exchange smiles, and she laughs before pointing toward the fridge. "In there. Can you toss the casserole dish with caramel in it?"

Opening the fridge, there's so many condiments. A carton of eggs and half a casserole dish of poisoned candy. He hesitates over the trash bag. "You want me to throw out the whole dish?"

"The whole dish."

He sets it into a bag, then walks over to her. She's scrubbing a beaker. "You wash, I'll dry?"

She hands him a dry rag. "Sure."

Chapter Thirty-Seven

One Year Later

Ben knocks on the door of Janine's office. It looks like a glass box with one sturdy black wall that holds a large modern print of colorful, squiggly lines someone called art and charged him an arm and a leg for. "You got a minute?"

Her mane of curly red hair pokes over the top of her monitor. She types furiously with an intense focus on the screen before looking up and stopping. "Yeah, what's up?"

Pulling up an upholstered red office chair, he sits across from her with his laptop. "I need your help with this because my calendar is fucked."

She grins at him and asks for the laptop with a flex of her hand. "He should have blocked the time off as busy, because now it looks like it's free. That's why people keep scheduling stuff on top of other stuff," she says, frowning at the screen. She clenches her jaw and grumbles a little, then yells, "Nathan!"

It brings a smile to Ben's face.

Within days of reporting Ana's disappearance, the keyboard cowboys of social media concluded that a man who loses a father-in-law and a wife in the span of a month and stands to inherit $250 million as a result is obviously a killer. They weren't wrong, but so far they couldn't prove it.

Despite his injuries and extensive evidence of the abuse Ben suffered at Ana's hand—witness statements, medical records, a police report—detectives were skeptical about how Ben explained his injuries. "She's five-eight, one-hundred twenty pounds, and you're claiming she did this to you?" one said, sliding a photo of Ben's bruised torso across the interview room table.

Ben expected nothing more. "What, you think I broke my own fucking ribs?"

They offered an alternative theory. He'd caught Ana having an affair and confronted the mystery man, then killed Ana. Ben didn't have to say a word, but he grinned to himself. No body, no battered mystery man, no signs of a struggle. Surely Ben would have gotten in a few punches of his own. "You're suggesting I single-handedly covered up assault and murder, despite three broken ribs and a collapsed lung, in a manner so thorough there was no evidence it even happened?" he asked, incredulously.

"You could have had help."

"From who? My sixty-four-year-old housekeeper?"

They had bupkis.

AFPK thought the publicity was attracting negative attention. They were careful to let Ben resign in lieu of being

terminated. They knew they didn't have cause, and in some people's minds were firing a guy who'd just tragically lost his wife. They paid him double for his partnership shares and agreed not to enforce their non-compete.

By that point, Ben was glad to distance himself from the King name. Ana's mother, Colette, led the charge against him as a talking head on every 24-hour news channel that would have her. Ben never liked that woman.

In an act of revenge, he had Chuck's secret box of naked actresses sent anonymously to a reporter at the *Los Angeles Times*. The news prompted dozens of victims to come forward. Chuck's bad behavior was the headline for a hot fifteen minutes, calling into question whether one of Chuck's victims was involved in Ana's disappearance.

Despite all the bad press, Janine never questioned Ben, never looked at him with suspicion. The day he left King, he filled a white banker box with things from his office and carried it out to find her packing up her desk right along with him. He almost teared up. It was an *oh captain, my captain* moment he appreciated so much he didn't argue when she insisted on starting as a business manager with a small partnership stake.

Ben and Janine shared an assistant, Nathan, who was fresh out of college. He was lanky and seemed to always need a haircut. His dark hair fanned just enough over the top of his ears to annoy Ben.

Now, Nathan lurches into Janine's office sheepishly with a notebook pressed against his chest.

"Do you know how to schedule a meeting?"

"Uh…"

Janine does nothing to soften her expression as she sighs with irritation. "Come over here and let me show you."

Ben bites his lip to hide a smile and sneaks out of her office. He walks through their reception area, where the letters D.E.M. are etched in glass and painted in red trim.

The shocks in his desk chair jerk and his abdominals seize up when he sits. "Ah, shit." He still has tenderness in his ribcage—Ana's final departing gift to him. He thinks he might be cursed to feel this pain forever.

Behind him are distant ridges of the Santa Monica mountains and a rocky terrain of low shrubs and palm trees. Natural light pours in from the many windows along the office walls.

Nathan walks into his office. "Mr. Deluca, I have Mr. Joe Sierra."

"Put him through."

Nathan looks frightened. "Um...he's like *here*."

The D.E.M. office isn't the most impressive place right now. They just moved in last month and most of the rooms are empty and unfurnished. It's not exactly a place that inspires confidence. He swipes up papers scattered on his desk and sweeps them into a neat pile, then takes a deep breath and strides out to the lobby.

"Sierra," he says through a confident smile. He's sweating under his bespoke Brioni suit.

Sierra smiles back and puts a hand on Ben's cheek. He hides his eyes behind tinted frames and a wide brim hat. "My boy," he says. "Nice place you got here."

"We're still moving in, but it's a great space. Lots of light." His mouth is dry and he swallows hard. "I wish you would have let me know you were coming. We could have rolled out the red carpet for you."

Sierra snorts. "Come on, don't worry about it. I figured I'm in town anyway, I might as well check out the new place. You got a minute?"

Ben gets an uneasy sensation in his gut. "For you? I'll clear my schedule."

They go into Ben's office, and he closes the door. He sits at the edge of his desk and Sierra sits on a white leather loveseat

against a floor-to-ceiling window, palm trees and neighboring rooftops behind him.

"What's on your mind?"

"Hey, I want to start with you. How you holding up?"

"I'm alright. One day at a time, right?"

"That's right. And you've got plenty keeping you busy. How's the little lady?"

A smile spreads across Ben's face. "She's incredible. I've never been happier." *Cut the bullshit and tell me what's going on.*

"I'm hanging it up," Sierra says like it pains him. "I'm gettin' old. I'm ready to retire."

Ben exhales his held breath and relaxes. The tension in his chest fades. He was worried Sierra came to tell him someone found the car or the barrel. Although, Sierra is D.E.M.'s biggest client. This news isn't good for business. He looks at Sierra like he's been stabbed in the heart.

"Joe," he says, his voice full of disappointment, betrayal.

A sarcastic chuckle escapes Sierra. "Come on, kid. Not to be insensitive to your situation, but you're not exactly hurting for cash these days. What do you need to whip the old workhorse for?"

In his experience, when the client needs him, he's a pal. When they resent him, he's a pimp. He feigns being offended. "Whoa, where is this coming from? I plan on working until the day I die, and that's exactly my point. Sure, you're plenty rich, but what about doing what you love every day?" Ben leans in like he's telling Sierra the meaning of life. "When you stop, you die, man. What are you going to do, feed your cows? You'll be bored in two weeks."

Sierra slumps in his seat like he's exhausted. "I've done what I wanted to do. I want to do something else."

"Okay. What'd you have in mind?"

Sierra shrugs, and Ben suspects he's actually here to figure that out. He opens his bottom desk drawer and retrieves a bottle of bourbon and two glasses. He sets the glasses on a coffee table in front of Sierra and pours them each two fingers.

"Alright, let's figure this out. Directing? Producing?"

"I'm sick of this town. The schedules. The bickering over script changes and call sheets. The egos. I'm over it."

Ben holds up his hands in surrender. "Got it, you're done with it. What about a business? You've got a brand. A whole vibe. You could buy a bourbon company. Who wouldn't want to buy bourbon from man's man like you?"

Sierra perks up and his eyes widen with surprise. "That's actually not a bad idea."

Shit. He was just spitballing. "But in the meantime, you have a lot of overhead, brother, that's just the reality. We can get you something animated, voice work. You can do it from Colorado. Feed your cows."

"Those'll be your cows one day."

"What are you talking about?"

"I'm leaving you the ranch."

It strikes Ben as an oddly timed declaration. He studies Sierra's face. There's something uneasy about him. It's weird how he just popped up unannounced like this. His gut tenses.

"Leaving me the ranch? What's gotten into you?"

"I can't leave it to just anyone. Ana's body's on the ranch."

Ben's pulse quickens. He lowers his voice. "What did you just say?"

"I said I can't leave it to just anybody. It's a ranch. I gotta leave it to someone who can afford to keep it up."

Did he say Ana's body? Ben can't be sure what he heard. In fact, he's been hearing a lot of strange things lately. The other night in bed, he swore he'd heard Ana's voice.

Pool acid, Ben, she'd said. *It doesn't dissolve bones you know*. It woke him out of a deep sleep. He sat straight up with a

cold chill running through him, then turned and shook Elyse. "Was that you?"

She rubbed her eyes, disoriented. "What?"

"The acid?"

"What are you talking about?" she grumbled.

She'd been asleep. It wasn't her voice. It was Ana, he knew it was. The sound turned his stomach. He had to get up and rinse his face with cold water, and it was nearly an hour before his heart calmed down enough to get back to sleep.

Sierra gives him an odd look. "You alright?"

Ben brushes it off. Maybe it's nothing. "You can't leave me the ranch. How's that gonna look?"

"Oh, relax. I had another lawyer write it all up. I ain't goin' anywhere anytime soon, at least I don't plan on it."

"Good. You start talking about giving things away, hanging it up. You got me worried. You coming out tonight?"

"Wouldn't miss it for the world."

After Ben leaves the office, it takes thirty minutes to drive five miles. He waves to the detectives parked on the street in front of his house on the way up the long driveway, then parks in the garage.

Flora is cooking in the kitchen. He takes a whiff of the air. The aromatics of onion and garlic fill his nose. "*Ah, la comida huele bien.*" The food smells good. He peers over her shoulder, and she passes back a spoon for him to taste. "*Mmm, muy rico.*" Very good. He kisses her cheek. "*¿Dónde están mis amores?*" Where are my loves?

"*En el jardín, como siempre.*" In the garden, like always.

He sighs. She really shouldn't be out there. He thinks he saw a drone fly over once, probably taking photos for whatever case they're hoping to build against him—or Elyse or Flora. He doesn't know yet. None of them have been charged with anything.

He walks out onto the terrace and through the path of stones to a clearing. Birds chirp in their quiet stretch of paradise. It's so peaceful. It's a shame they'll leave it behind, but it's like living in a haunted house. Everything reminds him of times he wants to forget.

When he finds Elyse, she's humming a tune and lost in thought, surrounded by lush greenery and vibrant blooms. She's bent, digging and plucking out weeds from the soil with baby Isla strapped to her breast in a sling and doesn't notice him sneak behind her.

"*¿Cómo están mis chicas favoritas?*" *How are my favorite girls?*

Elyse gasps and stabs her hand shovel into the earth, then looks up at him with one eye closed. "*Isla, Papi está en casa,*" she says in a high-pitched, singsongy tone. *Isla, Daddy's home.* Her hands and knees are covered in dirt. "Can you take her? My hands are dirty."

She lifts herself off the ground and dusts the dirt off her knees. He leans to kiss Elyse and sweeps Isla from her sling. She has her mother's eyes, and Ben is convinced she's the prettiest baby ever born. His lips are like a magnet to her fat little cheek as he cradles her in his arms.

"Dinner's almost ready. You getting cleaned up before people get here?"

Her hands brush against the fabric of her overalls. She wipes sweat off her forehead, streaking it with dirt. "You sure I can't just hang out like this?"

"In those sexy overalls? I don't know. I'd be worried Joe will try to make you wife number four."

She smiles at him. "I'm getting in the shower."

Ben follows behind her through the patio doors and into the house with Isla propped against him. Flora is wiping down the counter, and when she notices them, she smiles big. Isla is the love of her life. "Can you take her? I'm gonna help El upstairs."

"Of course, give me my chunky little princess."

It was only a few weeks after they buried Ana on the ranch that Elyse appeared in his office unannounced with an ultrasound photo. She sobbed against him, beside herself at the idea the baby was incontrovertible evidence of their affair, convinced having it would be the most irresponsible thing they could do in the middle of a highly publicized missing person investigation.

He'd sat at the edge of his desk and held her in his arms. "What if this is the only chance we get to be a family?"

"Everyone will think we killed Ana because of the baby."

"Who cares what people think? They can't prove anything."

The police had scoured the house on Tower Grove Drive and walked away with laptops, cell phones, journals and everything else they thought might be useful to find Ana. Eventually, they returned it all because they found nothing. Elyse and Flora had been thorough. Even the security camera server ended up drilled through and incinerated.

It didn't take long for them to talk to Elyse. All his calls to her the week before Ana's disappearance raised a red flag. Ben was adamant he would never deny he was the baby's father, so they admitted to the relationship. They asked Elyse about Ana and whether she knew anything about her disappearance. Her attorney had reenacted it for Ben, making his eyes big and fluttering his lashes. "I wish I could help you, gentlemen, but I know nothing about it."

Once the world knew Ben was a cheater and Elyse was his mistress, there wasn't any reason not to move in together. Just as their worlds should have been falling apart, they were the happiest they'd ever been. They were living together, he was waiting on her hand and foot throughout her entire pregnancy, and he loved it.

Elyse's dirt-covered overalls are on the bathroom floor. The glass stall is filled with steam. She's naked and wet. He quickly undresses to join her. "Jesus, look at you."

She looks at him with surprise. "Where's Isla?"

"Flora's watching her." Pulling her toward him, his hand finds the back of her neck and he lowers his mouth to hers. His hands grip her thighs, and her arms wrap around his shoulders. He lifts her, pressing her against the cold tile wall.

Her legs wrap around him and she hums against his mouth. "How was your day?"

"Better now. I missed you." He kisses her neck, her breasts.

"Don't. Isla wanted to nurse every two minutes today."

"Sorry," he says. He doesn't want to kill the mood, so he hooks his forearms under each of her knees to hold her in place but a pain cuts through him. He groans.

"Baby, put me down. You're gonna hurt yourself."

Goddamnit, Ana. The sexiest thing about the size difference between him and Elyse was his ability to toss her around like his plaything. But even with most of her weight against the wall, a dull ache resonates around his torso. He sets her on her feet, and she pushes him onto the shower bench, straddling him. Their mouths press together in open gasps as she settles onto him. She buries her head in his neck and kisses the tenderest spots beneath his ear.

"You smell so good," she whispers and every cell in his body jumps to attention.

Chapter Thirty-Eight

Stella arrives, the epitome of glamour with her Hermes bag tucked in the crook of her arm. She whips off her sunglasses and takes Elyse in. "You didn't just have a baby!"

"You bet I did," Elyse says, kissing Stella's cheek. "She's inside. I can't wait for you to meet her."

Ben is at the door eyeballing the gate Elyse made him install. Detectives are outside with a long-lens camera pointed up toward the house. He hooks an arm around Stella to greet her. "Our tax dollars are paying for this harassment. It's unbelievable," he says and kisses her cheek. "You look beautiful, sweetheart. Welcome home."

"I never thought I'd miss LA, but by the last month, I was so ready to come back."

"Well, Elyse hasn't been able to stop talking about you all week. She's been so excited. Haven't you, baby?"

Elyse nods. "We have so much to catch up on." She can barely contain herself.

They dine outdoors under string lights festooned between two pergolas that drip with gold and magenta bougainvillea. A long glass table with matching iron chairs that weigh about a hundred pounds apiece sits underneath. Elyse drags her chair closer to Stella across the travertine patio with a grunt.

The blue light of the pool casts an upward glow. Its dusk, and the twinkling lights of Los Angeles freckle the golden horizon far off into the distance, broken up by the silhouette of palm trees. Mambo plays over the outdoor sound system. The sounds of Spanish guitar and the pop of timbale repeat in a rumba clave. Horns cry out in mournful tones, and Flora sways to the rhythm as she sets out stacks of plates and cutlery.

Emerging through patio doors, Ben carries Isla in his arms. Stella gasps as Ben sits beside her. Isla looks at her with wide gold eyes and her head wobbles. He holds her steady in his big hands. Watching him with Isla fills Elyse with more love than she ever thought was possible. She swoons at how he makes his voice soft and light for her, cooing words of endearment in Spanish. *"Mira a esa gordita linda. Mi cariño. Te quiero mucho. Muah." Look at that pretty little chubby girl, my sweetheart. I love you so much.*

The doorbell rings, and Flora stops her dancing to answer it.

Stella makes faces at Isla, who looks on in confused wonder, her pacifier pulsing against her mouth. "Who is this crazy lady?" Stella sings.

Janine walks out onto the patio with a bottle of wine and waves to Elyse.

Ben nods to her. "Hey, kiddo."

"Stella, this is Janine, Ben's partner at D.E.M."

"Oh, we've met. You were an assistant at King, weren't you?"

"I was. A lot's changed since then."

"I'll say. I feel like I just introduced these two and now look." She smiles at Isla, sweetening the tone of her voice. "There's a pretty baby." Isla's eyes light up and her face twitches like she wants to smile.

Elyse hears a man's voice, and it takes a second for her to place it. Just as she does, Sierra walks out onto the patio.

"Who's ready to make some bad decisions?"

Ben turns to look at him and smiles. "Sierra."

He lowers Isla into Janine's arms, and she accepts with some surprise. He gets up to greet Sierra.

Stella leans over to Elyse. "Is that who I think it is?" She's undressing him with her eyes from his cowboy boots up to his hat.

"Oh, I should have told you. Sierra's joining us for dinner."

"Oh my goodness." She hurriedly fixes her hair and pushes her shoulders back. Elyse hasn't seen her flustered like this in a long time. "How do I look?"

"Gorgeous."

They sit at the table, passing around dishes of food family style. Ropa vieja, lechon, picadillo, rice, black beans, sweet plantains, and yucca. Ben holds up his wineglass. "This amazing feast was prepared by Flora."

"Thank you, Flora," Janine says.

"Yeah, thanks, Flora. This is delicious," Sierra chimes in mid-chew.

Stella sets down her wineglass and claps.

Flora smiles and waves it off humbly. "Made with love for all of you."

The Manchineel

The aromas of garlic and night-blooming jasmine carry on the cool breeze. It's dark except for the glow of the string lights above them and the windows of the house.

As Elyse hears the familiar sound of a slow bolero playing over the speakers, Ben gives her a knowing look. It's their song. He turns the volume up with his phone and then stands, pushing the heavy chair backward with his legs. He holds out his hand and she takes it.

Their guests' attention follows them to the edge of the patio, where he takes her into position and they dance close. He whispers along to her. "Slow. Quick-quick. Slow. Quick-quick. Slow." Congas, bongos, and timbales keep time against the lamenting wail of a trumpet. It's slow and romantic.

He sings along to her, slightly off key. *"Te quiero. Te adoro. Mi vida." I love you. I adore you. My life.*

Jessica Carrasquillo

About the Author

Jessica Carrasquillo is an attorney living in South Florida with her husband and two dogs. Drawing upon her observations of human nature, she crafts stories that explore the intricacies of love, justice, and morality. 'The Manchineel' is her debut novel.

Sign-up for updates:
www.jessicacarrasquillo.com